GARDEN
of
STONES

GARDEN of STONES

Sophie Littlefield

HARLEQUIN®
entertain, enrich, inspire™

Recycling programs
for this product may
not exist in your area.

ISBN-13: 978-0-7783-1352-6

GARDEN OF STONES

For questions and comments about the quality of this book, please contact us at CustomerService@Harlequin.com.

www.Harlequin.com

Printed in U.S.A.

First printing: January 2013
10 9 8 7 6 5 4 3 2 1

For Julie

1

San Francisco
Tuesday, June 6, 1978

REG FORREST LOWERED HIMSELF PAINFULLY into his desk chair, which was as hard, used and creaky as he was. The dark brown leather was cracked and worn, the brass nails missing in places. When he found the chair in the alley, he thought it had a certain masculine appeal, like something a hotshot lawyer might own. But it hadn't taken long for the thing to seem as shoddy as the rest of his office.

Reg flipped the corners of the stack of papers on his desk and sighed. The coffee wouldn't be ready for a few minutes yet.

Dust motes swirled in the first rays of morning sunlight, causing Reg to blink and then to sneeze. He had positioned his desk under the only window in the room, a filthy pane of glass at ceiling level that looked out into a corrugated-aluminum well half-filled with garbage and dead leaves.

Above the window well was the same alley where he'd found the chair, a narrow, stinking passage between the DeSoto Hotel and the building next door. Still, early in the morning, depending on the season, an errant sunbeam or two found its way down into the room, and for that small grace, Reg occasionally remembered to be grateful.

Beyond the office door, there was silence. The gym opened at seven, which was still a half hour away. He'd already unlocked the doors, but the half-dozen men who'd gather by seven would wait for him to come prop them open. They knew each other's habits. Early morning drew the shift workers, the boys getting in a few rounds on the bag after clocking out. Night security, deliverymen, dockworkers—they were quieter, as a rule, than the ones who came later. Other than the occasional grunt or curse, they had little to say as they worked through their circuits.

It had been several years since Reg himself had taken to the practice ring. He'd broken the same hand three times, and his shoulder was never right anymore. The ligaments in his back were for shit, and there was a scar like a zipper running over his left knee. He was fifty-nine years old and he'd spent three of his six decades here, in the basement of the DeSoto Hotel, building Reg's Gym up from nothing. Reg had paid in rough coin, but he wasn't complaining; the sounds and smells of this place were all he knew anymore, and if he spent more of his time locked up in this office with a calculator than on the floor these days, he supposed that was all right. A man slows down, in time.

A knock at the door. Raphael, his day manager, sometimes came in early and drank a cup of coffee with him. On days like this, when his aches and pains were more troublesome than usual, Reg could do without the conversation—at least until he'd had a chance to work the kinks out of his joints and was feeling more sociable. The only reason he came in to work this early was his insomnia: often stark-awake by three or four, Reg had nowhere else to go.

"Yeah. Come in."

He didn't turn. The only sound was the gurgling of the coffeepot. Reg squinted at the sheet on top of the stack and wondered if he needed to go to the eye doctor again. What had it been, two years, three, and it seemed like they were printing everything smaller all the time.

"Hey, Raphael, look at this invoice, will you, I can't make out the damn numbers—"

He jerked with surprise when warm hands covered his eyes. For a moment he was frozen, remembering the way his sister used to sneak up on him, half a century ago. She loved to put her small hands over his eyes and make him guess, little skinny Martha who died of scarlet fever before her seventh birthday; he hadn't thought of her in years. The hands pushed gently, tilting his head back, one of them cupping his chin to hold it in place. Reg squinted, trying to see who was standing above him, but he was blinded by the sun streaming in the window. Something cold and hard pressed against his forehead, and the last thing Reg saw was a face surrounded with a brilliant, glowing corona, like Jesus in the picture his mother had hung above Martha's bed.

2

San Francisco
Wednesday, June 7, 1978

PATTY TAKEDA WAS HAVING THE NIGHTMARE
again.

In it, she stood at the back of the church as the organist
finished the last few measures of Franck's "Fantaisie in C,"
watching her maid of honor approach the altar and execute
a perfect turn in her pink high heels. There was a pause as
the entire congregation waited breathlessly. Then the first
triumphant notes of the wedding march rang out, and everyone rose in their pews and turned toward the back, ex-
pectant smiles on their faces. Patty emerged from behind the
latticed anteroom divider. Step–pause, step–pause, a smile
fixed on her face.

But something was wrong. Audible gasps filled the chapel
and Patty looked down and discovered that she had forgotten to put her dress on. Or her slip, for that matter, or her

panties or strapless bra. She was completely naked other than her white satin pumps. She tried to cover herself with her hands, but everyone was watching, staring, pointing, and she turned to run back to the dressing room but the ushers were standing shoulder to shoulder, blocking her way, gaping.

Patty woke, shoulders heaving, sweat gluing her T-shirt to her neck, the sheets knotted around her body. She was breathing hard, but at least she was awake. Sometimes, when she had this dream, she ran around the church for what seemed like hours, never finding an exit.

The sound of the doorbell jarred her fully awake. Was that the sound that had broken through the dream? Patty groped for the clock on the bedside table, knocking the tissue box to the floor before she found it. Almost nine. Patty lay still and listened as her mother answered the door. She heard her mother's voice, and a man's, back and forth a few times—and then footsteps, through the house, down the hall past Patty's door, into the kitchen.

"...can offer you tea, if you like, Inspector," Patty heard her mother say clearly as they passed, and then the voices became indistinguishable again.

Inspector? Patty untangled the sheets from her legs and sat up in bed, rubbing her face. Why would a detective be visiting her mother's house? She pulled on the nylon running shorts she'd tossed on a chair the night before and was halfway to the door before she changed her mind and went back for her bra. It took a little searching—the bra had disappeared halfway under the bed—but Patty eventually found it and yanked it on, then exchanged the T-shirt she had been sleeping in for a fresh one from the suitcase on the floor. She sniffed under her armpits—not terrible. She really needed to unpack. She'd moved out of her apartment last week and she was staying here with her mother until the wedding, but it was only her third day off and she was still enjoying being lazy.

She peeked out the bedroom door, craning her neck to peer into the kitchen, and saw a man's polished brown shoe under the kitchen table. The rest of him was just out of sight. Patty grimaced and tiptoed across the hall to the bathroom. She washed her face and brushed her teeth in record time, pulling a comb through her hair and settling for a quick swipe of lip gloss.

When she entered the kitchen, she was feeling present-able, if self-conscious about her bare legs. The man stood and greeted her with a nod.

"Patty," her mother said. "This is Inspector Torre."

"Pleased to meet you."

"You too," Patty said automatically, taking the hand he of-fered, finding his grip surprisingly tentative. He was at least six, six-one, with the sort of beard that looks untended by lunchtime and thick, black sideburns encroaching on his jaw. Handsome, some women would no doubt think.

"I'm here to talk to your mother about the death of an acquaintance of hers."

"Who?" Patty quickly cataloged everyone in her moth-er's circle, a very short list. Besides work, Lucy Takeda went almost nowhere.

"Reginald Forrest. He was the proprietor of a commercial gym in the basement of the DeSoto Hotel."

Patty knew the hotel—a once-grand stone edifice about a quarter mile away, on Pine or Bush or one of those streets. A pocket of the neighborhood that had seen the last of its glory days. But she had never heard the man's name.

Lucy *tsk*ed dismissively. "Someone I knew a long time ago, in Manzanar. I haven't seen him in thirty-five years."

"But—" Patty looked from the inspector to her mother,

confused. Lucy never spoke about her time in the intern-ment camp. "Why on earth would you want to talk to my mother?"

Torre cleared his throat, looking slightly uncomfortable. "Someone claims to have seen someone resembling your mother in the vicinity of the gym around the time he died. We've got a time of death between five and seven yesterday morning, and this person places your mother there between seven and seven-fifteen."

"But that's—" Patty struggled to clear the morning haze from her thoughts. "My mom doesn't ever go over there."

"This person said…" Inspector Torre seemed to be search-ing for the right words. "That is to say, he described certain characteristics…. We asked around the neighborhood and several people mentioned Mrs. Takeda."

Now Patty understood his discomfort. "Characteris-tics…" Yes, people didn't quickly forget her mother's face. The pocked and shiny pink scars took up most of the right side of her face, extending from her right eye down to her jawline. They encroached upon her lower eyelid, pink and puffed and vertically clefted; the eye itself was milky and gave the impression of both blindness and acute vision, which was unsettling and put the observer in the uncomfortable posi-tion of having to find another place to focus his own eyes.

"The inspector talked to Dave Navarro," Lucy said indig-nantly. "And the Cooks!"

The faint beginning of a headache stirred between Patty's temples. Her mother had never had a great relationship with the neighbors—she could only imagine how those conversa-tions went. "I'm sorry, but this is, well, I don't get it," Patty said. "I mean, you weren't at the hotel yesterday morning, were you, Mom?"

"Of course not. And besides, Inspector Torre said it could also be a suicide," Lucy said. "It probably was."

"Why would you say that?" Torre asked.

"*You* said that. You said the stun gun or whatever it was—"

"Captive bolt pistol," Inspector Torre said. "Often used with livestock, but it has other uses. What I meant was, was there something about Mr. Forrest that makes you think he might have been suicidal?"

"How would I know?" Mrs. Takeda asked. "Reginald Forrest is an old man now. I'm sure he had his reasons."

"Was," Torre interjected. "*Was* an old man."

Lucy shrugged. She was in an odd mood, both irritable and nervous, Patty thought. "Wait," she said. "Can you just back up a little for me, Inspector? I'm sorry… I haven't had my coffee. I'm not sure I'm following what you're saying."

Lucy frowned, an expression that distorted her scars, and folded her arms over her chest.

"Sure." Torre reached for a notebook in his breast pocket, licked his thumb and started turning pages. "Janitor was buffing the lobby floor at about seven, seven-fifteen yesterday morning," he said. "He described you pretty accurately. Said you appeared flustered, that you were walking faster than normal."

"He doesn't know me," Lucy said. "How does he know how fast I walk?"

"*Mother.* Please."

"Your mother's neighbors, Mr. David Navarro and Cindy and Tom Cook, did say that she takes frequent walks around the neighborhood."

"How would they know where I walk? They're not my friends," Lucy said. "They've never liked me. Dave Navarro had a tree whose roots were choking the sewage pipes under my house, and we argued over it until he finally cut it down.

And the Cooks have a daughter who spreads her legs for every boy who comes around."

"Surely my mother isn't the only person you're interviewing," Patty said hastily, painfully aware of how caustic Lucy could sound to someone who didn't know her. She was a loner, but that certainly didn't mean she'd killed anyone, a point Patty feared might be lost on Torre.

He shrugged. "Sure, we've got a few people we're talking to. Forrest had a son from a first marriage—he's disturbed or retarded or something, lives in a group home. There's also a girlfriend. I don't suppose you can tell me anything about either of them."

"Of course not," Lucy snapped. Patty tried to telegraph *be nice*. "I told you I haven't talked to him in three decades."

"All right." Torre tucked the notebook back in his pocket. "Here's what I'm going to do. I'm going to give you a chance to think about Forrest, see if you remember anything that might help us out."

"From thirty years ago?" Damn, now she was doing it too—Patty instantly regretted snapping.

Torre turned his gaze on her. "So you live here with your mother, Patty?"

Patty resisted the urge to glare. "Only for a couple of weeks. I'm getting married. The wedding's on the seventeenth."

"Oh. Well, in that case, congratulations."

He stood and adjusted his jacket, his eyes traveling up to the shelf that ran the length of the wall separating the kitchen from the dining room, and Patty cringed inwardly. This was the moment that marked every newcomer's first visit to the house, the moment Patty had learned to dread so much that eventually she'd stopped bringing friends home at all.

Patty let her gaze follow Torre's, and tried to see what he saw, from his perspective—the gruesome tableau was as familiar to her as her mother's Corelle dish pattern or the fake-brick design of the kitchen linoleum.

All those eyes: wide and shiny, staring into every corner of the room at once. It probably seemed like there were dozens of them, but in reality there were only six or eight animals—squirrels and chipmunks and a pale little desert mouse, all of them stuffed and mounted so that they seemed to perch at the edge of the shelf, tiny claws curled around the edges of the painted board, hunching and crouching and tensed to jump, mouths open and leering, like so many gargoyles about to come to life.

3

Los Angeles
December 1941

EVERY DAY WHEN THE NOON BELL RANG, IT was the lunch monitor's job to stand at the front of the class and choose rows of students to line up, the quietest and most attentive first.

The teacher, for whom the ritual had lost some of its appeal over time—understandably, because she was at least a hundred years old—attended to her own tasks: gathering her purse and her lunch in its wicker pail, removing her glasses and placing them in the desk drawer, straightening stacks of papers. Unless the lunch monitor was utterly devoid of any sense of drama, she would drag out the selection, taking her time surveying the rows of eighth graders, and only after building sufficient suspense would she announce her choice.

Row three, you may line up.

And then the process would be repeated until everyone had lined up for lunch.

Each Monday morning, new recess and lunch monitors took up the yoke of duty, the schedule having been posted the first day of school. Lucy had waited more than three months for her turn. She had asked her mother to press her best blouse, the one with the tiny pleated ruffles around the Peter Pan collar. She had worn her favorite headband, the navy velvet with the small folded bow, and new snow-white socks. Lucy looked her best this Monday morning, and because she was Lucy Takeda, that meant she looked splendid indeed.

All through the morning she waited impatiently, forcing herself not to slouch in her seat. At last it was nearly noon. The teacher glanced up at the clock, and then looked thoughtfully at Lucy. She did not smile. Instead she closed her eyes and pinched the flabby skin between her eyebrows, frowning as though she had a headache. Then she opened her planner and ran her finger down the page. "The new hall monitor this week shall be Samuel McGinnis," she said without inflection. "The new lunch monitor shall be Nancy Marks."

For a second, Lucy was sure that she had heard wrong, that the teacher had made a mistake. Lucy had certainly not made a mistake—the date had been circled on the calendar at home for months.

Nancy Marks turned in her seat and gawped at Lucy, but she scrambled to her feet when the teacher snapped that she didn't have all day. It seemed that Nancy's voice held a note of apology as she chose Lucy's row to go first, but as the students filed to the front of the room, Nancy did not look at her.

"It's because you're a Jap," Yvonne Graziano said, not without sympathy. Yvonne and Lucy had been best friends since second grade. They huddled in the corner of the playground under an arbor covered with the canes of climbing roses gone dormant for the winter. Lucy had learned not to stand too close, or her angora coat would get stuck on the thorns.

Yvonne spoke with authority, since her eldest brother was in the Army Air Corps. He was stationed at March Field, but Yvonne's mother was worried that he would be sent to the front lines as soon as the United States entered the war.

"My dad says if there was ever a war with Japan, he'd sign up if they let him," Lucy said, fighting back tears. She'd managed to stay proud and aloof all through lunch, though she had little appetite for the boiled egg and apple her mother had packed. "He says he'd go fight if he could."

Yvonne nodded sympathetically. "My dad says your dad is one of the good ones. But he's too old."

It was true—Lucy's father was astonishingly old. His teeth were long and yellow, and his mustache was more silver than black. Behind his shiny round spectacles his eyes—though kind, always kind—were nested in wrinkles.

"But still, he's as American as anyone else." On this point Lucy was less certain, because her father still spoke Japanese occasionally. He read the *Rafu Shimpo,* a newspaper printed only in Japanese, and conducted much of his personal business in the shops along First Street in Little Tokyo. On their anniversary, her father took her mother to dinner at the Empire Hotel; he often brought her flowers wrapped in white paper from Uyehara Florist. Even their church, Christ Community Presbyterian, was mostly filled with Japanese families on Sundays.

Still, Lucy had no doubts about her father's patriotism. On the Fourth of July he studded the yard with tiny American flags, and he stood proudly for the national anthem at Gilmore Field when he took Lucy to see the Stars play.

Yvonne looked at her sympathetically. "That's good. But my dad says it's not going to matter much longer, if Japan keeps invading. He says things are bound to change."

Yvonne's words were as chilling as they were vague. *Change* was unimaginable. Lucy had grown up in the same house her parents lived in before she was born, a white two-story on Clement Street with black shutters and a porch with flowers spilling out of baskets hanging from the eaves, a nicer house than most of her friends lived in. Lucy had always had the same bedroom, the same bathroom with its pink-and-black tile and ruffled curtains in the window. The same walk to school—down Clement to the corner, crossing Normandie, and then three blocks to 156th—since the first day of kindergarten. The only changes in her life were the coverlets her mother made for her bed, the dresses hanging in her closet and the height of the two little twisty-branched trees in the front, which her mother had planted when she and her father were first married. Each year, they grew a few more inches, and Lucy knew that someday the tallest branches would reach the eaves.

Lucy knew that her father was worried too, though he refused to speak of the war while Lucy was in the room; when her parents listened to the radio after dinner, she was sent to her room to study. Of course, she snuck out and listened, anyway. And there were the newspapers: she couldn't read a single word of the *Rafu Shimpo*, but the headlines at the newsstand on the way to the market were impossible to miss. Hidden Tank Army Protects Moscow. Seven Vessels Sunk Off Italy. Still, how could the events unfolding in these far-off places possibly affect Lucy and her family a million miles away in California, where even now, in the middle of winter, the air was scented with citrus blossoms?

Two boys kicked a ball past them, coattails flapping. When

they saw Lucy and Yvonne, the shorter of the two skidded to a halt. "Thought you were supposed to be lunch monitor this week," he said, sticking a finger into his ear and scratching vigorously.

Lucy couldn't bear to look at him. Instead, she pretended to rub at a bit of dirt on the lid of her lunch pail.

"Thought *you* were supposed to be running home to your mama," Yvonne snapped. "I heard her calling you. She said you wet the bed again."

Lucy, buoyed by her friend's loyalty, blinked and smiled shyly. But as the boy ran off and Yvonne linked an arm through hers, Lucy knew that the changes had already started, and nothing in her power could stop them.

4

THAT DAY AFTER SCHOOL, LUCY INSTALLED
herself in the front parlor to wait for her father to come home.

She was tired of her parents trying to protect her from
things they thought she was too young to understand. Lucy
supposed that had been all right when her world was limited
to the bright-colored illustrations in her picture books, the
elaborate tea parties she held for her dolls and stuffed toys,
the swings and the slide at the playground in Rosecrans Park.

But she was in the eighth grade now, and her world had
been growing steadily for a long time. She'd read all the
books in her classroom and begun on the ones on her parents' shelves—the ones in English, anyway, most of which
belonged to her mother. Some were a little melodramatic
for her taste, but Lucy preferred to be bored and occasionally confused by Edna Ferber and Daphne du Maurier than
by *Madeline* and *Caddie Woodlawn*.

Consulting her mother about the future was out of the

question. Miyako Takeda wasn't like other mothers: she was quieter, prone to spells and moods. Withdrawn much of the time. Easily upset. And, of course, far more beautiful, which only made her seem more delicate, somehow.

Renjiro Takeda, on the other hand, would know what to do. He was a businessman, well respected, important. Lucy pretended to read—a book called *The Rains Came* that had been made into a movie that she was too young to see, in which a lot of people appeared to be falling in love with each other. The book was so confusing that she didn't intend to finish it, but it was as good as any, since she had too many things on her mind to pay attention to the words.

At last, when dark had fallen and Lucy could hear her mother moving about the kitchen getting dinner ready, the front door opened. Her father's face lit up when he spotted Lucy reading in the wing chair, but his smile didn't disguise his weariness. He had been looking tired much of the time lately.

"Hello, little one," he said, removing his hat and placing it on a high peg of the coatrack. He was a natty dresser and his hat was made of fine wool, smooth to the touch, its edges turned up slightly. Next he hung his topcoat, brushing invisible specks off its tight-woven surface. Lucy liked to watch this ritual, and she waited patiently until he finished. Only then did he turn to her and hold his hands out. Lucy leapt off the chair and put her hands in his, and he swung her gently around, something she suspected she was too old for, but couldn't bear to give up yet.

"I have something for you," he said.

"What, Papa?"

Her father pulled a small package wrapped in shiny white paper from his pocket. Lucy unfolded it carefully, revealing a mound of sugared almonds. Sometimes he brought candied lemon peel or crystallized ginger. He owned a business packing and shipping dried apricots, and he purchased treats for Lucy and her mother from the merchants and ranchers who brought their goods to the bustling business district.

"Don't eat them now." Her father's voice was teasing. "You'll have no appetite for dinner and then Mother will be angry with me."

"Thank you, Papa." Lucy carefully rewrapped the package. Then she took a breath. She had to talk to him now, when her mother wasn't listening. "Something happened today in school."

He laid a heavy hand on her shoulder. "You discovered you are actually a princess?" he pretended to guess, wiggling his eyebrows. "With a crown and a kingdom to rule?"

When Lucy was younger, her father would tell fantastical stories of apricots delivered by teams of white horses pulling wagons with silver fittings that sparkled in the sun, apricots so plump and perfect that each had a single green leaf attached to its stem, and he had to hire a pretty lady just to pluck the leaves and drop them into a basket, all day long. Lucy pretended to believe her father's stories long after she understood that they were invented. She knew they pleased her mother. More precisely, Lucy knew that her own happiness pleased her mother, that the tableau they made, the three of them, prosperous and modern in their kitchen with its sleek metal cabinets and green tiles, was an achievement Miyako could never bring herself entirely to believe in.

Already her father was moving toward the hall. Lucy knew he was anxious to greet her mother; he kissed her each evening as carefully as if she were made of spun sugar, and the smile he gave her was different from the one he had for Lucy. It was almost shy, if a father could ever be said to be shy.

Usually, Lucy liked watching her father kiss her mother, but tonight she had to talk to him first.

"Papa, be serious. I want to ask you about something. About the war."

That got his attention. Renjiro Takeda's shoulders went rigid, and he turned slowly to face his daughter. His skin was stretched tight across his face; the lines around the corners of his mouth and under his eyes looked even deeper. "There is no war," he said quietly. "Not in America."

"But there's going to be."

"Who told you that?" His voice hardened, and Lucy was afraid. Not of her father—he was never angry with her, he was always kind—but of what the shift in his mood signified. "Who have you been talking to?"

"Nobody. I mean, the kids at school talk."

"President Roosevelt will keep us out of the war. You don't need to worry." But he didn't sound as certain as Lucy would have liked.

"But Papa…I was supposed to be lunch monitor today."

Her mother's steps echoed in the hall; she was coming to see what the delay was. Lucy put a hand on her father's arm and spoke quickly, lowering her voice. "Papa, I was supposed to be lunch monitor but Nancy was instead, and Yvonne said it's because I'm a Jap and her father says things are changing and——"

But her father was cupping a hand to his ear and frowning, and she knew he was about to tell her to slow down and not talk so fast, to speak up so he could hear her. He was becoming hard of hearing; her mother teased him about it and threatened to buy him one of the new Dictograph hearing aids that were advertised on the radio.

"Dinner's almost ready!" her mother said, sweeping into the room. She'd touched up her lipstick as she always did before Renjiro came home, a slash of stark red against her fine, pale skin. "I made marble cake. And there's ham."

Lucy watched her father's expression change; neither of them had missed the faint edge to Miyako's voice, the fact that her smile was a little too brittle and her words a little too breathless. But the biggest giveaway was the cooking. Miyako was a good cook, but she rarely had the energy for more than a cursory effort. She was having one of *those* days, and Renjiro's outward calm faltered before he recovered and went to kiss his wife.

Many afternoons when Lucy came home and let herself into the house with the key she wore on a chain around her neck, her mother would be lying down, her room darkened, the drapes closed. On her bedside table would be a glass of water and a folded cloth. Occasionally her mother would wet the cloth and drape it over her forehead. Lucy no longer went into her parents' room on afternoons when the door was closed; her mother had asked her not to.

"You're thirteen," she'd said shortly after Lucy's birthday the prior year, before closing the bedroom door gently on Lucy's face. "Old enough to take care of yourself for an hour or two while I rest."

But sometimes, every week or two, there would be a day when Miyako's mood would swing in the other direction. She would have energy to spare. She cleaned and rearranged furniture, even though a lady came to clean every week. She tried new recipes and produced more courses than the three of them could eat. She met Renjiro at the door in her nicest apron and sat with him after dinner, talking breathlessly, her words chasing each other, instead of working on her embroidery by herself in the kitchen as she usually did. Nights like these were likely to end with the muffled sounds of Miyako crying in her bedroom, her father's voice a smooth blanket, his words unintelligible through the wall their bedroom shared with Lucy's. Long after they were finally silent, Lucy would lie awake in the dark, wondering what had made her mother so sad.

She'd missed the signs today, so preoccupied was she with what had happened at school. Now she saw her opportunity slipping away, the chance to ask her father what to do about it. Renjiro was ever solicitous of Miyako, and Lucy knew— without jealousy, with calm acceptance—that she was the lesser planet in her father's orbit.

She felt more and more discouraged as they worked their way through her mother's elaborate dinner. Miyako kept up a steady conversation, her sentences breaking off and starting over on entirely new subjects. She talked about a neighbor who had had something delivered in a large truck and a forecast she had heard on the radio that mentioned the possibility of hail and an article she'd read in a magazine about the first lady's social secretary, and a dozen other things, too many to keep track of. Renjiro seemed even quieter than usual, answering in Japanese as often as he did in English, something he usually worked hard to avoid. Several times he set his fork down without eating the food he'd lifted halfway to his lips.

After dinner, Lucy stayed in the kitchen, pretending to read again, as her mother cleaned up and her father fussed with the pipe that he smoked each night to help him digest his dinner, and finally her mother's stream of words began to slow down, like a music box that would soon need to be wound again.

Suddenly, a plate fell to the floor, causing Lucy to jump. In seconds, her mother was on her knees, and her voice broke as she scrambled for the fractured pieces.

"I'm so clumsy, I can't even hold a plate right—"

"No, no, it's all right, it's nothing, let me help you." Her father rose, setting his pipe down carefully. Then he paused, and slowly lowered himself back into his chair. "Oh. I'm sorry. Just a moment… Just give me a moment."

Lucy looked at him in alarm. His face looked grayish, his eyes wide and glassy. "Papa, are you all right?"

"Yes, yes, of course, I'm just… Help your mother, *suzume*."

"Yes, Lucy, get the dustpan."

Lucy obeyed, breathing a sigh of relief. Her mother was fine; she had managed to bring herself back from the brink to which her mood had driven her, and her father was simply tired. He worked so hard at the factory, with all the employees for whom he was responsible, all the trucks bringing the apricots, the crates carrying them away, beautifully wrapped and packed and bearing her father's name, all over the country. And she was her parents' *suzume,* their little sparrow, and as she knelt to help pick up the broken pottery, she tried to hold on to the warm feeling that came from knowing that here in her home, she was the center of something.

The week passed slowly. Nancy took her place at the head of the class each day at noon, and Lucy pretended not to care. The boys on the playground found someone else to taunt. Miyako's mood steadied, and when Lucy came home each day she found her mother embroidering in the parlor. She finished a rose-patterned scarf for her dresser and began a matching one for Lucy.

On Saturday Renjiro wasn't feeling well. The next morning, he stayed in his dressing gown to read the paper, and Miyako told Lucy that if she liked, she could go to church with the Koga family from down the street.

Lucy welcomed the chance to sit in one of the pews up front between the young Koga children, her hands folded on her lap as she stole glances around the congregation, knowing she was being admired. Rarely did a week go by without someone stopping her family outside the church to tell her parents how beautiful and well-mannered Lucy was, how much she resembled Miyako. And Lucy knew that she would receive even more compliments than usual after she spent the service seated between the squirming Koga boys, helping their mother keep them quiet.

She wore her navy coat with frog closures and her patent shoes and combed her hair until it shone. Lucy knew she was a beautiful girl, but for some reason this impressed adults even more than the other children in her class. Maybe it was because she had grown up with many of them, seeing each other every day. Now that she was fourteen, Lucy thought she could see signs of maturity in her face when she looked in her mother's vanity mirror—a narrowing of her cheeks, an arch in her brow that more closely echoed her mother's. Lucy wasn't particularly vain, but she had observed her mother carefully enough to know that beauty was a tool that could be used to get all sorts of nice things. The best fish in the case at the market, say, or a seat on the trolley on days when it was crowded.

As the reverend came to the end of one of his long and boring sermons and the congregation stood to sing the hymn, Lucy kept her eyes downcast as though she were praying. In reality, she was staring at Mrs. Koga's brown pump, noting smugly how dowdy the plain, unadorned shoe was compared to the dressy high-heeled pairs in her mother's closet. Lucy's feet were still smaller than her mother's, but soon they would be able to share—if she could convince Miyako that she was old enough for heels. By the age of fifteen, surely? These were the thoughts she was entertaining when the doors at the back of the church creaked open and two anxious figures burst inside, interrupting the listless singing of "Faith of Our Fathers."

Later she would remember the unfamiliar words repeated over and over by the adults all around her, *Pearl Harbor* and *torpedo* and *casualties*—but in the confusion inside the church, all Lucy could think about was that some unknown disaster had taken place and she was here, daydreaming, thinking selfish thoughts while her parents were over a mile away by themselves, her father ill and her mother barely able to take care of either of them. It was the first time Lucy understood that it would fall to her to help them if something bad had happened, the first time she realized that in some ways, her childhood was already far behind her.

Somehow, in the confusion following the news, Lucy ended up walking home alone. She imagined the Kogas realizing that she was missing, and feeling terrible about it— "How could we let that poor girl out of our sight?"—but even that was small comfort. She had a sense of foreboding, and though her shiny shoes pinched her toes, smashing them together, she hurried, almost running, her breath ragged in her lungs.

When she turned down Clement Street and saw the ambulance in front of her house, she was horrified but not surprised. She'd known from the moment the strangers burst into the church that tragedy had come for her—that no matter what other cyclones of disaster had swept the world that morning, one was bearing down directly on Lucy. Everything that led up to this day had been a portent: her mother's moods, the children's cruelty, the glassy look in her father's eyes—disaster.

Two men emerged from her front door as she ran toward her house. Between them they carried a stretcher bearing a figure covered with a blanket. Behind them, a woman came out onto the porch, holding the door—Aiko Narita, her mother's best friend.

Lucy ran to the stretcher and threw herself upon it. Her father's shoe jutted out underneath the blanket. If she could just get to him quickly enough, before they took him to the ambulance, there was a chance she could bring him back. If she touched his face, he might feel her hands and choose not to go. If she called his name, he might hear her, and understand that he couldn't leave them behind, not like this.

The two men didn't see her coming, and they were startled. One of them said a bad word. Lucy's fingers barely brushed the blanket when she was seized from behind and held in strong arms. She fought as hard as she could, but Auntie Aiko held her more tightly, and the men carried her father to the back of the ambulance, where the doors stood wide to receive them.

"No, no, no, Lucy," Aiko's familiar voice crooned in her ear. Lucy kicked as hard as she could, connecting with Aiko's shin; she tried to bite Aiko's arm but couldn't quite reach. She heard her own voice screaming, couldn't get enough air. "It's going to be all right," Aiko gasped, struggling to contain her. "It's going to be all right."

Auntie Aiko was a liar. Lucy knew that she wanted to help, but everything was wrong and Aiko wouldn't let go, and she saw her chance slipping away as the doors to the ambulance closed and after a moment it started slowly down the street. Aiko tried to carry her back up the steps into the house, but Lucy twisted savagely and almost managed to slip away. Aiko caught the hem of her coat and dragged her back. The coat's buttons popped off and went rolling down the sidewalk. One went over the curb, through the grate, and disappeared into the blackness below the street.

One more loss, and finally Lucy gave up and allowed herself to be dragged, limp in Aiko's arms. The button had been etched with the design of an anchor. They would never find another to match. The button would disappear in the muck and rotting leaves in the sewer, as the ambulance carrying her father's body was disappearing out of view.

5

THE DOCTOR HAD GIVEN HER MOTHER SOME-thing to help her calm down, which seemed to make her mostly sleep. Aiko had moved into the house and slept in Lucy's parents' bed. Lucy could hear her during the night, getting up to go to the bathroom or to get a glass of water. She missed the sound of her father's snoring. She missed everything about her father.

The funeral would take place tomorrow. Mrs. Koga had taken her yesterday to buy a suitable dress. She and Aiko had had a whispered conference in the parlor, and Lucy had taken the opportunity to slip into her parents' bedroom to check on her mother, something Aiko had discouraged her from doing.

Miyako had been sleeping with her hands folded under her chin, the covers pulled up neatly, almost as though she too were dead. Her face was smooth, her lips dry and pale, her eyelashes fluttering slightly as she exhaled. The flutter of the lashes was proof that she was still alive, at least. Lucy watched her for a moment and then tentatively touched her hand. It was warm. After a moment, Lucy went around to the other side of the bed and got in, lifting the covers carefully and inching slowly across until she was pressed up against her mother.

She burrowed her face into her mother's arm. She could smell her mother, an unwashed smell that was both unfamiliar and welcome. Usually, her mother smelled like perfume and hair spray and the cloud smell from the laundry. Lucy burrowed deeper, inhaling as much as she could, and wished that she could stay here, that Mrs. Koga would go away and Aiko wouldn't notice. She wished that she could stay here all night with her mother and maybe, in the morning, her mother would wake up and the first person she would see would be Lucy. She would look into Lucy's eyes that were so much like her own and decide to be brave for her. She would stop taking the medicine that made her so sleepy and send Aiko home, and she and Lucy would decide together what to do next.

But of course that wasn't what happened. Lucy had gone downtown with Mrs. Koga. She had nodded numbly when Mrs. Koga asked if the dress, the hat, the slip were all right, and when she got home Aiko had made a pot of bad-smelling soup with vegetables and thick noodles. Aiko's own husband had been dead since almost before Lucy could remember, and she was closer to Lucy's father's age than her mother's. Lucy supposed she might end up staying forever, now that her father was dead, and she wondered what would happen to Aiko's house and her two fat cats, one white and one tabby, who were never allowed outside because they killed the birds that came to the feeder Aiko had hung from a tree. The cats, the birds—Lucy supposed they would have to learn to fend for themselves now that Aiko had moved here.

A man arrived with a load of dishes and napkins and silver for tomorrow. Another brought a stack of funeral programs from the printer. They had a picture of her father on the front, one Lucy knew well since it sat in a silver frame on her mother's dresser; in the photograph, his hair was still dark and he wore a suit he no longer owned. The program was in both English and Japanese, and Aiko said that the readings had been her father's favorite. Lucy doubted that was true—she'd caught him napping in church more than once, and she was certain he only went to please her mother.

People would be coming to the house after the funeral. Lucy had attended two funerals already, so she knew what to expect: people would talk in quiet voices, and the ladies would make trips in and out of the kitchen, even though there would be hired help to do all the serving. The men would drift farther and farther from the women, until eventually some of them would be outside, huddled and smoking and shivering in the cold. Her mother would be required to talk to everyone, but at least she would be allowed to sit down, and a few words would suffice. No one ever wanted to talk to the grieving widow for very long. It was one of those things that grown-ups did that they obviously didn't want to do. There seemed to be so many of those, the more Lucy understood about growing up.

Aiko said that Lucy needed to stay at home for a while, that she could miss some school. Next week would come soon enough, she said. Lucy had asked if she could call Yvonne, but Aiko frowned and shook her head.

Something else was bothering Lucy. Aiko had moved the radio into Miyako's bedroom, where they listened to it after dinner, the sound turned down too low for Lucy to hear, even with her ear pressed to the closed door. Also, the newspaper was nowhere to be found. Lucy kept meaning to get up early enough to go out and get it from the drive, but each day she woke to find Aiko already up and busy around the house, the paper hidden away.

She thought of sneaking out, waiting until Aiko was in with her mother and slipping out the front door. She could walk to the newsstand; she had an entire piggy bank full of coins. She could buy a chocolate soda at the drugstore and read the paper. Only someone was sure to see her and insist on bringing her home. Everyone knew her father was dead; there was no way she could escape the eyes of the neighborhood.

Lucy filled the long and restless hours reading pages from her mother's books, the words lost to her as soon as she'd scanned each page. Instead, her mind turned over the words shouted in the church, the ones that had seemed to put in motion the terrible events that followed—and the words printed on the neat stack of programs on the dining room table.

Pearl Harbor. Torpedo. Casualties.
Renjiro Takeda, 1879–1941.

On the day of the funeral, Aiko never left Miyako's side. In the church, Lucy squeezed between them in the pew; at the graveside she allowed herself to be pressed against Aiko's wool coat, but she never let go of her mother's hand. Back at the house, though, they were separated. Someone had moved the red couch to the center of the parlor, and there was only enough room for Aiko and Miyako to sit.

Lucy stationed herself near the front door and gave herself the job of answering it. By doing so she could avoid going into the parlor with all the flowers surrounding her father's picture. His photo somehow made it seem like he was not only dead but fading from the house, memories and all, slipping away a little more each day.

Late in the day, when people were already beginning to leave, the doorbell rang one last time. Lucy opened it to discover two Caucasian men dressed in fedoras and black coats standing on the porch. They did not remove their hats. Neither smiled. For a moment Lucy thought they must be men her father knew from his business, perhaps other merchants from Banning Street, but surely they would have come sooner if they meant to pay their respects.

"Please get an adult," the shorter of the two men said. He had a large nose the color of an eraser.

Lucy said nothing, backing away from the door, and when the men followed her inside, she wondered if she should have asked them to stay outside. It wouldn't do to bother her mother or Auntie Aiko. This was the sort of thing a father should handle, but who could she ask? Lucy turned and hurried to the kitchen, where some of the men had been smoking and talking earlier, but they had dispersed and were standing in groups of two and three, collecting their wives and their coats, preparing to take their leave. There were only twenty or twenty-five guests left, perhaps a quarter of those who had filled the home earlier, and of those who remained, none were familiar to Lucy. Her father was not in the habit of bringing friends and associates home.

But the two strangers followed her into the parlor, and the one who had spoken earlier put his fingers in his mouth and whistled. Lucy was astonished, both by the sheer volume the man was able to produce and by his audacity. But before she could respond, the other one, a tall, thin man nearly as old as her father, clapped his hands and began to speak.

"Martin Sakamoto and Kenjiro Hibi. Please identify yourselves." Lucy saw Mrs. Hibi step forward uncertainly, searching the room for her husband.

"Martin and his wife left," someone said from the back of the room, and there was nodding and a murmur of agreement. The taller Caucasian scowled and muttered something to his partner.

They were holding something in their hands, small wallets containing badges that flashed gold. Lucy heard whispers of "FBI," and the worry that had had taken hold of her when she'd opened the door bloomed into full-scale fear. She edged along the perimeter of the room, trying to get to the red couch; her mother looked dazed, leaning against Auntie Aiko for support.

"See here, you can't come in here." One of the mourners, a man Lucy thought she recognized from one of her visits to see her father at work, stepped toward the FBI men. "This is a funeral. It isn't decent."

"Are you Mr. Hibi?"

The man hesitated, glancing over to Miyako's piano, where Mr. Hibi was standing with a plate in his hand. There was a half-eaten slice of cake on the plate, the pale green pistachio cream cake that someone had brought from the bakery. Mr. Hibi slowly lowered the plate to the shiny black surface of the piano. Lucy was shocked—no one ever set anything on the piano; her mother would not allow it.

"You'll come with us, sir," the shorter FBI man said.

"Where are you taking him?" Mrs. Hibi looked like she was about to cry. She hurried to her husband's side and took his arm, as though to hold him back. "Where are you taking my husband?"

"We just need to ask him some questions, ma'am."

Lucy had reached the other side of the room, and she made a run for it, dashing to the couch and crawling up into her mother's lap. She was trembling; she hadn't eaten anything since yesterday. Aiko had been too busy with her mother to make Lucy eat, and she hadn't felt like it. Now she felt as though she might faint. Her mother patted her back absently, and her hands were cool and dry.

Aiko stood. She was a small woman, but her arms and legs were thick and her hands were strong. "You must go now." Her voice trembled, but she took a step toward the FBI men.

"I'll come with you." Mr. Hibi pulled his arm away from his wife and didn't look back. "Leave this widow in peace."

But even this did not seem to shame them. Everyone watched in silence as they escorted him through the house. He looked back, once, and then they were gone.

Mrs. Hibi made a small mewling sound. Lucy's father, in his photograph, seemed to watch in sorrow.

Mr. Hibi did not return. Within days, other men had been rounded up and taken somewhere to be interrogated. No one knew where they were. None came home. The phone rang throughout the day and Lucy could hear Aiko's urgent voice; by eavesdropping carefully she learned that windows had been broken at the drugstore and several of the warehouses along East Second Street, only blocks from her father's building. Aiko asked Lucy to go to the store for her and then immediately changed her mind, and they went together instead. There was almost no one in the streets; the barbershop window held a large hand-painted sign that read, I Am an American. Lucy read the headlines as they passed the newsstand: 4,000 Japanese Die in Submarine Raid. Hong Kong Siege Is Begun.

The following Monday, Lucy was dressing for school when Auntie Aiko came into her room. Her face was pale and her eyes were red. Lucy knew she had been crying, which seemed strange to her because her mother had not cried since her father died. She'd barely spoken, barely eaten; she was like a shadow in the house, coming out when Aiko insisted she try to eat, bathing when Aiko led her to the bathroom.

"No school today," Aiko said. "We have work to do."

They went through the house room by room, taking everything that Lucy's father had brought with him from Japan, all the beautiful things that had belonged to his family: photographs, dishes, lacquer boxes, mother-of-pearl hair clips that had belonged to his mother, tiny ornamental dolls. There was a Bible printed in Japanese that Lucy had never seen him read, silk ribbons marking certain passages. There was an old set of calligraphy brushes and inkstones that Lucy had always wanted to play with but her mother had never allowed her to touch.

It took two days to find everything that had come from Japan, was printed in Japanese, or even hinted at Lucy's father's ties to the Japanese community. "They think we are sending messages," Aiko fumed, as she opened boxes containing old kimonos in gorgeous silks and added them to the growing pile in the parlor.

"Messages to who?"

"Whom," Miyako said. She barely spoke, and wasn't much help with the sorting and assembling. Her embroidery gathered dust in the basket, the hoops left too long on the linen leaving permanent circles that would not block out. Occasionally she would take an interest in some object, holding and examining it until Aiko gently took it back from her. Lucy was beginning to wonder if her mother was going crazy, since her conversation was limited to a few lucid sentences in the mornings as she picked at the toast Aiko forced her to eat. By evening she was almost entirely silent, and most nights she went to bed as soon as the sun went down.

"To whom," Lucy acquiesced.

"The emperor, I suppose. The Japanese army."

"But we're at war with them now. Why would we be sending them messages?"

Aiko's expression turned more bitter than Lucy had ever seen it. "It seems that some people have forgotten that we're Americans too."

"Well, *I* haven't," Lucy said fiercely.

But later, when the sun had set and the sky was slowly purpling over the rooftops, Aiko asked her to help carry the big pile of precious belongings into the backyard. She'd built a fire in the center of the sidewalk that led from the back door to the detached garage, and already Renjiro's old sheet music was burning.

"We have to burn it *all?*" Lucy asked, horrified. She had assumed the heirlooms were to be stored somewhere safe until after the war.

"Yes, and quickly too. The FBI has been to half the houses in Little Tokyo. It's only a matter of time before they come looking here."

"But they were already here. When they took Mr. Hibi away."

Aiko gave her a grim look. "At least they can't take your papa now. But we don't want to give them any reason to think we're not loyal."

The dolls, in the end, took the longest to burn, and as they did, they gave off thick, noxious smoke. The dishes had to be smashed with a hammer Lucy found in the garage, and the paint curled and flaked from the shards as they burned. When it was finally finished, she and Aiko came inside the house to wash and change out of their smoky, dirty clothes, tears mixing with sweat and soot on her face.

Lucy gasped when she saw Miyako sitting in a chair she'd

pulled near the back window. She hadn't bothered to turn on any lights as night fell, and her face was pale and almost luminous in the flickering glow of the dying fire. Miyako said nothing as Aiko pressed a hand to her shoulder and sighed, and Lucy wondered if her mother had ever even blinked as she watched the treasures burn.

6

THE HOLIDAYS CAME AND WENT. THERE WAS no Christmas tree, no tinsel, no candles in the windows as they had been in the past. Aiko moved back into her house on New Year's Eve, but she still visited almost every day. Lucy helped Aiko burn her own mementos from her childhood in Japan, and all the things from her husband's family. After that, Aiko's house seemed as bare and joyless as their own.

Miyako seemed to come out of her funk. "Time for you to go back to school," she said briskly the Monday that classes were to resume after the Christmas break. "No sense sitting inside forgetting everything you've learned."

The morning she was to return to school, Lucy tucked some money from her allowance into her pocket, planning to buy some iced cookies from the bakery on the way home. But as she walked past it, she was startled to see that the windows had been soaped and a sign read Lost Our Lease. The bakery was gone.

At school, Lucy ran to find Yvonne. She hadn't spoken to her friend since before her father died. It seemed like months had gone by, not weeks. There was so much to tell. Lucy didn't realize how much she had missed Yvonne until she spotted her hanging up her coat.

"Hi," she said, as nonchalantly as she could manage.

Yvonne looked at her, then quickly away. A red flush stole over her face. "I have to go," she muttered, and went to her seat. Lucy thought about following her, but the bell rang, and besides, Yvonne had made it clear: she no longer wanted to be friends.

The rejection stung. Lucy was wearing the same clothes the other girls did, carrying the same schoolbooks, bringing the same foods for lunch. She could say fewer than a dozen words in Japanese, and she couldn't read any at all.

At lunch, she walked uncertainly along the edges of the playground, her finger marking the spot in a book she'd borrowed from the library. She planned to sit under the arbor and read. She had no illusions that Yvonne would come find her there—none of the girls had even looked at her, much less spoken to her, all morning.

The boys were a different matter. "Dirty yellow Nip," one of them had whispered earlier, when she got up to sharpen her pencil. After that, Lucy had stayed in her seat, her face burning with embarrassment. Now, three boys—two from her class and one from seventh grade—approached her, and Lucy suddenly realized that the arbor was hidden from view. The teacher on recess duty would not be able to see her if anything bad happened. Hastily she gathered up her thermos and the waxed paper her sandwich had been wrapped in and tried to shove it quickly back into her lunch pail.

"Where you going?" one of the boys said. "Need to get back to your submarine?"

Lucy had heard the rumors about the Japanese submarines said to be patrolling the coast. Aiko said it was ridiculous, that Roosevelt would never allow them to get so close. Lucy hoped it was true. "I'm just reading," she mumbled.

"I heard your dad dropped dead. Was he a spy? Did he commit *hara-kiri?*"

"What?"

"You know——" The boy made a pantomime of stabbing himself in the gut.

Lucy felt tears well up in her eyes. She missed her father so much. Men had come by with papers for Miyako to sign—someone was buying the company, a man her father had done business with in the past—and Miyako had refused to answer the door until Lucy called Aiko and asked her to come over to the house. After that Lucy was afraid to mention her father, afraid of the effect it might have on her mother.

Lucy refused to let the boys see her cry, so she pushed past them, holding her book and the remains of her lunch. She had to shove against one of the boys with her shoulder to get around him, but to her surprise, he yielded easily.

"Ahondara," she said, under her breath. It was one of the few words she knew, something her father had said when he was angry about something. She'd asked him the meaning of the word long ago, but he'd only chuckled and said that maybe it was a good thing Lucy hadn't learned any Japanese.

Walking away from the boys, she hoped it meant something truly awful.

The odd rebalancing of Lucy's relationship with her mother continued as the weeks passed. Aiko was busy with her own affairs—she had a sister near the Oregon border whose twin sons were in their first year of college at

UC–Berkeley, and there was confusion over whether Japanese students would be forced to leave school.

Miyako made an effort: she began bathing, dressing and wearing makeup regularly again and wrote letters to all Renjiro's distant relatives to let them know of his passing. But when Lucy tried to tell her about the teasing she was enduring at school, she seemed to shrink from the news. "Oh, *suzume*," she said, laying her face in her hands and taking a shuddering breath. And so Lucy took back her words, swore she had exaggerated, and finally took to lying and saying that everything at school was fine.

With Aiko gone to see her sister, Lucy was able to come and go freely from the house. When her father was alive, she hadn't been much of a wanderer. Now she used the excuse of doing her mother's shopping to walk past Japanese-owned businesses, to see which were still occupied and which had boarded-up windows. She loitered near groups of men talking outside the barbershop, the drugstore, the tobacconist, and she heard the talk: Japanese were to be herded up like cattle, jailed, deported, tortured… No one seemed to know, but everyone had an opinion.

Late in February, she passed the newsstand and saw headlines screaming Japs to Be Sent Inland. With pounding heart, she bought a paper and read it on the way home. President Roosevelt had signed an executive order that excluded people from military areas. There were a lot of things in the article that Lucy didn't understand, but from the anxious buzz of people on the street, she knew it was bad.

This was one piece of news she could not keep from her mother. She handed the newspaper to Miyako and watched her mother read, her lips pressed together, a hand over her heart. She didn't move until she had read the entire article, and then she sighed and looked up to the ceiling. Lucy waited, hardly daring to breathe, until at last her mother spoke. "It's just me and you, *suzume*. Come here."

Lucy hesitated. She hadn't sat on her mother's lap since she was a baby. She knew her mother cherished her; Miyako knelt and kissed her before school each day and loved to comb and style Lucy's hair, patting her face when she finished. But Miyako was not the sort of mother one read about in books: she wasn't soft or round, she didn't wear an apron and she didn't invite embracing.

"Come," Miyako repeated, motioning Lucy to her lap with both hands. Lucy went. She climbed up carefully, afraid of hurting her mother's thin skin, her pale limbs, but her mother held her close with surprising strength. For a second Lucy remained rigid in her arms, and then she relaxed against her mother's breast and tucked her head under her chin, inhaling deeply, getting as close as she could. She felt tears well up in her eyes and was afraid she might cry—tears would stain the silk of her mother's blouse.

"My little Lucy," Miyako crooned, rocking Lucy slowly in her arms. "Just you and me. Your father has left us and now we must leave our home."

"No," Lucy whispered, frightened by the despairing words. She pressed more tightly against her mother. "They can't make us. This is *our* house."

Her mother laughed, a light, lilting sound that belied her mood. "Oh, my little *suzume,* you have the spirit of your father. He always promised me that everything will be fine. He said he would always protect me, that he wouldn't let anything bad happen to me ever again."

Miyako pulled away gently, and Lucy saw that she had gotten tears on the blouse, despite her best effort—the pale blue was stained dark in two tiny spots. But her mother either didn't notice or didn't care. She held Lucy's hands in hers and brought her face close. "I want to tell you that. That I can protect you. But the truth is, no one can. The war has come to us. If President Roosevelt says we must go, then we will have to go."

"But...where?"

Miyako shrugged her delicate shoulders. "What does it matter? Gone is gone."

Aiko was back in two days, bringing tins of walnuts from an orchard near her sister's house. Lucy cracked them on the back porch, sneaking bits of the sweet nutmeats as she worked, while the women talked in the kitchen. This time, they made it clear she wasn't to come inside until they were finished: they were taking no risks that she would hear.

The afternoon had been unseasonably warm—late February and already the thermometer edged close to sixty degrees—but as evening approached the sun dipped low in the sky and Lucy began to shiver with the cold. She was glad, for her mother's sake, that Aiko had returned, but she also felt a little resentful. When Aiko was around, Lucy had to concede the job of looking after Miyako, and the truth was that, now that she had no friends at school, being Miyako Takeda's daughter was the most—perhaps the only—special thing about her.

Lucy had always known that her mother was beautiful. Miyako Takeda's beauty was so remarkable that it was not considered improper to comment on it. "Your mother should be movie star," the fish man said as he wrapped their mackerel in paper. "Star in movie with James Cagney."

But it was only after Lucy started seventh grade last year that she had realized what should have been obvious: she looked exactly like her mother. Maybe her childish features had hidden the resemblance for a while, but when Lucy walked down the street with her mother now, she knew that the double takes and catcalls were meant for both of them. Her mother would not allow her to roll her hair or wear lipstick, but the resemblance could no longer be disguised.

Lucy knew that she still had some maturing to do before her transformation was complete. Where her mother's lips were sensually full, her own were still the bow shape of a child's. Her mother's eyes narrowed and tilted, elongated at the outer corners in a manner that suggested mischief, while Lucy's retained the wide-open look of youth. Miyako's fine cheekbones sculpted the planes of her face exquisitely: Lucy's had yet to become pronounced.

But there was no hint of her father in her face. Despite his success, his breeding—his father's father had been an important man in Japan, a respected merchant with several homes—Renjiro's appearance had been coarse, his skin pocked underneath his beard, his nose flat and his brow jutting. Lucy was proud to be his daughter, to be a Takeda. But she was very pleased that she resembled her mother.

Lucy knew little about the years between her mother's birth and her arrival, at the age of seventeen, at Renjiro Takeda's factory, where she applied for a job packing apricots into crates. She knew that Miyako was the daughter of farm laborers, and that her mother had died giving birth. Miyako had managed to stay in school until the tenth grade, had learned to sew and embroider and had earned money with her needlework. Something had happened when she was fourteen or fifteen—something terrible, something that had acted as a turning point in Miyako's life. She had left her father behind and gone to the city, where it had taken several more years—and these she never spoke of, so Lucy did not know how her mother had supported herself or where she'd lived—before she found herself in Renjiro Takeda's factory looking for work. Her father had loved to tell stories of how unsuited Miyako was to the noisy, backbreaking work on the line, how he promoted her to a position in the office after a week because he could not bear to see her distress. And then he had married her only a few months later.

Lucy sensed that life had punished her mother for her will to survive, that she had been tested and marked repeatedly, the scars cutting deeper each time they were opened. Lucy, and to some pale extent her father, were her respite and, on the very best days, her fleeting joy. But they were not her central truth. The core of her mother was fraught and dread-drenched, and Lucy feared that the loss of her father and the threat of upheaval were beginning to erode the fragile peace Miyako had molded from the ashes of her early years.

Lucy finished shelling the walnuts. The nutmeats filled the small bowl her mother had given her, the shells rustling in the tin. Lucy took a handful of shells and squeezed, harder and harder until their sharp edges cut cruelly into her palm, before flinging them onto the remains of the backyard fire, which winter rains had reduced to a lumpy, blackened scar on the sidewalk. For a moment Lucy thought she might throw the rest, the bits she'd worked so hard to pry from their shells, the delicate bowl, part of a matched set. Let them be lost, broken, ruined—what did it matter?

But inside the house was her mother, and no matter how fragile the strands that linked them, Lucy would do nothing to further erode her peace. She would endure and she would wait, and she would be ready when Miyako needed her.

7

ON A CHILLY TUESDAY A COUPLE OF WEEKS later, Lucy walked to the store with coins in her fist, thinking about the Nancy Drew book she was currently rereading. She'd discovered the series when she was ten, but the first time she read *The Secret of Shadow Ranch,* she'd missed all the clues. Now as she walked along, she thought about the way Carolyn Keene constructed the mystery, the clues layered in among Nancy's adventures. Nancy was brave, but she was also lucky, with her friends and her clothes and car and her handsome, dependable father. And she got to go to such interesting places, and war never intruded into her world, and she and her friends stopped the bad guys from getting away with the terrible things they'd done. Lucy thought she might like to be a detective herself, peeling away the layers of a crime until she figured out who the guilty person was. It was always a surprise, always someone you never would have guessed.

Lucy passed the boarded and broken windows, no longer sensitive to the ravages being inflicted on the neighborhood, but when she spotted a cluster of people around a lamppost in front of the movie theater, she stopped to see what the fuss was. The movie theater was one of the few places Japanese still went without fear; perhaps it was the darkness inside that made them feel safe. Had this too been taken away? Were they no longer welcome here?

Coming within a few feet of the crowd, Lucy saw that a sign had been pasted on the pole.

INSTRUCTIONS TO ALL PERSONS OF JAPANESE ANCESTRY

She craned her neck to read the smaller print below:

"All Japanese persons, both alien and nonalien, will be evacuated from the above designated area....

"The Civil Control Station will provide services with respect to the management, leasing, sale, storage or other disposition of most kinds of property....

"...transport persons and a limited amount of clothing and equipment to their new residence..."

Lucy felt cold fingers of dread creep down her neck. She turned away without reading the rest; Aiko had been predicting this day for a while now. Whenever she brought up the subject, Miyako blanched and begged her to stop. Now it was up to Lucy to finally make her understand.

She ran all the way home, and by the time she arrived, her lungs were burning and her feet pinched against the leather of her shoes. Somewhere, she'd dropped the coins without even noticing. She had not bought the tea that her mother had wanted. There would not be enough for tomorrow. But what did it matter?

Lucy burst through the front door and nearly collided with Aiko, who was standing in the parlor. For a moment neither said anything; Lucy could see from Aiko's eyes that she already knew.

Aiko knelt down and took Lucy's hand in hers. "I've already told her. Lucy... It's going to be okay. We'll put our things in storage. It's not forever. It's... It'll be like an adventure."

Lucy allowed Aiko to caress her arms, to keep speaking. The words blurred together as she nodded; what she most wanted was for Aiko to leave. She had to get to her mother. Had to see for herself what damage this latest onslaught had done.

At last Aiko released her and went to the kitchen, where Lucy could hear her rattling pots. Her mother had started the dinner before Lucy had left; Lucy supposed that Aiko would now finish it. The two worked well together that way. How many times had they cooked together in one or the other's kitchen? How many times had they taken the sun on balmy afternoons in the backyard, pruned the crape myrtles lining the street in front of both their houses, looked through magazines, listened to the radio, mended and darned and embroidered together?

But her mother needed her now. She crept down the hall to her mother's room, certain Aiko would tell her to leave her mother be. Slipping noiselessly into the room, she let her eyes adjust to the dark for a moment. But her mother wasn't asleep. She was sitting up in bed, propped up by pillows, with her arms folded across her chest and the blankets drawn neatly up over her lap.

"We're to be evacuated," she said to Lucy. "Come sit."

It was the second time in recent weeks that Miyako had invited Lucy into her embrace, and Lucy slipped off her shoes and clambered up onto the bed. She realized that her mother still slept in the same spot that she had when her father was alive, and that, as she crawled under the covers next to her mother, she was on his side of the bed. She wondered if it was true, what the pastor had said when he'd come to the house to pay his respects, that her father was able to look down from heaven and see them. She hoped so. Just in case, she fixed a smile on her face so that he would see she was taking good care of Miyako.

"Auntie Aiko says we can store our things."

Miyako frowned. "Maybe some of them. But, *suzume,* I have been thinking, we don't need so many things anymore. All this big furniture...all those clothes..."

She gestured at the heavy oak armoire, which was just a bulky outline in the darkened room. Lucy had always loved her parents' furniture, a matched set purchased when they had married. Another of the stories her father loved to tell: taking his young bride-to-be to the best department stores in Los Angeles—how shy she was!—and telling her to pick out anything she liked. She had never been inside Bullock's before that day, and the sales clerks were practically falling all over themselves to wait on her, assuming she must be some-one important, dressed in the finely tailored clothes she had made for herself.

"But you can't give all of our things away," Lucy whis-pered. The neat row of dresses, the drawers full of silken camisoles and slips, the bottles of perfume and the mirrored tray that held her cosmetics—what would her mother be without these things? "We can take them with us. The sign said. You just pack and the government..."

But Lucy wasn't at all sure what the government would

do for them. On the sign it had said something about storing household possessions if they were "crated and clearly marked." But this was the voice of the same force that broke down doors in the middle of the night, that cut slits in people's sofas looking for evidence of treason, that broke treasured records in half just because the labels bore Japanese words. How could they possibly be expected to care for Lucy and Miyako's possessions?

"We have a little time," Miyako said. "We will start tomorrow."

She raised her arm, making room for Lucy against her side. It was easy to fall asleep, listening to her mother's breathing. And when Lucy woke again—many hours later, in the middle of the night—she found that her mother had curled around her, holding her in the curve of her body, making a cocoon with her thin arms.

In the confusion and panic surrounding the evacuation order, Miyako and Auntie Aiko somehow managed to learn what goods could be packed to be sent along later, and what would have to be stored until after the war, and began to prepare. They were to report to the Methodist church on Rosecrans Avenue on March 22, bringing only what they could carry, but it wasn't clear what was to happen after that. The newspaper reported that the newly formed War Relocation Authority had secured land in the Owens Valley near the Sierra Mountains, and even now workers were building quarters for the thousands of Japanese Americans being ousted from their homes. But there were also rumors of people being sent to racetracks and fairgrounds all over California and forced to sleep in horse stalls, and no one could say for sure where anyone would be going on the twenty-second.

What *was* immediately clear was that the process would

be neither easy nor orderly. By the second day after the sign was posted, the local stores ran out of twine and luggage. Entire blocks in Little Tokyo were vacated, and speculators swooped in offering cents on the dollar for the ousted merchants' inventories. Soon, other men began going door-to-door, making offers for entire housefuls of family possessions. At first these offers were rebuffed, but before long frantic families began to realize that an insulting offer was the best they would receive.

After several days shuffling their belongings among ever-changing piles, Miyako and Auntie Aiko decided to be practical about what to store and what to ship. Into their boxes went bowls and pencils and writing paper, scissors and Father's gooseneck lamp and extra lightbulbs, pillowcases and serving spoons. For a long time, Mother did not pack her embroidery box. It sat next to a stack of dessert dishes on the table, waiting for her to decide, the thimbles and packets of needles and skeins of colorful floss arranged neatly in the lacquered box, the contents of which Lucy knew by heart even without opening the lid. She understood her mother's dilemma, because while the embroidery was beautiful, it was also useful; her mother only embroidered things one could use, like pillowcases and towels and bedcovers and tablecloths. In the end, the box was packed, which was only a fleeting comfort.

Lucy went across the street the morning they were to leave to return a hammer her mother had borrowed from Aiko to seal their crates, and found Aiko in tears.

"What's wrong? What happened?"

"Oh, oh. Lucy. I'm sorry." Aiko turned away from her and swiftly dried her eyes on a handkerchief. "I can live without all of this. But...Bluebell and Lily..."

Her cats. Of course. Bluebell and Lily trusted only Aiko;

despite Lucy's patient efforts, they never warmed up to her enough to allow her to pet them.

"I'm sorry about your cats," Lucy said softly. She touched the hem of Aiko's skirt. The fabric was stiff with starch and smelled like Aiko's familiar perfume.

"Oh, don't be silly." Aiko cleared her throat and forced a smile. "Mrs. Marvin down the street will take good care of them for me. Everything's going to be just fine."

But the men with the truck were late, and Aiko and Miyako were nearly frantic with worry by the time they finally pulled up to the curb. The bed of the truck was already so laden down with other people's belongings that Lucy didn't see how they could add any more, but the men lashed their boxes on top of the heap and drove away.

Lucy was wearing her best school dress and her good coat, and Aiko was wearing a suit and a hat with a small, glossy feather fanned out along the brim, but it was Miyako who people stared at as they walked through the neighborhood with their suitcases. Lucy knew that her mother took comfort in making up her face when she was feeling anxious; by painting and powdering her face, it was as if she created an extra layer to hide behind. Today she wore a simple olive serge dress with a matching coat, and had fixed her hair in an elaborate pompadour on top of her head. She was wearing a pair of dark sunglasses with pearly frames; they were too large for her face, but they made her look mysterious, unapproachable even, and Lucy knew that was the point.

It was chaos at the church. Caucasian volunteers sat at desks with long lists of names, and uniformed servicemen tried to organize the milling families and their belongings, but it seemed to take hours for their turn. They were given tags for their luggage and one for Lucy to wear around her neck, since she was still a child. Each family's tags bore their name, and Lucy thought it was sad that Auntie Aiko's suitcase was the only one bearing the name NARITA. Better that she should have been part of their family; better that she be a TAKEDA, at least until the war was over and they could come home.

At last, the assembled crowd was directed aboard buses, and the buses took them to the train station downtown. There were so many people, so many faces. Lucy searched the crowd for people she knew, but everyone from her neighborhood had become separated in the vast, milling throng. The string around her neck that held the tag pulled and itched, but she said nothing. The other children she saw were silent, their eyes wide. Even the adults spoke quietly, lapsing into silence whenever soldiers walked among them.

Lucy had never ridden on a train before, and as they pulled out of the station and everything familiar disappeared behind them, it did not seem possible that the boxes that her mother and Aiko had packed would be able to find them. How would their belongings find their way beyond the Santa Monica Mountains to the flat valley beyond, places Lucy had never seen? As the hours passed, she kept her face pressed to the train window, while her mother and Auntie Aiko talked in quiet voices. She saw orchards that looked like the pictures in her father's advertising brochures, and fields of strawberries and corn, little towns and ranches and children with no shoes waving madly as the train raced past.

At times, it almost felt like an adventure, except that the other passengers were silent and glum. Some cried, some slept, some talked in low voices. When a young soldier with acne freckling his cheeks told the passengers sitting next to the windows to pull down the blackout shades—even though it was bright afternoon—people complied without a word, and they were all plunged into darkness. Later, they were allowed to put the blinds up again, and someone had brought a box of oranges into the car, enough for everyone, and soon the air was full of the bursting scent of citrus.

Plump orange segments, bright and sharp on Lucy's tongue, a treat. Was this what life was to be like from now on? Monotony and confusion, other people's sadness and fear making it hard to breathe, punctuated by these small and unexpected pleasures?

In Bakersfield, they transferred from the train to waiting buses. Lucy clutched her tag and her mother's hand, as she had promised, and tried not to look at the watchful soldiers with their billed caps shielding their eyes, their gleaming guns. The bus was crowded and smelled of exhaust; people coughed and the soldiers in the front struggled to keep their footing as it rolled out of town and onto a road that followed a twisting mountain gorge. As the bus took steep climbs and hairpin turns, Lucy peering out at the breathtaking drop-offs outside her windows, there were quiet moans and the sound of retching from those afflicted with motion sickness. It wasn't long before the bus was filled with the stink of vomit.

It was night when they finally pulled off the road that bisected the flat valley between two mountain ranges. Somehow, in the miserable, fetid bus, Lucy had fallen asleep with her head in her mother's lap, an indulgence Miyako would not have allowed even six months ago.

When the bus groaned to a halt, a buzz of excited conversation rose all around them. Lucy pressed her face to the window. In the distance a mountain peak rose up into the night, illuminated by moonlight, snow topped and impossibly vast. It was the biggest thing Lucy had ever seen, bigger than anything she had ever imagined.

And laid out in either direction along the wide dirt avenue where the bus had stopped were long, low buildings like dominoes arranged on a table. Above them the sky was bigger than it ever was in Los Angeles, and dusted with so many stars that it looked like talcum powder had been spilled across it.

"Last stop," the driver said, perhaps joking; but after he cranked the doors open, it was several moments before anyone made a move. The air was cold here; while Lucy slept, her mother had covered her with a wrap taken from her valise. But the air that rushed into the bus was far colder. The soldiers, barking orders, made clouds with their breath.

"Are you sure this is it?" Lucy whispered, but her words were lost in the hubbub as people began to file off the bus.

"Wait," Miyako said, her free hand clutching Lucy's coat collar. The passengers exited and formed a milling crowd outside Lucy's window, illuminated by spotlights coming from two tall wooden towers. She searched for Aiko's familiar coat, but there were too many people, too many unfamiliar faces.

Eventually there were only a few stragglers on the bus. "Come on," the young soldier said impatiently, gesturing with the rifle he held in both hands. "Hurry up."

Miyako held both their suitcases in front of her, grunting with the effort of maneuvering them down the aisle. Lucy clutched her mother's coat and inhaled the smell of the wool. Descending the steps, Miyako accepted the help of a stranger in a jacket and tie, and Lucy couldn't help feeling sorry for the man, who apparently owned no warm coat. Once on the ground, she tested the soil with the toe of her shoe and found it sandy. The cold rushed under her skirt and the wind lifted her hair and swirled it around her face. It was as though the place was claiming her for its own, and Lucy stood rigid and fearful, not knowing how to resist.

8

San Francisco
Wednesday, June 7, 1978

FOR A MOMENT AFTER INSPECTOR TORRE LEFT,
the house echoed with the sound of the closing door. Lucy
stared thoughtfully at the cream-and-gray-plaid Formica
table.

"What the hell was that about?" Patty asked, when she
was certain Torre was well out of earshot.

Lucy shrugged. "You were here. You heard the same things
I did."

"That's not what I mean. You *know* that's not what I mean.
Who is this guy Forrest? Obviously, you knew him well
enough to remember him after all this time. Who was he?"

"Just one of the staff, Patty. And I hadn't thought of him
in ages."

"You didn't go see him the other morning?"

"No," Lucy said, but she didn't meet Patty's eyes.

"Not just the other morning, but ever. I mean, isn't that kind of a strange coincidence, that he lived a few streets over all this time?"

"Worked. He *worked* near here. I have no idea where he lived. And after the war, lots of people from the camps went to the cities. Those newsletters that come here, half those people are living in San Francisco."

Patty knew the newsletters her mother was talking about—stapled, folded affairs that her mother threw away without reading, the efforts of a group of former Manzanar internees who were trying to get what was left of the relocation center made into a memorial or a national monument. But Patty knew that Lucy would never seek those people out. She was a loner, content with her own company. It didn't matter that they'd shared an experience, a moment in history. It seemed as though Lucy would much prefer to erase the past completely.

"Mother, we have to figure this out. Someone thinks they saw you there."

For a moment Lucy looked as though she was going to say something—she bit her bottom lip and drew herself up in her seat—and then she merely got up and went to pour more tea. "It wasn't me. I was here, getting ready for work. Like always."

Like always, except that Patty had been asleep in the next room. She should have told the inspector that—that she had been here with her mother, that she'd confirm that at six o'clock Lucy's alarm had gone off as it always did, that she couldn't have been anywhere near the DeSoto because she'd been in the kitchen making tea.

Only she couldn't actually say for certain what had happened in her mother's little house until nearly ten, when she'd finally awoken to a throbbing headache and the sticky, foul taste of a hangover in her dry mouth. It had been the morning after her bachelorette party, scheduled midweek because that was when everyone could make it. Patty had had three glasses of champagne before switching to tequila and losing count—she may have still been a little drunk when she'd finally gotten up, honestly. A train could have barreled through her mother's house and she would never have noticed.

"Just tell me this," she said. "This man, Reginald Forrest, how did you know him?"

Lucy finished with her tea, pouring in the sugar and stirring until it was lukewarm, the way she liked it. "He had a job in the warehouses. All the supervisor positions—all the bosses—they were from the WRA. The War Relocation Authority. He was white, of course. He must have had a couple hundred men working for him, loading and unloading. The trucks came in every day—we used to watch them, us kids. We didn't have a whole lot else to do."

"That's how you knew him? Just from hanging around the camp?"

Lucy shook her head impatiently. "No. There were ten thousand of us living there, a few hundred staff. It was like a small city. It was impossible to know everyone. But he was different. He was good-looking back then. He wanted to be an actor, before the war, and when they put on shows in camp, he would help out, direct and guest star. He coached baseball too. Everyone knew him."

"Look, Mom..." Patty tried to keep the impatience out of her voice. "Maybe this is nothing, maybe they'll go talk to his son or his girlfriend or whatever and figure out who did this. Or declare it a suicide or something. But we have to be ready in case they come back."

It was the face, of course. There was simply no way to argue with someone who could describe Lucy's face. Either

her mother had been there or the janitor was lying. Both possibilities seemed absurd, but one had to be true. It was that simple. And Patty had to find out which—and why—before the detective did.

Maybe she could find this janitor, ask him questions. But as soon as she had the thought, Patty dismissed it. Why would a total stranger invent such a story?

Which left the other, far more uneasy possibility: that for reasons Patty couldn't begin to fathom, Lucy not only knew Reginald Forrest worked nearby but had gone to see him on the morning he died. If someone really had killed the man, her mother likely knew something about it.

Patty watched Lucy unload clean dishes from the drainer and put them away. How could she think her own mother could have killed someone? She could not recall a single moment of violence or even uncontrolled anger—never a spanking, never an altercation with a stranger or at work, barely a raised voice during all Patty's teen years.

But there was the dark history Lucy carried inside her and never shared. The horrors of the war years—being forced from her home and imprisoned, and then orphaned. Patty had never blamed her mother for trying to forget, but her secrecy had created a gulf between them nonetheless. It wasn't her mother's external scars that kept her outside Patty's reach, but the ones on the inside. What if they'd finally scratched their way to the surface? What if, after all these years, her mother's history had come back to haunt her?

After Lucy left for the grocery store, Patty rescheduled her appointment at the salon for the following week. The menu, flowers, place cards—all these details had been taken care of long ago. A chronic overplanner, Patty could coast all the way to the wedding if necessary, and everything would still run smoothly.

But none of that mattered anymore, anyway. She wanted to call Jay and tell him about the detective's visit, but he was in Atlanta for business, some important client the firm was pitching, and the last thing he needed right now was for her to drag him into a mess that might well resolve itself in a day or two. He'd taken the red-eye Sunday just so he could take her and her mom to dinner to talk about wedding details, like how the ushers would seat the guests since his family was so much larger than hers, and who would walk Patty down the aisle since she had no one to give her away. He'd been so sweet that night—she couldn't bear to interrupt his trip. It would wait until he was home.

With Lucy out of the house, Patty had a chance to collect her thoughts. She knew she wouldn't get anywhere with her mother; anything she wanted to know about Reginald Forrest she would have to find out for herself.

She got the phone book from the hall table. *Forrest, Reginald R.*—there he was, plain as day. On Oliver Street, number 225½; Patty pulled out a map and discovered that he lived only eight blocks to the west, dipping into the Outer Sunset, not the best neighborhood. She pulled her hair into a ponytail and put on her running shorts and shoes. She was just going for a jog, she told herself; what could it hurt to just take a quick look at his house from the outside?

When she found the address, she was out of breath and perspiring. The lot was overgrown, fronted by a row of palms shedding dusty brown fronds all over the sidewalk. The house itself was half hidden behind misshapen shrubs and overhanging branches. She located the house numbers, the metal 5 upside down on its nail, and figured Forrest's apartment must be in back.

Patty slowed to a walk and looked around; the street was empty. No one would notice, and she'd just duck in for a moment. The gate had lost its latch, but it squeaked as Patty pushed past, her feet crunching on dried leaves and pods.

A cracked and broken sidewalk led around the side of the house. Patty shoved branches aside and tried to be quiet. Someone could be home in the front of the house, despite its neglected appearance. She wondered if there ought to be police tape somewhere, draped across the door perhaps, or strung between tree trunks, but then again this was only where Forrest had lived, not where he died.

The backyard was tiny, a patch of dead grass separating the house from a leaning detached garage. Broken glass littered the garage window's sash and glittered on the ground below. A trio of disintegrating beach chairs was arranged around a rusted hibachi. A bony cat streaked past with something twitching in its mouth.

She tried the back door and found it locked. Peering through a grimy window, she saw a small kitchen with an old-fashioned fridge, a neat row of empty beer cans on a short strip of countertop, a healthy-looking houseplant trailing leaves from a macramé hanger in the corner.

"You the girl?"

The voice came from the side of the house. Startled, Patty whipped around and saw a pair of old, cracked-leather brogues, no socks, skinny legs. A figure emerged from behind the untamed oleanders: an old lady with gray hair clouding around her shoulders. She wore a man's work shirt and a skirt that hung on her hips. "You that girl?" she repeated. "Kinah's friend?"

Patty's heart had begun pounding the second the old woman spoke, but now she saw that there might be an opportunity. Maybe she could find out something about Forrest from his landlady.

"Uh…" she said, stalling.

"'Cause I expected you yesterday." A bit of spittle arced from the woman's mouth. Patty stepped back.

"I'm sorry I'm late."

"I found his boxes in the garage yesterday," the old woman continued, as though Patty hadn't spoken. "I called Kinah and I told her, you come get these or I'm going to throw them out. She acted like she was doing me a favor. The trouble he caused me, police coming around here—and he still owes me two hundred and sixty dollars. I suppose I won't ever see *that* money. You got a car?"

"Excuse me?"

"You're gonna need a car for the boxes. They're *heavy*. I don't want that junk on my porch."

Patty thought of Jay's car, his beloved red TR7. Its tiny trunk was already full of his soccer gear, and besides, he'd driven it to the airport and left it in long-term parking. "I thought I'd just take a look first, maybe, see what was there?"

The old woman frowned. "I told her I'm going to throw it out. I'm going to leave it on the porch, and if it isn't gone by tomorrow I'm going to put it in the can. Don't be knocking later when you come back—I got my bridge ladies coming."

"All right. I'm sorry, I didn't mean to trouble you. Can I just take a look for now?"

"Okay, but I have to get ready. I don't have time to stand around. You come back and take all that stuff, you hear? And tell Kinah to quit calling me."

The old woman stumped back up the path, and Patty raced to help her, holding back branches as best she could. Around front, the landlady made her way up the steps to the cracked and peeling porch, pausing at each step to drag her leg up, holding on to the rail with both hands. Next to the front door, Patty could see two water-stained cardboard boxes overflowing with junk.

"I don't know what's even in there," the old woman said, steadying herself with a hand on the doorjamb and breathing hard. "He had it down the cellar six, maybe eight years. I forgot it was there when the cops were here. I'm just glad he did it at work instead of in my house. I'd never get the blood out of the carpets."

"You think it was suicide?" Patty asked, sifting through a tangle of electric cords, a trophy, a metal stein with a beer logo etched on its surface.

"Mmm–hmm, that man was unstable. Him and Kinah, and before that, the other one. I forget her name. Besides, I don't know who'd take the trouble to kill him. He didn't have anybody else besides that simple boy of his, and he hasn't been around in a long time."

Patty wasn't really listening. She'd sifted through the first box and found nothing interesting, but in the second, stacked neatly along one edge, were two old photo albums. She lifted them out carefully, brushing off spiderwebs and dust, and turned them over on her lap. 1939–1940 was inked in neat block letters in Magic Marker on the cloth cover of the first.

On the second was written "MANZANAR."

9

Manzanar, Inyo County, California
March 1942

THE FIRST NIGHT IN THEIR NEW HOME, LUCY learned that the camp had a thousand different sounds.

Back in their house on Clement Street, night was the music of a small ensemble. The ticking of the furnace, the groaning of the old walls settling on their foundation, branches from the cherry tree scratching her window when the wind blew, and the squeaking of the floorboards and flush of the toilet when her parents got up in the middle of the night to use the bathroom. All these sounds blended together in a familiar way, soothing Lucy back to sleep whenever she woke.

But underneath the scratchy, unfamiliar blanket, Lucy shivered from the cold as noises intruded from every direction. A baby in the room next to theirs cried almost the whole night through, and Lucy heard every one of its mother's desperate, hushed whispers through the flimsy wall. She heard murmured conversations farther down the barrack. Her mother sighed in her sleep, and when she turned, the metal cot squeaked. Several times during the night, people went to the latrine, and then Lucy heard the door opening and closing, and muffled coughing as the night air filled lungs unaccustomed to such cold.

Deep in the night, the wind picked up, and sand flung itself against the barrack's walls and windows, the sound like an angry waterfall. Lucy could feel the rush of cold wind through gaps in the boards and then—shocking and sudden—grains of sand against her cheek. It blew up from the floor, from between the rough boards.

Lucy didn't think she would ever sleep. But somehow, she woke with sun streaming in on her face, her eyelashes stiff with tears.

Everything was terrible at first: there were long lines for every meal, and even when a two-shift system was put into place, there was always a wait. The food seemed merely unappetizing to Lucy, but for those accustomed to a traditional Japanese diet—especially the Issei, those born in Japan—it was practically inedible. One of the first meals featured canned peaches over rice, a combination many could not force themselves to eat, to the consternation of the Caucasian cooks, who could not understand that to the Issei the combination was as incongruous as ketchup on cake.

There was also the matter of vaccinations. Everyone was required to receive a typhoid vaccine. Done assembly-line style, the dosages given the children were so high that many were sick and feverish for days. Lucy lay in her cot, fading in and out of awareness, while her mother made repeated trips to the latrine to dampen a cloth for her forehead.

Every few days, a dust storm would pummel the camp. Fine grains swept through the cracks that had formed between the floorboards as they'd cured, and came in through the rough window casings and the gaps between the roof and timbers. The dust was cagey and relentless, and the evacuees scrambled to beat it back, stuffing the cracks with straw and strips torn from rags and anything else they could find. The more enterprising took to nailing lids from food cans in overlapping rows over the cracks. But these measures seemed only to renew the storm's efforts to find them. The fine grains felt like boulders when they found their way into one's eyes; they were gritty in one's teeth, sandy in one's ears and nostrils.

At night the sound of coughing filled Lucy's building. Everyone struggled to breathe, from the baby in the next room, whose condition was worsening by the day——her mother waited outside the temporary hospital most mornings to beg the harried doctors for medicine——to the old man at the other end of the hall who sounded like furniture being roughly pushed across a floor.

But by far, the worst of the privations was the public latrine.

On the morning after their arrival, Miyako took Lucy's hand and they ventured out of the barrack. There were sounds of conversation up and down the row of rooms, but Miyako waited until she was sure no one else was in the hall before they left their own room.

"I will not meet my new neighbors before I have had a chance to freshen up," she vowed fiercely, gripping Lucy's hand so tightly that it hurt. She had a folded cloth, their toothbrushes, a comb and a tiny cake of soap in a small box that she'd had the foresight to bring for that purpose, and she had wrapped a scarf around her head and donned her dark sunglasses. Privately, Lucy thought she looked even more like a movie star in this getup, but she doubted her mother would take the observation as a compliment.

They walked the short distance to the latrine with sand blowing up under their skirts. The dust storm of the night before had settled, but sand still blew and the wind was cold on their faces. Though it was late March, the temperature had fallen below freezing the night before, and there was a rime of ice on a puddle leaking from the plumbing pipes leading into the latrine.

And there was a line. As they got close, they heard the intense, agitated conversation among the women already waiting.

"Wait, *suzume*," Miyako murmured, holding Lucy back. Lucy knew her mother was loath to intrude on others' conversation; her reticence was more imperious than shy, but she was not a naturally outgoing person. This was a subject to which Lucy had already devoted a fair amount of worry: how would her mother make friends here, if in all their time on Clement Street she'd made only one? Yesterday, after they were processed at the main office, they discovered that Aiko would be living far from their block, nearly three quarters of a mile away, sharing a room with an elderly woman and her unmarried grown daughter. The entire camp was a square mile with thirty-six blocks, and they said that ten thousand people would be living there by summer. Lucy was afraid they would never see Aiko. If her mother did not make new friends, she would be all alone.

The ladies at the door of the latrine ranged in age from a young mother with a baby on her hip to a hunched, elderly crone being supported by a younger woman—a daughter, perhaps, or a daughter-in-law. Lucy strained to hear what they were saying, but the wind prevented her from making out the words.

"Mother, I have to *go*," she whispered urgently.

Miyako frowned as the door abruptly opened and two

women came out, their faces downcast, and hurried down the road in the other direction. Those waiting gave them a wide berth.

A second later the smell hit Lucy. The women near the door took a step away from it, before one of them resolutely walked up the steps. A moment later, the others followed.

"Mother," Lucy pleaded. She was afraid that she couldn't control herself much longer, that she might urinate right here outside for everyone to see.

"All right." Miyako's voice was thin and worried. They went inside, Miyako never letting go of her hand.

Inside, the stench was overwhelming, and Lucy's stomach roiled. On the floor, dark runnels of murky liquid and sewage flowed freely from the toilets, all but one of which had overflowed. The line to use the remaining toilet was a dozen women deep, all of them trying to avoid the waste that seeped across the floor and through the cracks. They stood with their backs to the last working toilet, giving the only privacy they could.

Sitting on the toilet, an elderly woman was crying, tears running down her cheeks while she tried to shield her face. Her shame was palpable, her misery absolute. Next to Lucy, Miyako gasped.

Lucy would never forget what her mother did next. Miyako, who couldn't bring herself to speak to a stranger, who walked past the greeters at church without a word, who never attended a tea or a card game or a club meeting, took the folded cloth and handed Lucy the toiletry box. She walked across the foul-smelling room, ignoring the row of curious strangers, and handed the cloth to the old woman, not meeting her eyes, unable to avoid stepping in the waste. The woman murmured a few words and took the cloth, unfolding it and draping it over her head, obscuring her face completely.

After that, Lucy and her mother waited their turn with the others. No one spoke; everyone bore the shame of the lack of privacy in silence. When it was their turn, Miyako allowed Lucy to go first. Her relief was immense. Afterward, she washed her hands and waited with her back to her mother. She had never seen Miyako unclothed—even last night her mother had waited until Lucy was in bed to undress. It was dawning on Lucy that all their privacy and modesty was to be taken from them in this place, but she was determined to give her mother all the dignity she could.

The wave of evacuees that swept Lucy and her mother into Manzanar was among the first, but within days, the earliest to arrive felt as though they had been there forever. Each day brought busloads of dazed families. Lucy learned to read in their faces the cycle of emotions as they came to understand what their new life entailed. Astonishment, dismay, horror, desperation…and slowly, slowly, the deadening of the features that signaled acceptance.

Six families to a barrack, each in a room that measured twenty by twelve feet. Surplus cots and scratchy blankets from the first war. Instead of walls, raw wood dividers that didn't reach the ceiling. Curtains instead of doors. Tar paper, unfinished wood, gaps and cracks in walls, floors, roofs. Freezing desert nights, impossible blowing sandstorms. Plumbers were recruited from within the ranks of the interned to work on the latrines, but problems persisted, and soon there was a grapevine among the women about which blocks' latrines were working.

There were toilet-paper shortages. Food shortages. Staff shortages. Still, as the days wore on, bits of scrap started turning up from the construction going on all over the camp. Boards were turned into shelves. Packing crates were turned into dressers and tables and even chairs; curtains were fashioned from bedsheets; men whittled and women knitted, anything to pass the time.

In Manzanar, words took on new meanings. Lucy learned to use the word *doorway* when what she was describing was the curtain that separated each family's room from the hallway that ran the length of the drafty barrack building. In short order they developed the habit of stamping on the floor to announce a visit, since there was no door to knock on, but they still called it *knocking*. Even *building* did not mean what it did back on Clement Street. At first the evacuees thought the barracks were unfinished, with their tar-paper walls and unpainted window casings and plywood floors, but it turned out that these humble edifices were what the government meant for the internees to live in for as long as the war raged on.

The dirt avenues filled with people, the crowds extending all the way to the razor-wire-topped fence that encircled them. Already Lucy had lost her way to her barrack several times, finally learning to orient herself by the mountain in the distance and the guard towers, entirely too close, in which soldiers peered down at them all day long, and from which searchlights projected at night, crisscrossing the bare dirt streets in dizzying patterns.

Slowly, people began to absorb the fact that Manzanar was their home for the foreseeable future. Signs of domestic life began to appear: bright garments hanging from clotheslines, children's toys left on stoops, and all kinds of makeshift innovations meant to turn the tiny cells into homes. Women adorned walls with pictures torn from magazines. Men scavenged bits of cast-off trash to create everything from decorative fences to wooden doormats to aid in the never-ending struggle to keep the dust out.

After two weeks, Lucy's paper name tag still hung from a nail above her cot. She saw the way her mother looked at it, in the afternoons when they waited for dinner. Miyako's mouth got small, her lipstick lips disappearing in a trick where she rolled them inside, and her eyebrows went up until they met the faint line in her forehead.

Lucy had learned to read her mother's thoughts through her facial expressions. Manzanar seemed to have turned Miyako even further inward, until she barely spoke at all, spending her time sitting on the edge of her cot, her hands resting lightly on the embroidered coverlet she had brought from home.

Miyako asked Lucy why she kept the tag, and Lucy said she liked seeing their name, TAKEDA, written out in big black letters on the strip of cardboard.

After her father's business was sold, the sign that read TAKEDA PACKING in bold black letters was removed from the building by the new owner. The next time Lucy and her mother passed the building, in a busy industrial area of the city several miles from their house, Lucy cried when she saw that it was missing. Now she wondered if her mother believed she kept the tag because it reminded her of him, but the truth was that, as the weeks and months passed, Lucy's memory of him was becoming like a drawing, all mustache and spectacles.

Anyway, this was not why she kept the tag. The real reason was much simpler.

Before they came to Manzanar, Miyako often reminded Lucy that other children had far less than she did. That she should not talk about her Madame Alexander doll with her patent-leather shoes, or her View-Master or her paints and easel or the jewelry box on the tall dresser in her room, because the other children at her school did not have as many nice things and it would make them feel sad if she talked about them.

But here, in Manzanar, they had only the things they carried with them. Lucy had her paint box. She had *The Mystery at Lilac Inn,* because her mother had made her choose only one of her Nancy Drew mysteries and it was her favorite. On Lucy's bed was the spread that her mother had embroidered with daisies. She had a box of colorful hair ribbons. Four things that belonged to Lucy alone.

The tag made five.

10

WORD GOT AROUND THAT MIYAKO HAD NO husband to protect her, and she could no longer walk freely in the streets without suffering unwanted attention. Adolescent boys followed her; men made catcalls and rude invitations as she walked to the laundry, the ironing house, the general store. Even the wizened, broken-toothed Issei who crouched under the barracks' eaves, out of the wind, watched her unabashedly.

Men had watched Miyako in Los Angeles too, but they were covert about it there, glancing over a hymnal at church or letting their gaze linger too long at Miyako as they held the door for her at the post office. But here in the camp, the conventions of polite society were unraveling. Overwhelmed families were fracturing. Gangs of young men, bored and emboldened, roamed the camp. Men fraternized with each other in the evenings, drinking smuggled liquor and smoking.

Miyako wore her sunglasses and wrapped her hair in scarves and kept her chin held high, but the strain showed in her hollow eyes, her lack of appetite. She went out less and less, refusing even the invitations from the other women in the block to attend church, to join in efforts to spruce up the barrack, to share precious hoarded tea.

Aiko came to visit one warm afternoon in April. She had surprised those who knew her by being one of the first to take a job. All the internees were encouraged to work, but unskilled workers were paid eight dollars per month, a sum that made Miyako curl her lip contemptuously since, as she told Lucy, she used to spend more than that on hats alone. Still, most people jumped at the chance of a job, any job at all; former merchants labored as mess-hall workers; artists toiled alongside ministers in ditches and warehouses. Those lucky enough to have a skill that was in demand—doctors, nurses, teachers, dentists—were paid for their labor the sum of nineteen dollars per month.

Aiko had secured a position in the net factory inside Manzanar, which made camouflage nets for use by the troops fighting overseas. The nets were made by weaving strips of fabric through a large mesh that was suspended from the ceiling twenty feet high, and the workers had to wear masks to prevent the fibers from aggravating their lungs, but the pay was better than most jobs available inside the camp—and more important, Aiko said she liked to stay busy.

"You need to get outside," she chided Miyako, as they had tea in Lucy and Miyako's room. The porcelain tea set that had belonged to Renjiro's mother was one of the few luxuries Miyako had shipped to Manzanar. "You're even more pale than before!"

It was true; most people spent time outside in the sun, from sheer boredom and a desire for a change of scenery, if no other reason, but Miyako stayed in her room nearly all the time. Lucy herself had developed lines where the sun browned her skin below her sleeves from roaming the avenues and building sites from breakfast until dinnertime.

"You need a job," Aiko said decisively, ignoring Miyako's protests. "Soon Lucy will be in school, and then you'll have nothing to occupy your time at all."

The start of school was imminent and unavoidable. Lucy had enjoyed her freedom from the classroom, but already evacuee parents were organizing classes and nursery schools. Each block had a barrack set aside for use as a recreation center, and some of the men were building simple tables and benches for the children to use. There were rumors of classroom materials arriving any day, and donations of used textbooks, paper and other supplies had been made by churches.

Lucy had no wish to return to a classroom—her final days in school in Los Angeles had left a sour taste. Besides, she was learning to relish her freedom, the ability to leave their barrack in the morning and return whenever she felt like it, sometimes taking her lunch in other blocks' mess halls. She'd met kids from all over, compared experiences with children whose families fished off Bainbridge Island in Washington or grew produce in the central valley or attended schools in Sacramento much like hers. She moved from group to group with ease, but it was her own company she kept the most, because Manzanar had stoked in her the explorer's spirit that she had only begun to discover in the weeks following Pearl Harbor.

As she watched workers put the finishing touches on the auditorium being built near the entrance one day, she noticed a sign posted on the newly constructed façade. It advertised for boys to serve as runners, delivering documents and mail all around the camp. Interested parties should come to the main administrative office.

"I'm going to the library, Mama," she said the next morning after breakfast, hoping Miyako would neither notice nor remark upon the extra care she'd taken getting dressed: she was wearing her best skirt and blouse and had rubbed a little rouge into her cheeks and borrowed her mother's pearl brooch, which she shielded with the strap of her book bag until Miyako shrugged and turned away; then she slipped the bag from her shoulder and left it lying on her bed. She'd mentioned the library because she thought it was least likely to draw an objection—in fact she *had* been a frequent visitor to the trove of donated volumes ever since a few volunteers had begun collecting and cataloging them in a block rec hall. "I'll be back in time for dinner."

Lucy practiced her speech on the walk to the main administration building. Sure, they wanted boys—that just meant that she would have to be particularly convincing in her appeal. In her experience, even allowing for the bitter disappointment of the loss of her turn as lunch monitor, girls were more adept at all the tasks at her old school than boys, who were far more prone to cutting up and slacking off. Here, at least, no one could deny her the job because of her race. Taking a deep breath, she straightened her skirt and collar, tucked her hair behind her ears and went inside.

A woman wearing half-moon glasses looked up from her typewriter and gave Lucy an efficient smile. "May I help you?"

"Yes, please. My name is Lucy Takeda and I would like to apply for the job of courier that you are advertising."

The lady raised her eyebrows and looked Lucy up and down. "I am sorry, but Deputy Chief Griswold is hiring boys only for that position."

At that moment a tall, sandy-haired man stepped out of an office in the rear of the building. "Did I hear my name?" he asked in a friendly voice. "Well, hello, young lady. Is there something I can do for you?"

"Yes, sir, I would like a job as a courier. I know that you are looking for boys, but, sir, soon we will be in school and you will need additional help to take care of all the deliveries that pile up during the day."

Deputy Chief Griswold's smile widened. "Is that so?"

Lucy risked a glance at the secretary, whose fingers were still above the typewriter keys. "Yes," she said hurriedly. "And also, girls are smarter than boys, and so there is less risk that I will fall behind in my studies if I work for you."

The chief laughed out loud, a booming sound that filled the office. "Well, Mrs. Kadonada, what do you say to that? Mrs. Kadonada has a boy about your age who is already working for us." He winked at Lucy, and for a moment she was afraid she'd just insulted the secretary and ruined her chances at the job, but then Mrs. Kadonada laughed too.

"I might agree with you sometimes," she said, not unkindly. "My son is fifteen—how old are you?"

"I am fourteen. I was in eighth grade in Los Angeles. I made very good marks there."

This was not entirely true, but Lucy figured there was no way the administration would know that. Besides, she never had trouble understanding the material; she just got bored and allowed her mind to wander. If she had a job to look forward to—a chance to get outside rather than being cooped up all day—she was sure she could do better.

"What's your name, young lady?"

"Lucy Takeda."

"And how long have you been at Manzanar?"

Lucy counted quickly in her mind. "Five weeks and three days."

"You know your way around pretty well?"

"Yes, sir."

"Tell you what, Mrs. K," the deputy chief said. "Let's give this girl a try. See what she's made of."

Already the secretary was reaching into her in-box for a stack of letters. Lucy felt the first stirring of excitement and anticipation that she'd experienced in a long time.

The job was a welcome break in the monotony of camp life. Mrs. Kadonada and the other steno workers gave her memos, letters, packages and signs to be delivered to every corner of the camp: to the various administrative buildings and the staff quarters, the net factory, the warehouses, the motor pool and garages. Lucy delivered papers to every block captain and block recreation center; to the volunteer-built churches throughout the camp; to the theater and fire station and the various makeshift nursery schools and classrooms that were springing up throughout the camp. On the other side of the camp, more than a mile from the administrative buildings, were the temporary hospital and the Children's Village for the children who came from orphanages in Los Angeles and San Francisco.

Lucy loved everything about the job, from the neat stacks of papers with their mimeograph smell and purple ink, to the packages and envelopes postmarked from as far away as Washington, D.C. She loved the stamps and ink pads that Mrs. Kadonada sometimes allowed her to use on incoming mail, the small postal scales, the Teletype and adding machines.

But most of all, Lucy loved walking along the avenues, admiring the gardens created by the internees. Seed was provided for victory gardens, but even before the first shoots grew above the soil, the outline of traditional rock gardens began to appear between barracks. Children were put into service to find smooth, round stones down in the creek, and boys carried boulders for the older men whose designs mimicked the gardens they remembered from childhoods spent in Japan. Former gardeners joined forces with stonemasons and landscape designers to create large pond gardens and landscapes reminiscent of towering mountains, but there were also tiny patches of leaning stones set carefully on raked sand, sources of serenity in the midst of the chaos of camp. Young men, impatient and bored and desperate for something to do, learned the principles of the *Sakuteiki* as their elders selected and set stones and borders; it was not uncommon to see men walking with their eyes cast down, searching for the perfect stone.

Lucy waved to the gardeners as she made her deliveries. She loved how the gardens grew and changed with every passing day, how bridges, paths, arches, even "waterfalls" of pebbles slowly emerged from the dusty earth. The gardens were evidence that beauty could exist even here, that meaning could be found in the humblest objects.

She didn't meet Mrs. Kadonada's son until her second week on the job, because they had opposite shifts: he worked in the mornings, and played baseball in the afternoon when Lucy worked. Baseball fever had seized the camp, since there were so few recreational opportunities, and already there were half a dozen leagues. Jessie, according to Mrs. Kadonada, was a crack first baseman, and his coach, Mr. Hayashi, couldn't spare him from the thrice-weekly practices.

But on Thursday, when his team ceded the practice field to other boys' teams, he showed up late in the afternoon as Lucy was returning from her final run of the day. Lucy's first glimpse of him was a figure disappearing at a run around the side of the administration building; a moment later he was back, a squirming, laughing toddler slung over his shoulder. Lucy knew this had to be Mrs. Kadonada's son; not only was he about her age, but he was wearing a Padres baseball cap. He was tall, with a wide grin and a little gap between his front teeth.

When he saw Lucy he stopped abruptly, his grin disappearing, and the little boy tumbled to the ground, coughed with surprise and then started to wail.

"You're fine," Jessie said without looking, and the boy wailed more loudly. A moment later, Mrs. Kadonada hurried out of the building, looking worried.

"Jessie, what on earth have you done to him?"

"He's fine, Mom, he just tripped."

Lucy kept her face impassive; she wasn't about to challenge his story. Besides, there was something intriguing about a boy who would lie before being properly introduced. She shifted subtly, putting a hand on her hip the way she'd seen the high school girls do when there were boys around.

"Is that right." Mrs. Kadonada's skepticism faded when the little boy's tears trailed away and he dusted himself off. "Come here, Bunki, let me see your hands. Oh, no, you're filthy! Jessie, where did you take him?"

Jessie shrugged. "The creek."

Mrs. Kadonada sighed and shook her head. "Lucy, this is my son, Jessie. And this is Bunki Sugimoto, our neighbor. Jessie was supposed to be watching Bunki while his mother does the wash."

"I *did* watch him!" Jessie protested, but he looked directly at Lucy and winked. She felt her face flush with something other than embarrassment.

After that, Jessie occasionally lingered after his shift long enough to run into Lucy—especially if she got there early. If Mrs. Kadonada noticed, she didn't say anything. Mostly, Jessie would toss his baseball in the air and grin and Lucy would pretend to be interested in the newspapers, which were delivered in a twine-bound bundle. When he left, he always said the same thing—"See ya, Luce"—and Lucy would give a half wave. No one else had ever called her Luce, and she thought she might like it.

Those first few minutes of her shift were the best. But as five o'clock neared, her spirits began to sink, and once the vest was hung in the closet next to Mrs. Kadonada's wool coat and she was on her way back to Block Fourteen, Lucy's feet dragged. She dreaded finding her mother in bed late in the afternoon, purple circles under her eyes. Sometimes her mother refused to come to the dining hall and Lucy would have to bring her portion back to the room and coax her to eat. Their barrack neighbors were bewildered by Miyako; since they had stopped trying to include her in their outings and socializing, they seemed to have grown suspicious of her.

One afternoon when the temperature had passed one hundred degrees, Lucy came out of the admin building after her shift to find Jessie sitting in the shade of the porch. When he saw her, he got to his feet and jammed his hands in his pockets. "Hey, Luce. Want to walk down to the creek? It's cooler there."

"But it's almost—" Lucy stopped herself. She was about to point out that it was nearly dinnertime, but that only meant that they'd have the creek to themselves. And being alone with Jessie was an appealing idea, even if it meant she missed dinner. "Never mind. Sure, I'll go."

On the walk through camp, cutting between the warehouses and garages and the security fence on a path that was becoming well-worn, they passed a few kids, stragglers rac-

ing to make it home before the dinner bell. By the time the tree-lined bank came into view, they were alone. Jessie was in the middle of a rambling recounting of a series of grueling drills his coach had recently instituted when he suddenly reached for Lucy's hand. He didn't miss a beat, but his fingers twined with Lucy's and she felt her face flame with something that was both less and more than embarrassment, as she lost track of the conversation.

"Wait," Jessie said, suddenly coming to a stop when they were halfway across the weedy clearing that fronted the creek. "Hear that?"

At first Lucy didn't know what he was talking about, and then the faint sound of laughter reached her ears, coming from down in the creek bank. Deep voices—men, not other kids.

"I've seen them down here before," Jessie said. He didn't let go of her hand, but his face took on a calculating look.

"Are they from your block?"

"They aren't from anyone's block, Luce. They're staff. WRA guys."

"We should go, then," Lucy said, unease prickling her skin. She kept as far away from the staff men as possible, other than Deputy Chief Griswold, who was unfailingly polite to her. The soldiers were larger and louder than Lucy's father or most of the men from her old neighborhood, and the military police all looked alike—unsmiling and angry—in their caps and uniforms. Even the warehouse supervisors and the deliverymen seemed threatening, if only because they were constantly barking orders at the internees and yelling at any kids who got underfoot.

"No, wait." Jessie's sly expression bloomed into a grin. "Come watch this."

And before Lucy could protest, he'd grasped her hand

more tightly and pulled her along at a sprint toward a bank of trees with branches arching down toward the brackish creek. Lucy knew that she could wriggle out of his grip and escape if she wanted to, but it wasn't only exertion that made her short of breath. Being with Jessie was exciting, never more than when he defied the rules.

When they reached the trees, he pulled her against him behind a leaning cypress, the tree blocking the view down to the creek bed.

"Take a look," he whispered against her ear, his breath hot and tingly. "Don't let them see you."

Lucy leaned cautiously around the trunk, her face pressed against the rough bark and Jessie's hand resting lightly at her waist. Her heart pounded in her chest so hard she was sure he could feel it.

Five men sat leaning against rocks or cross-legged in the silt, smoking. While she watched, one threw a spent cigarette into the brown water that eddied lazily around a downed, dead tree. This late in the summer, the flow was reduced to a trickle, and the men had taken advantage of the tame current to cool a tub of beers that was anchored in place with a pile of flat rocks. The men were barefoot, the sleeves of their undershirts rolled up in the heat. Their uniform shirts and hats, along with caps and shoes and socks, were strewn along the dry bed. A small pile of personal effects included watches, wallets and cigarettes.

"—I told her the blonde was her *sister!*" one of the men exclaimed loudly, prompting a round of guffaws, the punch line of some drunken joke. The men slapped their knees and drank from their bottles and wiped their mouths with their arms, the conversation taken up by several of them at once.

Lucy ducked back around the tree and found Jessie watch-

ing her expectantly. He didn't take his hand away from her waist.

"Who are they?"

"Staff. Fat cats." Jessie grimaced. "The guys in charge. See that big guy? That's Mr. Van Dorn. He's a section supervisor, but all he does is take smoke breaks and order everyone around. And those other guys are almost as bad."

Jessie's contempt felt dangerous and strangely thrilling, but before Lucy could respond, he leaned close and said softly, "When you see me turn around, run like hell. I'll catch up."

"Jessie!" Lucy whispered fiercely, grabbing the tails of his shirt tightly in her fist. "What are you going to do?"

"Nothing. Just a prank."

"Don't—"

But then something so unexpected happened that Lucy stopped protesting.

Jessie kissed her.

It was brief—only a fraction of a second. His lips, brushing against hers, were warm and silky and slightly damp, and his eyelashes fluttered against her cheek, and Lucy was so startled that she lost her grip on his shirt, and before she could react, he bolted down the creek bank, whooping like an Indian. His sneakers skidded over the loose gravel and the men's heads whipped around in surprise.

Lucy put her hand to her mouth, touching the place he'd kissed her, a strange heat keeping her immobilized in a kind of liquid trance until she saw Jessie leap over the men's beer stash and land on a rock a few feet from the men's abandoned clothes. The rock slipped under his feet and for a moment he teetered, and Lucy was sure he was going to fall. Two of the men scrambled to their feet and one of them swiped Jessie's arm as he danced out of the way, regaining his balance just in time.

"Run!" he yelled, and Lucy obeyed, spinning around just after she saw him grab something off the ground and take off, the two men in hot pursuit behind him while their companions hollered encouragement.

Lucy ran as hard as she ever had, straight for the edge of Block Five. In seconds, Jessie had caught up with her. He grabbed her hand and they rounded the corner of the women's latrine, nearly knocking over a mother and her little girl, and then they ran straight through a kitchen garden, Lucy trying to avoid stepping on the squash vines that wound between the rows.

She was laughing along with Jessie when they finally slowed.

"They won't follow," Jessie said. "They're too drunk and slow."

"How do you know?"

He shrugged, never taking his eyes off her. "I've done it before."

"Jessie!" Lucy was genuinely shocked. "What if they come after you?"

He snorted. "They'll never know it was me. We all look alike to them."

Lucy considered for a moment. "Well, what did you take?"

Jessie beamed as he dug in his pocket and pulled out a nearly full pack of cigarettes. Lucy gaped.

"All that—for *cigarettes?*"

Jessie flipped the pack and caught it before he shoved it back in his pocket.

"It's all about getting away with it," he said, grinning his splendid grin, and when he took her hand again, it felt like the most natural thing in the world.

11

THE OPENING OF THE JUNIOR AND HIGH schools had been rumored for weeks, but delays in the arrival of civilian teachers, as well as the completion of the buildings, had slowed things down. Lucy had mixed feelings. Mrs. Kadonada had already told her that she could continue several afternoons a week, as long as she kept up with her studies. But Jessie was quitting the courier job, since he'd have time only for school and baseball—and he was a grade ahead of her. Lucy would see him only at lunch and recess, if then.

Jessie came to the office near the end of his shift a few days later and announced that practice had been called off because one of the younger boys had fainted in the heat.

"I'm glad you stopped by, actually," Mrs. Kadonada said. "There's someone I'd like the two of you to meet."

The door to the back offices opened and several people emerged with the director of education, himself a relative newcomer.

"Lucy, Jessie, meet our new first-grade teacher, Mrs. Purcell. And her daughter Irene—she's in the same grade as you, Lucy."

"How do you do," Mrs. Purcell said tightly. She was a plain woman, short and squat in a brown shirtwaist dress, but her daughter was lovely, with hair as pale as milkweed silk and two rows of ruched grosgrain ribbon around the neckline of her dress.

"They've come all the way from Kansas City," Deputy Chief Griswold said, rubbing his hands together, a gesture that Lucy had come to understand signaled his impatience; he was anxious to get back to work.

"We've been in Reno this week. We stayed in the Golden Annex and I got to go in the Bank Club," the girl said proudly. "I had a Shirley Temple and they have these little cakes—"

"That's quite enough, Irene," Mrs. Purcell interrupted.

The girl merely shrugged, snapping the gum she was chewing. Lucy blinked in surprise—she was not allowed to chew gum, because Miyako considered it an appalling habit.

"Lucy, I was thinking, why don't you show Irene around this afternoon?" Mrs. Kadonada said. "There's really not much to deliver, and Jessie can take care of it in the morning."

"Oh," Mrs. Purcell said dismissively. "That's very nice. Very much appreciated. Only, there is another member of the staff with a daughter Irene's age—"

"Mrs. Swift." Mr. Griswold supplied the name, avoiding meeting Mrs. Kadonada's gaze.

"And her daughter. I just thought, the two of them, they might have...more in common."

"Betty Swift is only eleven," Mrs. Kadonada said. "Surely—"

"She and Irene will be going to school in Lone Pine together," Mrs. Purcell said pointedly. "With all the other staff children. There's to be a bus. Really, I think that maintaining some degree of…separation is for the best."

She exchanged a cool glance with Deputy Chief Griswold, who cleared his throat uncomfortably.

Lucy felt sorry for Mrs. Kadonada, who looked as though she had been slapped. But it was Jessie who spoke.

"Nice meeting you, Mrs. Purcell, Irene. Come on, Lucy, we're going to be late. Bye, Mom."

He turned around and headed for the door without even saying goodbye to Griswold, and after a split second's deliberation, Lucy followed him. Behind them the screen door slammed, and then they were out in the full force of the sun.

"Just what we need in this place," Jessie said. "Another stuck-up white girl."

Lucy had seen a few kids playing near the staff apartments, riding tricycles and playing in a sandbox that had been constructed for them inside the borders of the staff gardens. But she hadn't noticed anyone near her age. "Why, are there others?"

"Yeah, Mom keeps trying to make me meet them when they come in to do their paperwork. Even though they don't want anything to do with us—or at least their parents don't."

Lucy was silent for a minute, remembering the way Yvonne had treated her in the days leading up to evacuation. "You think it'll be better when the war's over?"

Jessie shrugged, his hands jammed in his pockets. "Guess it depends on whether people ever figure out we're not the enemy. I wish they'd let us fight—I'd enlist."

"You're not old enough!"

"I *will* be," Jessie said fiercely.

"Well, I wouldn't. Why would I volunteer after they locked us up in here?"

"You better not let anyone hear you say that. They'll send you to Japan and you'll have to swear the emperor is a god."

Lucy made a face. "I don't speak any Japanese, so it doesn't matter—I won't know what they're saying."

They were walking down the wide firebreak road between blocks, the sun beating down on them. It was still half an hour before lunchtime, and already Lucy's forehead was slick with perspiration and her cotton blouse clung to her skin. Being with Jessie always made her feel even warmer than she already was. Ever since he kissed her, she had replayed the moment over and over in her memory, but there hadn't been another private walk, another chance for him to hold her hand. Maybe he wasn't interested anymore. Maybe he'd found some other girl.

"So where are we going, anyway?" she asked, as casually as she could.

Jessie laughed. "I just said that to get us out of there—I didn't want to get stuck with that girl."

Lucy took a breath and tried not to sound nervous. "Want to have lunch in our block today?"

"Sure."

He sounded happy enough with the idea, and Lucy congratulated herself as they walked toward Block Fourteen. But a surprise waited outside their barrack: Miyako was standing in the shade of the overhang, dressed in her best suit. Her peplumed jacket nipped in at her tiny waist; the skirt grazed her knees, not quite daringly. It was a shade of blue called *cerulean,* according to her mother, evoking June skies and the spray of waves. Miyako had released her hair from its careful paper twists, the curls blooming at her forehead and highlighting her fine features. Lucy couldn't remember the last time she'd seen her mother dressed up, and she looked both radiant and a little lost.

"Lucy!" she said when she spotted them. "Thank heavens. I was just coming to look for you. Hello," she added, almost as an afterthought, nodding at Jessie.

"This is my friend Jessie Kadonada," Lucy said uncertainly. "I invited him to have lunch in our mess hall."

"Very nice to meet you," Miyako said distractedly. "Lucy, where is my makeup box? I have an interview!"

Lucy blinked with surprise, then chagrin. She'd snuck her mother's cosmetics box the day before, putting on a little lip-stick and eyeliner before leaving for her shift, and when her mother stirred in her sleep, she'd stuck it under her bed and forgotten it. "Oh—I'll get it for you."

She raced into the building and pushed aside the curtain, then got on her knees and retrieved the small box. She had pulled her bedcovers up in the same haphazard way she usu-ally did, and now she wished she had done as her mother nagged her to do, and made it up neatly, in case Jessie came inside. In fact, her entire half of the room was a mess, and there was no time to do anything about it.

Back outside, her mother was chatting amiably with Jessie.

"I was just telling your friend that Mrs. Narita has found something suitable for me. There is to be a dress factory, right here in the camp. They will need experienced seamstresses. Oh, thank goodness, you found it." She took the box from Lucy and gave her a nervous smile. Then she surprised Lucy by saying, "Do I look all right, *suzume?*"

Lucy blushed, embarrassed by the ludicrousness of the question. It was like asking if the sun was bright enough or if the distant mountains were tall, and she hoped Jessie didn't mistake the question for false modesty.

"You look very nice," she said softly. Miyako didn't need makeup, with her flawless, pale skin and perfectly arched brows, her glossy upswept hair. The deep shade of her suit complemented her coloring perfectly, and a stranger would miss the subtle evidence of her apprehension. In fact, the flush of excitement and nervousness hinted at something else entirely, something sensual and sly, her beauty provocative, her eyes brimming with intimations.

"Thank you, dear. I am hoping to get a position making patterns, what do you think of that? Skilled work, nineteen dollars a month."

"Wow," Lucy said. That was almost the highest pay grade. Auntie Aiko must have pulled some strings. Recently, Aiko had begun spending time with a man who was a member of the community council, a widower in his sixties named Roy Hamaguchi who had owned a grocery store in Victorville before the war—perhaps he had used his influence. "When can you start?"

Miyako laughed, a feathery sound that Lucy had not heard in a long time. "Let me get the job first! But I know they need to hire people fast. Aiko says they have received thirty-eight industrial sewing machines."

Lucy felt a stirring of hope. Her mother's sewing skills were legendary. Though Lucy's father was happy to buy Miyako all the clothes she wanted from the best stores, she loved to sew her own, combining bits from different patterns to make something wholly original. She favored Vogue patterns, especially the Schiaparelli and Lanvin designs suitable only for experts, and modified them to suit herself. A fitted jacket might be composed of six separate pieces in the front and back alone, not even counting the sleeves or placket or collar.

"Where will the job be?" Jessie asked.

"They're setting up a building in Block Four, near the warehouses. They're bringing in a man from the garment industry. From New York."

"Why does he want to come all the way from New York?"

"They don't have enough workers, because of the war." She gave them a final smile and turned to go inside. "Well, I had better go finish getting ready. If I don't hurry, I'll be late."

"It was very nice to meet you, Mrs. Takeda," Jessie said formally.

Lucy watched her disappear into the building, trying to quell her nerves. It was the first time her mother had surfaced from her isolation since they had arrived in Manzanar, the first time she'd breached the still surface of her ennui. But Lucy had learned long ago not to trust these bright moods. They never lasted. The glorious hope would shrivel and crack, and Miyako, as stunned as anyone to discover that she was still the victim of her own mind, would slip back into despair, into the darkened bedroom, into the cell of their room in Block Fourteen.

Much later Lucy would learn the official terms, diagnoses that sought to explain these ripe, dangerous, easily shattered moods. Depression was Miyako's known world; mania her occasional frenzied escape. But for now Lucy just saw that Miyako had swung, like the heavy pendulum at the Griffith Observatory high above the Hollywood Hills, to the edge of the orbit of her life, where it felt as though she might break away and go hurtling through space.

"Gosh, your mother's pretty," Jessie said.

"I know. I mean, thanks."

"You look exactly like her," he added, and Lucy felt the warmth creeping along her skin, evaporating her worries. "Come on. I'm starving."

After lunch, a chaotic, noisy affair punctuated by the shrill shrieks of the little boys Lucy sometimes babysat, Jessie suggested walking over to the ball fields. "We can check out the competition."

When they arrived at the stands, however, a little group had already taken the best seats: Irene Purcell, along with half a dozen other Caucasian teenage girls. Lucy recognized some of them from her delivery route, though she'd never exchanged more than a word or two with any of them. When they saw Jessie, a couple of them waved.

"Do you know them?" Lucy asked.

"A little."

"Hey, Jessie," a pudgy redhead called. "Want to sit with us?"

"Nah, it's okay. We're not staying. Got to be somewhere else."

Lucy smiled to herself, her annoyance at the girl's flirting overshadowed by the way Jessie had said *we,* the ease with which he included her in his fibbing.

"Oh, are you working?" another girl said. "I can't believe you guys work for them anyway when they don't pay you. It's like you're their slave."

Lucy didn't respond, even when she noticed Irene smirking at her. She wondered what the girls would say if they knew that her father had had his own factory, that once, on her birthday, he'd arranged for the toy department at Bullock's to devote a clerk and the doll counter to her while she picked out a dozen outfits for her birthday doll and a wardrobe lined with genuine China silk to store them in. That her father had driven a gleaming Mercury, which, after his death, was stored in the garage and then sold for a fraction of its worth to the men who came to the neighborhood in the final desperate days before evacuation.

She wanted to let it go, wanted to believe she was unaffected by their casual cruelty. Tried to remember that she was the daughter of Miyako Takeda, famous in her neighborhood for her perfect complexion and tiny waist and mysterious smile. And that Jessie had chosen *her,* not any of them. But still, their condescension cut deep.

"You have a thing," she said to the redhead, tapping the corner of her upper lip.

The girl blinked. "What?"

"A…smudge or something. What did you have for lunch? It looks like gravy."

The girl blushed furiously and rubbed at her mouth. Lucy stared directly at Irene and smiled, deciding that even if she couldn't always keep them from getting under her skin, she would never let it show.

On the other side of the ball field, there was an equipment shed built from wood salvaged from barracks construction, and behind it someone had built a pair of long benches with rough notched legs. Here Jessie and Lucy sat, out of sight of the players and the observers in the stands, and Lucy lit her first cigarette using the book of matches Jessie offered her.

Jessie watched her. "Have you smoked before?"

Lucy considered trying to pretend she had, but she knew there was more to smoking than met the eye. Instead she shrugged and puffed as she lit the cigarette, holding it between her index and middle fingers, as she'd seen the older girls do.

The smoke was intriguing and shocking at once. She felt it travel down her throat and willed herself not to react. She held Jessie's gaze and closed her mouth on the smoke and tensed all her muscles, curling her toes and stiffening her shoulders against the cough. Her eyes watered and she held her breath and in a moment the urge passed.

Jessie smiled.

After a while, they ground the cigarette butts into the dirt. Lucy liked the way the toe of her shoe felt twisting into the fine soil, crushing the filter.

"Have you had a boyfriend before?" Jessie asked. "Back in Los Angeles?"

Lucy knew she was supposed to be coy, to play it cool. *Who wants to know?* she could imagine the high school girls saying, or *What's it to you?*

But it wasn't like that with Jessie. When he kissed her, it had felt…important.

"No," she said, her voice barely more than a whisper. "You're my first."

This time when they kissed, Lucy forgot about everything that was wrong. When Jessie's arms were around her, he was all there was in the world.

Lucy stood on a chair to drape her blouse over the partition and air out the smoke. She meant to take down the blouse before her mother got home, but when Miyako returned a little after six o'clock, Lucy was dozing, her finger marking her place in a book she'd borrowed from the lending library.

"I got the job," Miyako said. "I already started working, they asked me to begin right then and there. You should see the sewing machines, Lucy—they're brand-new. They can hold a thread cone this big."

She held her fingers six inches apart, her voice filled with wonder as she talked about the machines, the converted barrack, the bolts of yard goods wrapped in paper and stacked along the wall, the cutting tables with the heavy scissors, and the bins on the floor for collecting scraps. "Nothing is to be wasted," she said. "Some of the others are piecing the scraps into a quilt. They're going to use surplus wool as batting."

"Do you like the other ladies?"

"They're fine. I have more experience than all of them except a lady from Bakersfield. Miu something. She worked in a children's garment factory." Miyako sniffed, dismissive of the others' skills or irritated at being bested, or both.

"And your boss?"

Her mother's mouth pulled down faintly. "My *supervisor*. Mrs. Driscoll bites her nails. We will see what she knows of sewing."

Lucy turned away, heeding her mother's imperious tone.

"And Mr. George Rickenbocker. The businessman from New York," Miyako went on. "He was there. He walks among the tables, watching us work, like this." She clasped her hands behind her back, and did a pantomime, walking the length of their tiny room between their beds. "He is an important man, *suzume*. A big boss."

"Won't he be going back to New York soon? To run his company?"

Miyako wrinkled her nose. "He will be staying here for several months to establish the business. He has taken an apartment in the staff quarters. We'll see how he likes the desert, after his fancy New York City life."

Lucy watched her mother talk and gesture. Miyako could be witty, even saucy, when she was in her best moods. Maybe this job would be good for her; maybe she would make friends. She still had a chance to be normal, to shrug off the cloak of isolation she'd pulled around herself since they'd arrived in camp. Lucy thought of the clusters of women in the ironing house, gossiping and laughing over their work, or even fussing over sick children together. Sharing moments of levity and of grief. Wasn't that the way a woman's life was supposed to be?

As if sensing her thoughts, Miyako placed her hand on

Lucy's cheek. Lucy was startled to realize that she had grown in recent months; she was almost at eye level with her mother.

"You must be careful during the day, when I am working," her mother said, the levity suddenly gone from her voice, the familiar unease tightening her features. She cupped Lucy's face and stared intently into her eyes. Lucy wanted to grasp her mother's good mood and cling to it, but Miyako's mind followed its own ever-changing rhythms.

Still, her mother's request came from nowhere. Since their arrival in the camp, it was Lucy who had ventured out each day: enduring the freezing cold, the stinging dust storms; waiting in line at the mess hall to get food for both of them; buying her mother licorice or packets of hairpins at the general store when Deputy Chief Griswold occasionally gave her a dime. Lucy was careful in the way of someone who knew that she could not leave the square mile, surrounded by razor-wire fencing, in which she lived; who never forgot that in the towers above them, armed soldiers stared down and watched her movements.

Staring into her mother's eyes, with their long, thick lashes and perfect swipes of eyeliner, Lucy understood that even on her worst days, her mother loved her deeply and would stop at nothing to protect her.

"Yes," Lucy whispered. "I will be careful."

Her mother tightened her grip, her fingernails digging into the soft skin beneath Lucy's chin. "You must," she said. "You *must*."

12

PATTY SIPPED AT HER GLASS OF CHENIN BLANC, her third. She hadn't been much of a drinker before Jay. She hadn't been much of *anything* before Jay, just another single girl in the city, waiting for a man to come along before making any real life decisions.

When Patty was younger, she had allowed herself to imagine what it would be like when she met that perfect man, the one who would see in her what everyone else was missing. As the years of awkward dates passed and boyfriends came and went, she began to wonder if the right man for her even existed. Jay—thank God for him—had come just as she was beginning to give up.

It had taken until she was nearly thirty-two, but she had found him, introduced by friends at a raucous house party that she had been on the verge of escaping. Jay got her a beer and led her out on the rickety wooden deck and pointed out the houses of famous people far off in Pacific Heights, then admitted he'd made the whole thing up to impress her.

Jay was only thirty-nine and already an associate partner, and he reveled in his family's pride in him. Jay wanted children—two, three, *four* of them!—and he called her mother Mrs. T. and brought her flowers from the BART station whenever he came over. Jay fixed whatever broke at her mother's place, and he was the best thing that had ever happened to Patty, by far.

And yet she couldn't bring herself to tell him what she'd found in the album. It was too big, too confusing, too frightening, and she was hardly ready to face the implications herself.

Instead, she kept drinking. She was buzzed and she knew it. Her mother had gone to bed early, claiming not to have slept well the night before. So much for her mother's day off, their planned mother-daughter day. By the time Patty returned from her trip to Forrest's house, her mother was in the backyard in her big straw sun hat, weeding. Patty poured her a tumbler of iced tea and went outside to chat, but Lucy was focused on getting the small rock garden cleared of the matted chaff that accumulated during the spring rains. After a few failed attempts at conversation, Patty gave up and went back inside.

She'd opened the bottle of wine to go with the Chinese takeout she had ordered, but Lucy had declined. Now, the dishes done and her glass topped off, her mother's bedroom door closed and the house silent except for the hum of the dishwasher, Patty retrieved the album labeled MANZANAR from her room and brought it to the kitchen table.

She stared at the photograph mounted on the first page. In it, a hard-built, square-jawed man in his thirties reclined in a metal chair, holding a beer bottle in one hand. On his knee sat a young Japanese woman in a slim skirt and high-heeled pumps and a blouse with a rounded collar. She appeared to balance effortlessly, her legs pressed tightly together, his big, meaty hand resting at her waist. The image was an arresting study in contrasts—the woman's delicate beauty and vulnerability measured against the man's raw, almost predatory energy, but it was the caption that made Patty catch her breath.

Miyako Takeda and Internal Security Officer George Rickenbocker. August 1942.

Miyako Takeda was her grandmother.

Patty allowed herself to absorb the image for a moment. Her grandmother was beautiful. Head-turning, drop-dead gorgeous. But what was her picture doing in an album that had belonged to the dead man? Who was the officer who held her against him in an uneasy embrace? And most importantly—had Lucy lied about her relationship with Reginald Forrest?

Even if Miyako's presence in the album was a chance coincidence, Patty still found it suddenly far more difficult to believe her mother's denials about going to see Forrest. And the possibility that Lucy was lying filled Patty with dread.

Patty stared at her grandmother's perfect, heart-shaped face, trying to find any resemblance among her, Lucy and herself. But there was none. Miyako possessed an elegance that seemed all the more striking given the vulnerability of her pose in the photo. Patty would give anything to be able to pull that off, the way the angle of her calves lengthened and accentuated her legs without calling attention. Lucy was plain, even before you took into account her disfigurement: her body was thick and shapeless, her hair chopped straight in a wash-and-wear style, the good side of her face fleshy. Patty had always struggled with weight herself, and for the most part kept the extra pounds at bay, and she was conscientious about her hair and makeup. She figured she was a seven on a good day, a solid five when she didn't try. Average. Jay called her beautiful, but Jay was kind.

Turning the pages of the album, she found Miyako in half a dozen other photos, all of them from a series of gatherings in 1942 and early 1943. Patty couldn't deny the likelihood that her grandmother and the dead man had known each other. Her heart raced as she flipped page after page. When she reached the end of the album, she took a long sip of her wine before turning back to the start.

In the first photo, Miyako's face was pensive; she seemed to be staring at someone outside the photograph to the right, and her lips were slightly parted as though she were whispering a confidence. Meanwhile, Rickenbocker's head was thrown back in what appeared to be raucous laughter.

In other photos, she posed with several other Japanese women, all of them young, all of them pretty. They wore bright lipstick smiles and cheap beads at their necks, their hair twisted and curled. The final photograph in the album was labeled Valentine's Day 1943, and it showed a man identified as Benny Van Dorn with his arm slung around a short, plump girl's shoulders, looking drunk and leering at the camera.

Benny Van Dorn. Something clicked in Patty's mind, a stirring of familiarity, and then it came to her: Benny Van Dorn was a member of the San Francisco Board of Supervisors. She was pretty sure he represented her mother's district, in fact. Could it be the same man? The age was about right. She remembered the election because Van Dorn had narrowly beaten a candidate who was enmeshed in a high-profile bribery scandal.

Lucy had never mentioned the election, or Van Dorn, for that matter, but then again her mother had no interest in politics. Still, if it really was him, that was *two* people from Manzanar who lived nearby in San Francisco, and her mother had never spoken about either of them. Patty's stomach twisted with anxiety. There was something here, some connection between all these people and Forrest's death.

The background of many of the photos was a cramped office, the most arresting feature of which was the snow-topped mountain rising far in the distance outside the window. Young men, all of them white, and half a dozen pretty, young Japanese girls crowded onto a sofa and chairs. A Japanese boy of twelve or thirteen appeared in a couple of the photographs. Only he and Rickenbocker wore civilian clothes; the other men wore military-style uniforms.

Reginald Forrest was in only a couple of the photos, and Patty didn't even spot his name among the captions until her second pass through the album. He was a pleasant-looking young man with a handsome if bland face. In one of the shots, he was caught in profile, almost as though he had been turning away from the photographer at the time of the snap. In the other, he posed between two other men holding bottles of beer.

The album seemed to chronicle a series of parties and get-togethers that had taken place over six months at Manzanar. Patty doubted that fraternizing between the staff and internees was sanctioned or even allowed, and she wondered who arranged and hosted these events. Most of the girls looked as though they were there by choice, their pouty smiles and provocative poses suggesting they enjoyed their role. Miyako was the exception. Compared to the younger girls, she seemed far more sophisticated; her clothes were elegant and fit her well. She eschewed their cheap baubles and low-cut blouses, but in every photograph of Rickenbocker, he had eyes only for her.

After going through the pages twice, Patty set the album aside and picked up the other one. It chronicled Forrest's life leading up to the war. The last pages held his official War Relocation Authority staff portrait and a group photo, thirty or so men and a few women posing in front of half-built rows of barracks, with the spectacular mountains in the distance. The rest of the pages were filled with publicity photos and magazine clippings from before the war. Forrest had appeared as "Boy #2" in a film called *Frontier Stagecoach,* and what appeared to be a slightly bigger role—"Officer Timmons"—in *The Last Princess.* Small parts, evidence of a film career that never got off the ground before the war and didn't continue afterward. Whatever Reg had done since 1943, it had ended here, with his gym, his small life, his shitty apartment. His volatile girlfriend and crabby landlady.

Patty went back to the first album, to the one photo where Reg posed with two other men, their arms slung casually around each other's shoulders. The caption read, "Reg Forrest, George Rickenbocker, Benny Van Dorn and Jessie Kadonada."

There he was, barely visible in the background, the young boy who appeared in some of the other photos, sitting at the edge of the couch, head down, prying the top off a bottle. Patty wondered what he was doing in the midst of these gatherings, like a mascot of sorts.

Patty closed the album and slid it to the center of the kitchen table. Her grandmother had apparently known Forrest quite well at the camp, though if these parties were illicit, maybe it wasn't surprising that Lucy didn't know about them. Or maybe Lucy was ashamed of her mother's behavior. Was it possible her mother had a boyfriend? Patty's grandfather had died before the war; she didn't remember ever seeing a picture of him.

Tomorrow, when her mother got home from work, Patty would show her the photos and ask her some questions. But first, she would need to find out a little more. What had happened to her mother during the war? How had she met Patty's father? What happened to him?

Patty stood up and had to grab the counter as dizziness unsteadied her. She got the pad of paper that her mother kept by the phone, and a pen, and as she sat down, she poured the last of the wine into her glass. Then she started to make a list.

In the morning, Patty looked at the piece of paper from the night before, her handwriting more florid and loopy than usual. Certainly messier than when she was sober. She pushed the hair out of her eyes, feeling the beginnings of a headache, and drank a glass of water before studying the list.

George Rickenbocker—Miyako?
Reginald Forrest (Dead!!)
Benny Van Dorn—Same one?
Jessie???
Girls?
Miyako Takeda. Pretty. Shoes. Thin.
Mom? Did she?

Patty sucked in her breath, staring at her handwriting. She remembered writing the list the night before, sounding out the name Rickenbocker and drawing the line to signify the relationship with Miyako. She did not remember the rest, especially that last line.

Did she?

Her drunk self wondered if her mother had killed a man. What did her sober self think?

An hour later, teeth brushed and her hair pulled back in a tight bun, Patty sat with the phone cord threaded through her fingers, drinking the remains of her coffee over ice. She had been on hold long enough for her heart to stop pounding, long enough to doodle a series of cubes on a notepad, carefully shaded, their sides tapered in vanishing-point perspective, just as she had learned in high school art class. She was so absorbed in the drawing that when the man came back on the line, his throat clearing startled her.

"Miss Stapleton?"

"Yes?"

"Sorry about that, it took me a while to find the right reel. So. That's *Van Dorn, V-A-N* space *D-O-R-N*. Benjamin."

"Yes. I mean, I can't be positive, but Benny's not short for anything else, is it?"

"No—no, I don't think so," the man said. He really was very nice; in fact, Patty thought they might be having a little phone flirtation. She forgot for a minute the very serious nature of what she was doing, that she was betraying her mother and possibly committing a crime. "Benjamin Van Dorn. And George Rickenbocker. And you need this by when?"

"Well—the article is supposed to run this Sunday." Really, Patty had no idea how long it took to write a newspaper feature, or what happened once it was written. "And I need to turn it in by tomorrow. If I can."

"That should be no problem. I can probably call you in about an hour."

"That's really nice of you. Seriously."

"Well, your taxpayer dollars at work, right?" He laughed. He seemed remarkably jolly for a government employee.

Patty thanked him and settled the phone back in its cradle, surprised her ploy had worked. She had said she was fact-checking for an article, but it didn't seem like citizen records should be that easy to consult. And it was true that all she was trying to confirm was that it was the same Van Dorn, because that was about as far as she had gotten. And she'd asked about Rickenbocker too, with the vague idea that if she got more information on him, she might be able to look him up somehow. Her grandmother's lover. He could easily still be alive. Odds were slim that he was local, but still…

Patty's thoughts tumbled and churned, her hangover making them difficult to organize. Finding Rickenbocker, even asking her mother about him—it wouldn't help them build a stronger case to convince Inspector Torre that Lucy had nothing to do with Forrest's death. Patty's curiosity might even uncover information she didn't really want to know, dark truths about her grandmother and the war years. Still, she had a vague idea that the other men in the album might have the key to the connection between Reg and her mother… if there was one.

While she waited for him to call back with the information, Patty made a halfhearted effort on the wedding favors. She gathered the edges of an organza circle with a running stitch, stuffed it with birdseed and tied a ribbon to hold it shut. Each favor took way longer than it should and was mind-numbingly boring. By the time the phone rang, she'd only finished three.

"Well, I have a little bad news for you, Miss Stapleton." He sounded genuinely regretful, and Patty's stomach tightened. "Benjamin Van Dorn's middle name is Walter. But George Rickenbocker died while he was at the Manzanar Relocation Camp. It happened on March 2, 1943—I'm looking at the report right now."

Patty stilled, her fingers midtwist around the phone cord. "How did it happen?"

"Well…I guess I can tell you, since it would have been in the papers—nothing you couldn't find yourself with a little digging. He was killed with a pair of sewing shears—stabbed in the throat. The killer was a resident of the camp. She left a note confessing to the crime."

Patty swallowed, foreboding suddenly making it hard to breathe. "What was her name?"

"Miyako Takeda. Says here she hanged herself the next day."

13

Manzanar
July 1942

AFTER A FEW WEEKS AT HER NEW JOB, SOME-
thing changed in Miyako. Lucy had gone to dinner alone one
night after waiting through the first meal shift for her mother
to return from work. She'd finally given up and gone to eat
with the second shift, but when she returned, she found her
mother sitting on her bed, still in her good clothes.

"Where have you been?" Lucy asked, setting down the
plate of food she had brought home for her mother.

"Mr. Rickenbocker walked me home." She rubbed her
forearms as though she was cold, despite the fact that the temperature had climbed to almost a hundred degrees that day.

"Why?"

"Because it was getting dark."

"People walk in the dark all the time."

This was true; the path to the latrines was lit through the

night, both by the bulbs wired to the buildings and by the searchlights that regularly swept the streets from the guard towers. But it wasn't even dark yet. The last glow of twilight still came through the window.

"I didn't ask him to," Miyako said tensely. "But he is our boss. I work for him, Lucy. I cannot refuse his offer to see me home."

Lucy remained silent as Miyako got up and began removing the pins from her hair, dropping them into a little dish on the dresser, her hands flitting with manic energy. Then she examined herself in the mirror, inspecting her flawless skin as though looking for a blemish only she could see. There was something unsettled about her appearance, but Lucy couldn't put her finger on it. Her lipstick was faded but still in place; her stockings had no runs, a small triumph in this time of scarcity, and yet something seemed out of place.

"Does he walk other ladies home too?" she asked in a small voice.

"How would I know?" Miyako asked grimly. "I don't have time to watch them all day."

"To watch *who* all day?"

"Mr. Rickenbocker and the others." Miyako glanced at Lucy. Her eyes were bright, her expression brittle. Her mood was shifting again, right before Lucy's eyes. "The other men. His friends."

"What friends? You mean, in the dress shop?"

Miyako *tsk*ed with annoyance. "No, *suzume*. Why would there be men in the dress shop? Mr. Rickenbocker has friends on the security staff, and they gather at the end of the day near our building. Sometimes, outside in the afternoon, to smoke."

Lucy thought of the men she and Jessie had spied on down by the creek, their drunken laughter carrying through the hot afternoon. She'd seen them a few other times after their shifts were over, playing cards in folding chairs pulled into the shade or driving around in the command truck, whistling at pretty girls. They'd never given her a second look, and Jessie's words echoed in her head: *We all look alike to them.*

"He spends a lot of time with that section-two supervisor. Tall man with a neckline like this, from fat." Miyako drew her hand across the back of her neck and Lucy knew instantly who she was talking about. Supervisor Van Dorn, from the creek. He wasn't fat so much as overdeveloped, with muscular arms and a massive chest. Lucy had seen him throw packets of Life Savers into the crowd of boys playing baseball, laughing when the candies fell to the dusty ground.

That night, the anxious flutter of her mother's hands and the memory of the red-faced soldiers scrambling after Jessie kept Lucy awake long into the night, wondering how they would escape the notice of the camp staff until the war finally ended and everything went back to the way it was supposed to be. George Rickenbocker. Benny Van Dorn. Lucy had no way of knowing, at that moment, that someday those names would be seared into her memory.

Miyako started coming home late several nights a week, missing dinner and smelling like cigarettes and the whiskey Lucy's father used to drink. On these nights she would say little and go straight to bed, pulling the covers up over her shoulders even though the room was stifling. By morning she would disappear entirely, hidden in a cocoon of sheets. She never went to the mess hall for breakfast anymore, saying that the ladies made tea at work.

Lucy's courier services were only required a couple times a week now that the deputy chief had hired a second assistant. Lucy took over all the household tasks—the washing and ironing and cleaning that her mother seemed too exhausted to do herself. Lucy didn't mind the work; it kept her at home where she could keep an eye on Miyako and monitor her comings and goings. But she missed spending her free time with Jessie. She went to his baseball games whenever she could, and he came by early to walk her to school, but they hadn't been able to be alone together since the afternoon they'd kissed behind the equipment shed. Lucy felt torn—her feelings for Jessie were stronger than ever. But so was her worry about her mother.

She decided to go see Miyako at work, unannounced. Maybe that way she could see for herself what was happening, maybe she could solve the mystery of what was slowly draining the life from her mother. When Jessie's practice was canceled one afternoon, she seized the opportunity to ask him if he would go with her.

"I'm worried about her," Lucy confessed. So worried, in fact, that she had been afraid to visit alone, not because she feared getting in trouble, but because she didn't know what she would find. Perhaps it would be nothing—and in some ways this was the most frightening possibility of all, for it meant that Miyako's slow downward spiral was a product only of her own mind. And Lucy had no idea how to fix that.

But if something else was going on—and if Jessie was by her side, helping her figure out what to do—then maybe it wasn't too late. Maybe it could be fixed, and they could go back to that brief moment in time when there had been hope, when Miyako had been poised and beautiful and excited about her job, when Lucy had been able to imagine a future for both of them.

Jessie glanced at her carefully. "Is she sick?"

"Why do you ask?" Lucy said, too quickly. Her mother

had been losing weight, and the circles under her eyes were deepening. Were people beginning to notice?

"No reason. Just...I heard my mother talking to some of the other ladies."

"Talking? About what?"

"About your mom."

Lucy could sense Jessie's hesitation. "Just tell me!" she pleaded.

"It's nothing, really, just—Mom knows a couple of the women who work with her. They say she doesn't talk to anyone. That she's standoffish."

That, at least, Lucy understood—it was the reputation that her mother had always had. Still, she felt that she had to defend her mother to Jessie. "She's just really shy."

Jessie didn't seem convinced, and Lucy knew there had to be more, but they had almost reached the dress factory.

"Listen, Jessie...it's just, I think something might be going on at work. I just want to check on her."

"You mean like they're working them too hard or something?"

"I'm not really sure, but I don't think they'll let her take a break just to talk to me, so...see, I brought this."

She dug in her pocket and pulled out her mother's small pillbox and showed it to Jessie. "I'll just say she forgot her asthma medicine."

"I didn't know your mom has asthma."

"She doesn't. I need an excuse that sounds important. What do you think?"

"I think it'll work." He gave her the smile he reserved for her alone, the quiet grin that seemed to promise she could depend on him, and Lucy's trepidation lifted a little.

Lucy took a deep breath and tried the door to the building. It wasn't locked, so she slipped inside, Jessie following right behind her. Inside, the air hummed with the sounds of the sewing machines and the chatter of the women working at the cutting tables. A plump, gray-haired woman wearing glasses on the end of her nose looked up from the nearest table and asked if she could help them.

"My mother is Miyako Takeda," Lucy said. Several heads turned, the women clearly curious. Caught staring, they quickly returned to their work.

"I have her asthma medicine. She forgot it this morning, and if she doesn't take it she'll get sick."

"I'm sorry," the lady said, setting down her pinking shears and dusting off her skirt. "Miyako has been called away. You can leave the medicine with me."

"Called away?" Lucy echoed. "Where?"

The lady glanced nervously down the service hallway at the end of the room. "She had an errand for Mr. Ricken-bocker," she said at last.

"Oh. I'll just... Maybe I can come back a little later."

"I really don't mind giving it to her, dear."

Lucy couldn't give the woman the box, because it was empty. She hadn't planned for this scenario. She thought either she would see her mother right away or, if she wasn't in the main room, she could use the pillbox to gain access to wherever she was working. "No, she, she..." Lucy stammered, the woman staring at her curiously. "She's very strict. She won't let me give it to anyone else."

She thanked the woman, averting her eyes from her appraising gaze, and turned to go. As soon as they were outside, she pulled Jessie toward the side of the building, her body trembling from a buildup of nerves.

"I don't understand," she said. "Where would she have gone?"

"Do you want to wait for her to come back?"

Lucy hesitated, considering her options. "Maybe we could look around?" she finally asked. "That lady…she was looking down the hall. Maybe that's where they went."

"Where? You mean the other end of the building? That's where the trucks pull up. I bet it's just storage and shipping down there."

"Yeah, but she acted like she knew where they were and didn't want to say."

"Okay." Jessie touched her arm lightly. "If you want, I can stand out by the street and block the view so no one can see you by the window."

Lucy couldn't help thinking of the schemes Nancy Drew was always coming up with in situations like this. "You'll be my distraction?"

"Sure. Whatever you need."

Lucy gingerly approached the side of the building, treading carefully in the landscaping. The windows along the short wing were propped open to allow as much air as possible to circulate inside the hot rooms. Lucy rested her fingertips lightly on the sill of the closest window. Behind her she could hear Jessie's tuneless whistling, and felt reassured; anyone passing by would focus on him, not her. But inside the room there was nothing but a pair of empty handcarts and a long metal bar against the wall, from which hung a row of finished garments, wrapped in paper and ready for shipping.

A flash of movement caught her eye. There—at the end of the room—a small anteroom, the door partway open. It took Lucy a moment to process what she was seeing, gray and white moving together until she realized it was two people she was looking at, not one, pressed up against a utility sink, partially obscured by the door. A man, his arms wrapped around a woman who seemed to be struggling silently, trying to extricate herself from the embrace, her blouse pulled free from her skirt, her hair falling from its carefully pinned chignon. Lucy heard a small grunt as the woman tried to push the man away.

Her mother.

Lucy gasped as she recognized her mother's glossy hair, her tiny pearl earring, the near-white nape of her slender neck. She struggled harder, but the man was undeterred. His arms, roving across her back, came to rest on the curve of her buttocks and he squeezed and kneaded while his mouth traveled along her throat, burrowing into the V of her unbuttoned blouse. "Stop," she heard her mother say, but it sounded more like a question. "Someone will hear you."

"Let 'em," he grunted, and abruptly he released her backside and seized her wrists, pushing them up above her head. He clasped them in one large hand and pressed them against a pipe that ran along the ceiling, mashing them against the metal, while his other hand groped the front of her blouse, tugging the fabric up.

Lucy covered her mouth with her hand to keep from making any further sounds and backed away from the window. The last thing she saw before she turned away was her mother's face, completely empty of expression or emotion, eyes uplifted to the ceiling, as the man pushed the white cotton of her blouse up above her breasts, exposing the thin cotton-lawn camisole that Lucy had watched her put on that morning.

She stumbled away from the building, her feet tracking through the gravel and crushing the flowers, almost falling as a wave of nausea passed through her. She choked down bile, the horrible taste burning her throat, and pushed her hair away from her eyes. No, no. *No.*

Jessie was tossing his baseball, throwing it high above him and seizing it on the way down with a swipe of the wrist, still whistling. "Hey," he said when he caught sight of her. "See anything in there?"

Lucy sucked in a breath, composing herself as well as she could. She kept her face turned away so he couldn't see how upset she was and fell in step beside him.

"Nothing," she said. "Just a couple of empty carts. Guess they went somewhere else."

That night Lucy watched Miyako undress, holding a book in her lap and pretending to be reading in case Miyako looked in her direction. Her mother's white blouse was wrinkled where Rickenbocker's hand had crushed the fabric. One strap of the camisole was broken, the silken ribbon dangling from the metal clasp. Miyako's hair had been repinned, but strands of it hung loose in the back, curving against her white neck. There was a faint purpling along the tender inside of her arms. Bruises. Lucy thought she could make out the imprint of individual fingers.

"Oh, Lucy, I almost forgot," her mother said dully, after she had put on her nightclothes. Her speech was slow and thick, an effect which on recent evenings Lucy had chalked up to fatigue. "I brought you something."

She opened her pocketbook and pulled out a tiny glass bottle and handed it to Lucy. There were real French words on the label, and the bottle was two-thirds full of straw-gold perfume. Lucy sniffed it: flowery, powdery.

"Where did you get this?"

Miyako shrugged. "Mrs. Driscoll, she says she no longer cares for it."

"But why did she give it to you? Why not some other lady?"

"To reward me, I suppose. The other ladies make so many mistakes."

Lucy sat so still it felt as though she was turning to stone from the outside in. She was sitting on the edge of her bed wearing her pajamas and a pair of socks knitted by an old lady from their block and traded for one of Miyako's embroidered runners. Now that autumn had arrived, the nights were turning chilly.

You can't say it out loud, she told herself miserably, as Miyako eased herself under her bed linens as though they weighed a thousand pounds. The tiny exhalation she made when her head finally rested on the pillow was like the puff of silken seeds when a milkweed boll bursts. *You can't let her know you know.*

But Lucy closed her eyes and breathed in and betrayed herself. "Did *he* give it to you?"

The silence that followed was weighted with unbearable tension, and Lucy opened her eyes to see that Miyako had pushed herself up on her elbow, her cotton gown hanging off her bony shoulders.

"Who?" Miyako whispered.

"That *man.* Mr. Rickenbocker. At your work. I *saw* him. I saw you with him. In that room. His hands all over you and—"

Abruptly Lucy was sobbing, unable to get enough breath to continue. Miyako threw off her covers and rushed to kneel next to Lucy's bed. She wrapped Lucy in her arms, and Lucy pressed herself against her mother's warm skin, her beating heart. She let her mother hold her and imagined they were somewhere else, back in their house on Clement Street, sitting together on the red settee waiting for her father to come home.

After a very long time, Miyako pulled back from Lucy. Her face was pale, her skin so thin it looked as though you could tear it with a fingernail. "What you saw, Lucy. I didn't want— If there was any way I could—"

But Lucy knew that already. Who could willingly go with a man like that, with a voice like gravel and grabbing, bruising hands? Obviously, the man had chosen her mother for two reasons—because she was the most perfect, the most beautiful—and because he *could,* because his power was great enough that she could not say no.

"But can't you quit your job? Can't Auntie Aiko ask Mr. Hamaguchi to talk to him?" she begged.

"I don't know, I don't know," Miyako murmured, and she encircled Lucy again with her arms and rocked her. "I'll find a way, *suzume,* there has to be a way."

Within days it seemed that she had. Each morning, Miyako left for work before Lucy woke, and she returned home before Lucy got home from school. As the days went by, she seemed to regain some of the vitality she'd lost. Most nights she brought work home with her, and Lucy would find her hand-sewing a zipper in place or hemming the full skirt of a party dress.

The bruises faded.

Lucy brought plates of food back to the room after every meal and encouraged Miyako to eat as much as she could, a second piece of toast or a cold slice of potato. It seemed to be working. She was gaining back some of the weight she had lost, her clothes no longer hanging on her thin frame.

For weeks, Lucy saw little of Jessie. Other than school and her job, she spent all her time at home with Miyako. Her schoolwork suffered and she turned down invitations from the girls in her class. All her focus was on her mother. Miyako slipped silently through the days like a pale fish swimming far below the surface, a shadow among the lily fronds, and Lucy watched intently for the rainbow flash of brilliance that would signal her mother's return.

The Indian summer days faded to the chilly, gray skies of November. Lucy was given a coat from a large box of winter clothes donated by a Sacramento church. A tag sewn into the lining was embroidered with the name Tabitha E. Davis. It was too large, the sleeves extending past Lucy's wrists to her knuckles. Miyako promised to tailor it, but every night she was occupied with her piecework.

Baseball practice tapered off, the leagues between seasons, and Jessie met Lucy after school almost every day. She didn't realize how much she had missed him, and she stole moments away from Miyako to be with him. They held hands on the porch of the mess hall after dinner; they kissed behind the recreation hall as the moon rose above the mountains. During the day, it was almost impossible to find privacy in the camp, not even a small patch of dirt where they could be alone without children playing, ladies talking, old men tossing stones. But at night it sometimes felt as if they were the only two people in Manzanar.

One night Lucy and Jessie stayed out late watching the reflection of the full moon shimmering in the creek, looking like a glittering disk of silver. Lucy said it was the most beautiful thing in the entire camp. Jessie pulled her close against him and whispered against her neck as he kissed her. "You are, Lucy. You're the most beautiful, at least to me."

Later that night, Lucy watched her mother sleep in the moonlight that streamed through the window. Her shoulder was so thin, her breathing impossibly shallow. Thoughts of Jessie got her through nights like these, when her worries about her mother threatened to crush her. Jessie was all she needed. As long as she had him, everything would be all right.

14

AS WINTER BLANKETED THE CAMP, JESSIE BEGAN to pull away. At first it was just a sadness that shadowed his face, a bleakness that quickly disappeared when Lucy spoke his name. But one day he wasn't waiting for her after school; then it was three times in one week. He said he needed to work on his fielding before the winter league started up, but when Lucy looked for him on the fields, he wasn't there. He made plans with her and failed to show up; later he would apologize, but he never offered an explanation. When they did spend time together, he was preoccupied and silent.

"Please, just tell me what I did," she pleaded one day after waiting for forty-five minutes outside his barrack for him to come home. "If you're mad at me—"

"It's not you, Lucy, I've told you that," he snapped, sliding his bat bag off his shoulder. Then he added, more gently, "I had batting practice."

"I looked for you at the fields."

"I was there," he insisted, but he wouldn't meet her eyes.

One night after dinner, while her mother was sewing a row of tiny pearl buttons on a fitted bodice, Lucy went out for a walk with a vague plan to go by Jessie's block and see if he happened to be around. The night was cold, but Lucy knew that Jessie was occasionally driven outside in the evenings by the noise and demands of his two little brothers. It was a long shot, and Lucy brooded as she walked the long stretch up C Street and over to D, zigzagging through the victory gardens, wondering what she could say that would get Jessie to open up to her.

It was her intense focus that kept her from noticing the figures approaching behind her. Footsteps crushing frost-dead plants startled her out of her thoughts, and suddenly two men appeared beside her. Lucy was astonished to see that one was Mr. Van Dorn, and the other was Reg Forrest.

Reg Forrest was something of a celebrity in the camp. Now a warehouse manager, he'd been an aspiring Hollywood actor before the war. He hadn't landed any big roles yet, but he was even more handsome in person than he was in the publicity photo someone had posted in the general store above the rack of movie magazines. There were rumors that he'd been in a television ad for Swift meats, though no one had actually seen it aired. He had wavy blond hair and a cleft in his chin like Cary Grant's, only not as big. He was tall and broad shouldered and he smiled a lot and many of the girls claimed to be in love with him. Reg was friendly enough, and he helped coach the junior high baseball league and had directed a performance by the drama club.

Lucy was mystified and a little frightened. Lots of people used the victory gardens as a shortcut, especially now that the soil was turned under and frozen, but at the moment there was no one else about. The afternoon had turned cold and the air damp, and people were keeping inside. The oil heaters had been cranking around the clock for several weeks now, and tendrils of greasy smoke wound up out of the barracks roofs.

"Hello there," Reg said, in a friendly enough voice. Van Dorn said nothing, keeping his hands jammed in his pockets.

Lucy wondered if something terrible had happened—an accident, someone in the block, her auntie Aiko, even her mother. But would they send these two to tell her? More likely it would be someone from the block.

"We have a message for your mother," Reg continued. "I'm hoping you'll deliver it for us. Tell her George misses her."

Lucy's heart was pounding so hard in her chest that she didn't trust herself to speak. All around her were neat rows of turned earth, a few winter lettuces and the tops of radishes showing above the soil. The melons and beans and sunflowers had all been turned under after the first frost, and here and there a few dead stalks poked out of the earth.

Night had blanketed the camp, and lights burned in the windows of the barracks all around them, but they seemed very far away. Too far to call out; too far to summon help. Lucy's hands ached with cold because she'd left her mittens somewhere, and hadn't got up the nerve to tell her mother yet. Van Dorn stared silently out across the broad avenues toward where the mountain's shape was visible, the bright snow a beacon above the horizon. Reg put his hand lightly on her shoulder. For a moment it rested there and Lucy held her breath; then he squeezed.

"This is very important," he said, his fingers finding the tendon that ran along the base of her neck and digging in. "I'm going to ask you to repeat it. Tell your mother, 'You have a lovely daughter. George looks forward to your next visit.'"

"I don't..." Lucy whispered, blinking tears. Her legs felt weak and a small amount of urine dampened her panties.

"I would like you to repeat that back to me," Reg said kindly, but his fingers continued their pressure. Lucy's arm twitched.

"You have a lovely daughter," she whispered. "George looks forward to your next visit."

Immediately the pressure was released and Reg was patting her coat gently. Lucy felt a tear roll down her cheek, splashing to the ground, where she imagined it would freeze by morning. She wanted to rub her nose on her sleeve, but didn't dare move.

"You'll tell her," Reg said softly, and he and Van Dorn began backing away. "Go on home now."

Then they were gone. She heard their footfalls behind her but did not dare turn around to see which way they went. She waited until it was silent, the only sound the rushing of the wind, and then she walked home as fast as her trembling legs could carry her.

Miyako's face, when Lucy repeated the message, went blank.

Lucy could see the toll the past few months had taken on her mother, the fine lines and dark smudges around her mouth and eyes. It was as though she were no longer living, but a life-size porcelain figurine.

She cupped Lucy's face in her hand, just firmly enough to force her to meet her gaze. "Did they touch you?"

"Yes," Lucy said, remembering the astonishing force of Reg's forefinger and thumb digging into her flesh through her coat and sweater. "I mean no."

Miyako stared at her for a long time but asked no further questions. When she finally let go of Lucy's face, she touched her three times: on the bridge of her nose, on her lips and on her chin; and then she drew several strands of Lucy's hair through her fine fingers. Lucy, unaccustomed to such tender gestures, stood frozen.

"You're cursed, just like me," Miyako whispered. "But I will fix this."

After a final caress she went back to her side of the room and began to undress. Within moments she was in her bed, the covers pulled up over her head, while Lucy wondered where in her body the curse was hidden and when it would fight its way out.

15

DECEMBER CAME. THERE WAS TROUBLE IN THE camp between the older Issei—those born in Japan—and the next-generation Nisei. Many of the old people still wore the stunned expressions that they'd arrived with, unable to speak enough English to communicate with the Caucasian staff. Some of the younger men were anxious to join the service, to prove their loyalty—but others were driven by darker impulses: resentment over their incarceration, over the loss of their property and livelihood, over educations interrupted and voices ignored. There were clashes over loyalty and duty, fights and accusations and simmering tempers.

Lucy, increasingly lonely, immersed herself in her schoolwork. It came easily to her, and it helped her to ignore the chaos around her, to temper the loss of Jessie and her worries about her increasingly distant and frail mother. Her marks were high; her teacher often singled her out for praise, holding her papers up for the other students to see, but Lucy's pride was dampened by the distraction of the turmoil all around the camp.

Nothing got resolved. Tempers flared and fights broke out and one night the military police surged inside the gates to quell a riot. Lucy stayed inside her room with her mother, while outside the shouting grew deafening and something— a stone, an ax—struck the side of the building. Their neighbors were out there, the men and boys from their block, while inside the women comforted the children and clutched broomsticks and paring knives and prayed the conflict would not reach inside. Lucy pressed her hands over her ears, shut her eyes and wondered what Jessie was doing, if he was outside in the melee, if he would have the sense to stay out of the worst of it or if he would welcome the chance to fight.

By the next morning, one young man had been killed, and an eerie sense of calm descended on the camp. The wind kicked up and dust blew through the abandoned streets. Finally, it was time for breakfast, and people ventured from their barracks, heads down and hurrying. The staff were already out in force, patrolling the streets, posted at the auditorium and rec halls to prevent another round of fighting from breaking out. News traveled slowly at first, building to a crescendo inside the mess halls.

Lucy ate by herself amid the din. When a sudden hush fell, she looked up from her cereal and saw that Reg Forrest had entered the room. He'd evidently been pressed into service to help keep the peace, and he wore one of the MP's pressed uniform shirts. A baton hung from his belt. He walked around the perimeter of the room, hands behind his back, saying nothing, a strange smile fixed on his face. Lucy put down her spoon, her appetite lost. A few hundred feet away, in the guard towers that loomed over the camp, soldiers watched every inch of the fence, their fingers never far from the triggers of their guns—but somehow Reg's presence was even more chilling.

Lucy slid closer to the family whose table she was sharing, hoping that she could escape Reg's notice by pretending to be one of their children. But Reg had already spotted her. He walked directly toward her table and Lucy felt the filament that connected them grow taut. She sat up as straight as she could and forced herself to meet his gaze.

"Well, well, little Lucy Takeda," Reg said, nodding to the family Lucy was sitting with. They blanched and slid away from her. "Good to see you up and about, looking fit as a fiddle this morning."

Lucy wondered what response he was looking for, what words would make him go away.

"And your mother? I trust she is well also?"

"Yes," Lucy said quickly, though in fact Miyako had resumed her late-night outings two or three times a week, and sometimes didn't come home until Lucy was already asleep. On those nights Lucy occasionally woke to find her mother kneeling on the floor next to her bed, her head resting on the edge of the mattress. Miyako was losing weight again, and she sometimes clutched herself around the middle as though she was in pain. She wore long sleeves and high collars, but even so, Lucy had spotted bruises on her skin.

"But—" he made a show of looking around the room, assuming an exaggerated expression of concern "—I don't see her here. She isn't forgetting to eat, is she?"

"No...sir." Lucy hated the papery tone of her voice, the tremor in her hands that betrayed her fear.

"Because you gotta eat, keep your strength up, times like these." Reg squared his shoulders, his broad chest and powerful arms filling out his uniform shirt and tapering to the trim waist and muscular legs. Reg was rumored to have a punching bag and weights in his apartment rather than living room furniture; this only added to his allure among the young women in camp.

Lucy nodded faintly, unable to think of a response.

"You know…it's been awfully nice to see her around again. The boys sure missed her. Your mother's a class act." Reg made a gun from his thumb and forefinger and pretended to shoot Lucy with it, making a clicking sound in his throat. He winked and finally turned and walked away, completing his tour of the mess hall before leaving to haunt other corners of the camp.

The couple she was sitting with exchanged a worried barrage of words in a mixture of Japanese and English, but Lucy didn't listen. Her appetite was gone. She carefully wrapped two slices of bread in a handkerchief and headed back to her room, knowing she'd have to work hard not to let her face give her fears away.

16

THE RIOTS WERE FOLLOWED BY A RELENTLESS wave of cold. The new year came without incident, people cowering in their rooms under whatever warm clothes and blankets they were able to find. Donations from churches and deliveries of surplus clothing from the first war supplemented the meager belongings the internees had brought from home, and the oil heaters burned constantly, but it seemed as though no one was ever warm enough. There was only one heater per barrack, a barrel-shaped thing that could not produce enough heat for the entire building.

The business of the camp continued unabated. Deputy Chief Griswold promoted one of the full-time couriers to clerical assistant and asked Lucy to help out again a few days a week after school. If Mrs. Kadonada was aware of the distance between Lucy and her son, she was too discreet to mention it, but it seemed that she was especially solicitous as she gave Lucy stacks of letters and mimeographs to deliver.

She asked after Miyako with no apparent irony, and for that kindness, Lucy was grateful. She wondered if Mrs. Kadonada understood that her errands in the frozen camp were preferable to afternoons alone with her thoughts in a warm room.

One Friday afternoon, Mrs. Kadonada gave Lucy an envelope stamped CONFIDENTIAL and addressed to Reginald Forrest, Property Manager, Warehouse One. Ordinarily such a delivery would only be handled by an adult courier; exceptions had to be approved by Deputy Chief Griswold. But the full-time courier was ill, and the deputy chief had left early to visit his fiancée in Sacramento for the weekend, so Mrs. Kadonada gave the envelope to Lucy and told her that, after she delivered it, she could consider herself finished for the day.

Lucy tried to tamp down her apprehension as she walked through camp. Since the day after the riot, she'd had no direct contact with Reg or Van Dorn, and she'd glimpsed George Rickenbocker only once, at the wheel of a truck going too fast down Avenue C. Over the holidays, Reg had agreed to guest-direct one of the holiday programs. His photo was featured in the *Manzanar Free Press,* playing Santa for the orphans in the Children's Village, handing out gifts sent by church groups.

Lucy knew that it was impossible that Reg had changed, that a cruel and dangerous side of him hid underneath the glib public exterior. But this was only a simple delivery. She would find Reg, get his signature, thank him and leave; and that would be the end of it. This was what she told herself over and over as she walked, the cold wind reaching under her dress and through her woolen tights.

But when she arrived at the warehouse, it was locked. Lucy's heart sank. Many of the offices closed early on Fridays, especially when bad weather threatened. She couldn't return to the office with the letter; Mrs. Kadonada had said it was imperative that it be delivered today. She had to find Reg.

She would start with his apartment. Lucy walked past the garages, through the decorative gardens and benches at the edge of staff housing. Trying to ignore her skittering apprehension, she rounded the outside row of barracks. When she arrived at his door, marked with a metal plate stamped with his name, she knocked before she could lose her nerve.

There was no response. As she tried to decide what to do next, a young man in an MP uniform came around the corner, his gait uneven. When he saw Lucy, he gave her a sloppy salute.

"Well, hey there, girlie."

"I am looking for Mr. Reginald Forrest to deliver this letter," Lucy blurted, holding up the envelope.

"That's a funny coincidence," the man said, his words running into each other. "I was just with him. Check in the motor pool office." He began fumbling at a door with a key, muttering under his breath. He was drunk, Lucy realized with growing unease. But she'd come this far; she had to try.

The front door of the motor pool office was locked, but Lucy followed the sounds of laughter around the back of the building. A slant-roofed addition housed the desks where the mechanics processed WRA paperwork and requisitions. At this hour, it should have been empty, but light leaked from the slats in the window blinds.

Lucy knocked on the door. Inside, voices rose in shouting and laughter, and no one answered. A tumbleweed rolled nearby, swept in by the winds, and Lucy felt the cold seep into her ears. As she stood there deliberating her next move, the wooden door pitched open and a man stumbled out.

"Oh Jesus, girl, where'd you come from?" he said. He had one hand on his crotch, which made him look both vulner-

able and menacing. Lucy didn't recognize him; he was wearing civilian clothes, stocky, and ruddy-faced.

"I have a letter for Mr. Forrest," Lucy said in a high-
pitched, formal voice, averting her eyes from his hand
fumbling at his belt. "From Mr. Graves of the Minidoka
Relocation Center." This she knew only because she had
read the typed return address, but saying it made her feel
more official. The door was on a spring, but before it closed
she glimpsed two Japanese girls inside. They wore bright
lipstick and tight sweaters and leaned against each other on
a sofa, clutching drinks and giggling. One looked vaguely
familiar, a girl who played the ukulele in the variety shows
and lived far on the other side of camp by the hospital, Block
Twenty-eight or Twenty-nine.

"Well, have you ever heard of knocking?" the man said.
"Reg isn't here, haven't seen him in a while. Maybe you
ought to just take that letter back where you got it. In or
out, make up your mind, I've got to drain the pipes so I'm
going to recommend you choose in."

He staggered along the side of the building, still fumbling
with his pants, and Lucy realized that he meant to relieve
himself against the wall. There was nowhere to go to escape
watching him urinate, so she caught the door just before it
clicked shut and slipped into the room, jamming the letter
into her coat pocket.

"Well, lookee what the cat dragged in," a man said from a
chair tipped back against the wall. Lucy smelled burning wax
and the unpleasant aroma she remembered from her father's
glass of whiskey, and the faint scent of vomit, and realized
everyone here was drunk. Off to the side was a table laden
with liquor bottles and a bowl of pistachios; broken shells littered the table and the floor. "All the way from across town."

Lucy took a second look at the man, too massive for the

chair in which he sat, and belatedly recognized Deputy Assistant Director Van Dorn. For some reason the notion made her blush, even though her overwhelming emotion was fear—fear of being found out, fear of being trapped here with these older girls, fear of things she couldn't name. She turned around, thinking she might retreat before anyone else noticed she was there, but one of the young men had stepped between her and the door.

"Not so fast," said a tall man standing at the table, pouring from a bottle into a short, squat glass held by a slight Japanese girl. The girl had her hand on his arm, her face tilted up to his. She stood with one foot, clad in a frayed silk pump that had seen better days, insinuated between his, her thighs rubbing against his legs.

The man pushed the girl away as though she were a low-hanging branch, and Lucy saw that it was George Rickenbocker. She would have known it was the man she'd seen with her mother in the storage room from his expression alone: he had the handsome, broad face and slicked-back dark hair of the characters in superhero comics—Superman or The Flash—but his smile was both amused and hungry, his eyes narrowed and appraising. "You're Miyako's girl, aren't you? Fellas, look here, we got another little apple didn't fall far from her mama's tree."

The girl plucked at his sleeve and said something breathy and high-pitched, and he batted her hand away. "Go on home," he snapped, not bothering to look at her.

"But I don't—" She got out only a few syllables before Rickenbocker seized her wrist and twisted it. She shrieked when he yanked it up behind her back, and he gave her a little shove toward the door when he let her go.

"I *said* go on home." His voice was deadly cold. "Get your coat, now, and go."

One of the girls on the couch leaned forward, her elbows on her knees, which were parted in a way that Lucy knew would horrify her mother. She whispered something to her friend, who closed her eyes and laughed. The slight girl stared at them beseechingly, but they refused to look at her. One of the MPs wordlessly fetched a green cloth coat from a pile on the coatrack and tossed it to her. She fumbled and it fell on the floor, and she had to bend down to pick it up. When she stood, there were tears in her eyes, but no one—the man, the girls, the MP—looked at her. Only Lucy watched her struggle to get her arms in the sleeves, and when their eyes met, the girl's face contorted into an expression of fury. Then she was gone, the din of the party resuming before the door had closed all the way.

"Do you know who I am, little girl?" Rickenbocker demanded. Lucy looked more closely, at his thick, dark hair tinged with silver, the hard line of his jaw. "Your mother and I are good friends. George Rickenbocker, at your service."

Lucy could manage only a small nod. The frayed edges of her composure ripped the rest of the way, and pure fear rushed in. This was the man who owned her mother's evenings, who bruised her thin arms and could crush both her hands in one of his, who ran his hard, bristly jaw along her vulnerable, pale neck.

Rickenbocker went back to pouring his drink. He set down the glass and picked up a second, poured an inch into that one. He lifted the glass to his nose and sniffed, swirling the golden liquid inside. Van Dorn was watching, along with the others. Two, three, four of them, young men who all looked alike in their uniforms. Their faces were flushed and sweaty, and their shirts pulled loose from their pants. They watched and smiled, and she felt her face burn.

"I have to go," she stammered. "I have to..."

But she couldn't finish her sentence. The man who stood between her and the door folded his arms over his chest. She took a step toward him, but he didn't budge. She stepped to the right, and he did too.

He was not going to allow her to pass. She was trapped.

"Sit down here," Rickenbocker said, pulling an empty chair away from the wall, his voice unctuous, slippery. "Have a little drink."

He handed her the glass, and when no alternative revealed itself to her, no ally to help her escape, Lucy sat with her legs pressed tightly together.

"I don't think I—" she whispered, willing Rickenbocker to realize that she was just a child, of no significance or value to him.

"Drink."

She put the glass to her lips, hands shaking, and took a tentative sip.

She expected the drink to taste bad, but she wasn't prepared for the burn, the way it gouged at her throat. She almost gagged, but forced herself to close her throat around the fire and lick the residue from her lips before she set the glass down on the table. The taste seemed to coat her mouth on the inside and burn her tongue. She wished for ice, for a slice of the soft bread they served in the dining hall, something bland, something to wash the burn away.

"You're just the spitting image of your mother, aren't you," Rickenbocker mused. He regarded her like a man at a museum contemplating an exhibit. "I can't get over it. You see this, Van Dorn?"

Van Dorn nodded without looking. His attention had swung back to the girls. A game of cards was laid out on the table; one of the girls rolled four dice and shrieked at the result, and Van Dorn clamped a meaty hand on her thigh, pushing her skirt higher. Her giggle turned to a high-pitched trill, half excitement, half panic.

Rickenbocker paid no mind. He stared at Lucy, his eyes bright and glowing, a cigarette stuck to his lower lip as though it had been glued there. "Hard to believe. She must have had you when she was fifteen years old."

Lucy forced herself to return his gaze. She cataloged each of his features, from the faint scar that bisected one sandy eyebrow to the slight bump on one side of his nose to his squarish, large teeth.

"Your mama ever tell you what a nice time she has here?" one of the MPs said. He had been lurking nearby, as if hoping for an invitation to join in the conversation. "She's a true mystery of the Orient, that one. Don't give an inch to anyone."

"Hey," Rickenbocker growled, and the MP flinched. "Did I say you could talk to the girl?"

Van Dorn pulled himself up out of the sofa and muttered something in the MP's ear, steering him away with a hand on his shoulder, leading him to the card game. It was something less than an invitation, if not quite a threat. Rickenbocker seemed oblivious to everyone else in the room; he regarded Lucy as though trying to decide where to move a book on a shelf.

Moments ticked by. Everyone drank, the girls' long white throats exposed when they lifted their cups to their lips, the men taking great gulps and wiping their mouths on their shirtsleeves. Lucy's face was hot under Rickenbocker's scrutiny, and she looked away, unable to sustain eye contact. "I have to go," she tried again, and stood shakily, clutching the folds of her skirt in one damp hand.

"I bet you're almost done growing," Rickenbocker said, shifting slightly on his feet so he was directly in front of her.

She had a view of the buttons of his shirt—plain mother-of-pearl, sewn with tan thread. He knelt down before her on the floor, and she could feel his hot breath on her face, and smelled liquor and sweat.

The MPs and Van Dorn studiously avoided looking their way, the conversation faltering for a second before surging back with forced gaiety. Lucy looked down on Rickenbocker's close-cut, thick hair, focusing on the strands of silver, her mouth dry.

"This is really quite unexpected," he said softly. Then he reached for her.

For a fraction of a second, Lucy thought he meant to shake her hand, but before she had time to react, he had seized her skirt, fanning out the cotton. His other hand slid down, past the hem, skimming her knee and settling at the widest part of her calf, encased in thick tights. She could feel the warmth of his hand through the knit material, the pressure of each individual finger. Then he squeezed, and she made a small sound of surprise. He squeezed harder.

It didn't hurt at first, exactly, though it was surprising how much power he had in his hand. But then he kept increasing the pressure slowly, watching her face with his lips parted, breathing shallowly, until Lucy gasped with pain. Only then did he abruptly let go.

"You get home now," Rickenbocker said, rising gracefully and stepping aside so she could pass. "I'm sure we'll be seeing each other again soon."

Lucy backed away from him with the shape of his hand burning on her skin. She thought of the bruises that she had seen on her mother's arms and knew she'd bear his mark by morning.

She stumbled into the darkness outside and the door slammed shut behind her. The wind howled and she blinked as fine grains blew against her face, her eyes adjusting to the darkness. She set off for Block Fourteen, moving as quickly as she dared, trembling too badly to run.

But the street wasn't entirely empty. She had gone only a block when a figure came flying toward her with unfastened coat trailing behind like wings. Lucy knew even before she was swept into her sobbing embrace that it was her mother.

"How did you know?" Lucy whispered against Miyako's neck. And then she remembered the look on the slight girl's face, her expression of pain mixed with hatred. The girl had gone to Miyako. The girl had told because she wanted revenge.

"It doesn't matter," Miyako whispered. "What did he do? What did he do to you?"

"N-nothing," Lucy stammered. She could still feel where his fingers dug cruelly into her soft flesh. She would find a way to hide the marks from her mother, until the bruises faded.

But Miyako moaned, pressing Lucy even tighter against her. "You must tell me," she begged. "You must."

"He..." A tremor racked Lucy's body and she felt that she might vomit. She couldn't stop thinking of his hands. The way they slid up her leg, as though he meant to keep going until he'd burrowed a path through her, until he'd torn her flesh from bone. "He said he was sure we would be seeing each other again soon."

"No, no," Miyako wailed, over and over, her cold lips against Lucy's ear, and Lucy wrapped her arms tightly around her mother's neck, breathing in her sweat, the smell of her fatigue.

A searchlight swept past them and then returned, bathing them in a harsh, yellow pool of light. Lucy froze, the terror of the guards' invisible nighttime reign seizing her breath.

She hated the lights, and over the months she had learned to evade them on her nighttime walks. She knew to stick to the less-traveled paths, use the shelter of buildings whenever possible. But now she and her mother were exposed, crouched in the middle of the street, huddled in each other's arms, and the light lingered, looking its fill, mocking them.

Finally it swept away, apparently satisfied, flashing its sickly arc elsewhere, looking for the innocent, the hapless, the defenseless. Night surrounded them once again, Miyako's keening cries carried away on the wind.

17

IN THE MORNING, LUCY WOKE ON THE FLOOR
beside her mother's bed. Miyako had not wanted to let go
of her, and Lucy lay in her arms until she finally heard her
mother's breathing grow steady with sleep. But even exhaustion was not enough to help her fall asleep in the narrow cot,
and in the end she pulled the covers off her own bed and
made a pallet on the floor.

A storm had come through during the night, and a thin
ray of winter sunlight now slanted through the window.
Lucy hurried to fold the bedclothes, afraid she would miss
breakfast and the chance to bring her mother something to
eat. She had fallen asleep in her clothes, and didn't bother
changing now, knowing that underneath her tights were the
marks George Rickenbocker left on her flesh.

She was pulling on her coat, struggling with the buttons,
when she discovered the envelope in her pocket. Reg's letter. Her breath caught as she remembered the vow Mrs. Ka-

donada had extracted from her: "You must make sure he gets this today," she'd said, giving the letter to Lucy only after she promised. If Mrs. Kadonada found out the letter never made it to him, Lucy might lose her job.

"All right," Lucy whispered to herself. "I can do this. I can."

The breakfast line was almost closing, and she begged for a bowl of Malt-O-Meal and a glass of milk. Back in the room, Miyako still slept, and Lucy pulled the covers more snugly around her mother's shoulders before she left again, setting the food on the small side table.

Lucy hurried through camp, keeping her eyes on the road ahead of her, not wanting to see or speak to anyone until the task was done. On the way, she had a conversation with herself, trying to build her courage. Perhaps Reg didn't associate with Rickenbocker and the others much after all; perhaps that night with Van Dorn, when he'd pinched her skin and made her promise to deliver the message, had been a one-time-only affair. It was possible that he didn't even know the meaning of the message he'd been given to deliver. That seemed far-fetched, but then again, stranger things happened all the time. Alliances in the camp shifted and faded. The day after the riot, when he'd spoken to her in the mess hall—maybe she'd misinterpreted that as well; maybe the threat she heard in his voice was only the product of her imagination.

Arriving at Reg's door, Lucy felt the muscles of her face tighten. Her pulse quickened and her thoughts scattered. Still, it was daylight. There were plenty of people about—if she cried out, someone would hear. She would not go inside his room. She would hand him the letter, or—if he was out—she would slip it under the door. Maybe that would even be better—except that Mrs. Kadonada would ask for the signed receipt, and Lucy wasn't sure she could lie convincingly.

As she deliberated with her hand on the letter in her pocket, the door opened in front of her, and there was Reg, filling up the frame, saying something over his shoulder.

Then he saw her.

"Oh," he said, clearly startled. His expression shifted and went opaque, and Lucy remembered the way he'd looked at her that night in the winter garden, the morning in the mess hall. She knew she had not been wrong to fear him after all. "Lucy. What are you doing here?"

Lucy backed up as Reg stepped out onto his small porch, pulling the door shut behind him. But not before Lucy caught a glimpse inside the apartment.

Jessie was sitting on the bed. He was wearing no shirt, and no pants either, just white cotton drawers and a pair of dark socks. What was he doing there? He looked right at Lucy, this boy who had been hers for all these months, who had held her hand and told her jokes and kissed her, but he didn't appear to see her. His eyes were wide and vacant, and he clutched the mussed blankets on either side of him. His lips moved but he made no sound.

Reg took Lucy's arm rather a little harder than necessary and pulled her away from the door.

"Jessie came by this morning for a little help with his swing," Reg said easily. "What with the winter league starting up and all. Bet you didn't know I played in the minors, did you? I was a utility player for the San Bernardino Padres for a couple seasons. Gave it up for Hollywood, but I still remember a thing or two."

Lucy wanted to protest, to demand to go back, to talk to Jessie. Something was terribly wrong. All along, Reg had been more dangerous than all of them, worse even than Rickenbocker.

"He's a bit shy about it, actually," Reg went on, his tone

almost jovial. "Doesn't want Coach Hayashi to know he's getting any extra help. You see how it is, don't you?"

She couldn't form words, couldn't force her horror and revulsion into syllables. With each step she took away from his apartment, she was betraying Jessie, but she couldn't help herself.

"So what can I do for you? You didn't come to see me for baseball help, did you? Unless they're putting dames on the teams these days!" Reg laughed as if this was one crazy, unpredictable world they shared and he was happy to have someone to commiserate with about it. "Of course, the same deal applies to you. I show you my famous knuckleball, the secret stays with us." He released her arm finally, now that they were clear of the block of apartments, and winked at her.

"I don't. I don't play." Lucy reached in her pocket and pulled out the letter, creased and folded now. "I, uh, have a delivery for you. I need your signature."

"A letter, eh? Well, what do you know." Reg took the envelope from her and examined it, front and back, taking his time. Then he took a pen from his breast pocket and scrawled his name on the receipt with a flourish before tearing it off and handing it back to Lucy.

"It'll be okay, you know," he said, smiling indulgently, almost conspiratorially. "War's hard on everyone. But it'll end, you'll see. And then you can forget all about this place."

Lucy shoved the receipt in her pocket and turned. After a few steps, she broke into a run, but she could not go fast enough to escape the sound of Reg's laughter behind her.

18

PATTY AND LUCY WERE JAMMED INTO A TINY booth along the side of the restaurant, which was packed with workers from the surrounding buildings. They should have gone somewhere quieter, but this place—breakfast twenty-four hours a day—was her mother's favorite. After they ordered, Patty took a deep breath. Now that she finally had her mother's attention, she wasn't sure where to start.

She reached into her shoulder bag for the photo album and awkwardly opened it to the first page: Miyako on Rickenbocker's lap. She held it up for her mother to see, glancing around the restaurant nervously. But really, what did it matter who saw? The people in the photo had been dead for thirty-five years.

"I went to Forrest's apartment," Patty said. "I found this. I know Grandma killed George Rickenbocker."

Her heart was pounding and her eyes hurt. She had noticed this morning that her face was looking sallow, the skin under her eyes sunken and purplish.

Lucy said nothing at first. Then she reached across the table and took the album from Patty's hands. She turned the pages slowly, her expression unreadable. A couple of times she touched the photographs of her mother tenderly. Finally she closed the album and hugged it to her chest.

"There are some things I didn't tell you," she said. Her eyes glistened and her voice was hoarse, and Patty wondered if her mother was about to cry. If she did, it would be a first.

But somehow, the possibility failed to move Patty. She wasn't sure what kind of reaction she had expected from her mother—denial? regret?—but she was suddenly angry. "How could you lie to me all those years?"

"I didn't lie, I just didn't—"

"It's lying, when you let me believe—"

"How did you find out?"

"I called the Department of the Interior. They keep all the records."

Lucy nodded. "I always wondered where they ended up."

"*Mother.* Don't you get how serious this is? If the cops find this... All these connections lead right back to you. And your mother was a *murderer.* Don't you think—"

"*Patty.*" The rebuke was sharp, especially coming from Lucy, who never raised her voice. Diners at neighboring tables glanced their way. "I am very sorry that I never told you about any of this, but please don't talk about your grandmother that way. She was... You never knew her. But she did the best she could."

The waiter appeared, bearing their lunches, balancing the plates high above the diners' heads. As he began to lower them to the table, Lucy stopped him. "Pack those up, please. We'll be taking them to go." The waiter sighed and retreated.

"I'm sorry, I know you have to get back to work."

Lucy shrugged. "Maybe I'll take another afternoon off."

Patty started to dig in her purse for her wallet, but Lucy reached across the table and stopped her. "I will buy."

Patty watched as her mother stacked bills and coins. She always left a ridiculously large tip. She said it came from working as a motel maid, that once you had to count on other people's generosity, you learned to be generous yourself.

As Lucy counted out twenty, thirty, thirty-five percent of their bill, Patty slipped the photo album back inside her shoulder bag, where it weighed more heavily than ever.

When they got home, Lucy set the take-out containers on the counter and disappeared into her bedroom. She emerged a few minutes later with an old tin box covered with a design of roses and the logo for a soap company. She set it on the kitchen table and took a deep breath, almost as though she was afraid to open it.

"I haven't looked at any of this stuff in years," she said softly, prying off the lid. Inside was a stack of yellowed papers and photographs curling with age. A faint dusty scent rose from the box as Lucy dug through carefully and took out a small square photo.

"This is my school picture, the year I went to Manzanar. I was fourteen."

Patty took it carefully, touching only the edges with her thumb and forefinger. "You always said you didn't have any pictures of yourself." Then, catching her breath: "Mother…"

The girl in the photograph was perfect. Her smile was serene yet mischievous, her glossy hair falling perfectly around the curve of her jaw. Her eyes sparkled beneath long lashes and her teeth were even and white. Her velvet hairband and round-collared blouse were suitable for a child, but already there were unmistakable signs of impending womanhood in the swell of her cheekbones, the curve of her lips.

Patty glanced from her mother to the photograph and back. There…in the profile of her mother's good side, in the shape of her eyes, she could see the shadow of this girl.

Lucy sifted through the papers in the box. "Here's one from Manzanar. I'd won a prize, for history."

In this one, Lucy posed with a plain, skinny woman in front of a map tacked to a white wall. She stood with her hand on her hip, grinning at the camera with an expression that could only be described as provocative. Her hair was longer and curled in the style of the forties. She wore a simple skirt and cardigan, rolled socks and black shoes, and she was turned slightly away with one foot pointed toward the camera, her chin tilted flirtatiously. She was a girl on the cusp of womanhood, and her resemblance to the photographs of Miyako was startling.

"You were…gorgeous."

"Yes," Lucy said, without a trace of self-consciousness. "It was a long time ago."

"What's this one?" Patty lifted a snapshot from the box. In it, her mother, a little older, stood between two lanky, blond teenagers, a boy and a girl. But this was her mother after the accident; the transformation was astonishing. Her scars were dark and jagged, her hair cut short and badly. She was wearing a shapeless dress that was too big for her. No one in the picture was smiling.

Lucy took the photograph from her. "They worked at the motel in Lone Pine too. They came with their mother on weekends. I don't remember their names, but the girl and her mother cooked, and the boy worked on the grounds."

"Were they your friends?"

Lucy shrugged noncommittally. "They were the only other young people I ever saw, so I spent a little time with them."

A connection clicked in Patty's mind. Her mother had always said that Patty's father was a boy from Lone Pine, someone she didn't know well, someone who didn't matter. She refused to say more about him, and Patty had always secretly assumed that her mother had been taken advantage of in some way, that her conception had been against her mother's will.

Could this be the boy? She looked closely at the picture, at the boy's sunburned, broad face, his worn overalls, his somber expression.

Lucy took the photo back and placed it carefully in the box. Then she fitted the lid back in place. "It was so long ago, Patty, I doubt they even remember me anymore."

"I wish…" But what did Patty wish, exactly? Of course, she wanted to settle this business with the police as soon as possible, to clear her mother's name. But there was more. She wished Lucy had shown her these pictures long ago. She wished she'd met her grandmother before she died. And now that she had seen the wholly unsettling image of the girl her mother had once been, she wondered if she really knew her mother at all, and it seemed that discovering that truth was a dangerous thing to wish for.

"I don't know if I can tell it right after all these years," Lucy said, as though reading her thoughts. "Sometimes things get mixed up in my memory. But I'll tell you the best I can."

19

Manzanar
February 1943

LUCY WENT TO SCHOOL EARLY ON MONDAY and waited, shivering in the cold, outside Jessie's classroom. She had gone to his baseball game on Sunday afternoon and watched the whole thing, standing up against the chain-link fence, gripping the links so hard they left red marks on her fingers. He never looked her way. His expression never changed, not when he was crouched at the plate, or when he lunged to catch a grounder, or even when his team won the game four to zero. Afterward he left so fast that she wasn't able to catch up with him.

As kids arrived, blowing icy breaths on their way into the classroom, she started to wonder if Jessie would come to school today. Finally, as a teacher struck the brake drum that improvised as a school bell, he came jogging along the path, his book bag banging against his hip. He barely slowed when he saw her, bounding up the steps two at a time.

"Leave me alone," he muttered in a low voice. "Don't talk to me."

Lucy put her hand on his arm as he tried to pass, and he flinched—but at least he stopped.

"Jessie…what happened?"

"It doesn't matter. Just forget you ever saw me there. I'm serious. If you don't—bad things will happen."

"Bad things?" Lucy echoed.

"Just forget it, okay? Quit asking me!" Jessie wrenched his arm free, and Lucy saw that his eyes were puffy and rimmed with red. "You can't help me."

"Oh, Jessie—what did he do to you?"

He raked his hand through his hair and exhaled in frustration. His face was ashen and drawn; it looked like he hadn't had much sleep. "Nothing, just… *Nothing*. He was helping me with my stance. He used to play semipro. That's all it was, okay?"

Jessie had to know she would never believe the lie. They knew each other too well, had shared too many secrets. Lucy longed to touch him, to hold him and brush the hair from his brow the way she had a dozen times before, but his anger scared her.

"We have to tell someone," she said urgently. "Mr. Hamaguchi, he's on the community council, he can—"

"He can't do *anything*," Jessie snapped. "Forrest is friends with all of them—everyone who matters. He told me—"

He bit down on his words, staring off at the mountains, shaking his head.

"What? What did he tell you?"

"Only the truth. That no one would ever believe me over him. Look, Lucy, if you care about me at all, you have to let this drop. Just pretend you never saw anything and things can go back like they were before, okay?"

Lucy might have refused; she might have threatened to tell someone herself, promised she would stay by his side no matter what, but at that moment his teacher came outside and Jessie was gone, darting inside with the speed and agility of the baseball league champion he was, and Lucy walked slowly to her own classroom.

Lucy tried to talk to him one more time, at lunch. She approached their regular table with her tray, but Jessie got up and moved to another table. When she followed, he turned around and brandished his tray between them.

"I told you to leave me alone," he muttered in a low voice. "Don't talk to me. If you don't leave me alone, I'll... I'll..."

Lucy was devastated, but she was also angry. All she wanted was to talk, to understand, and he kept pushing her away. "You'll do what? How are you going to stop me?"

Jessie's hand was at her throat before she could blink, their trays crashing to the ground. He circled her neck with his hand but he didn't squeeze hard, mostly just shoving her into the table. Lucy's shin banged painfully against the edge of the seat and she pushed his hand away, only to have him fall against her. He made a sound like an animal as they tumbled to the floor together. Lucy struggled underneath him as teachers came running and other students yelled and tried to pull him away, but in the end Jessie rolled off her himself, backing away from her on his hands and knees, an apology in his haunted eyes.

In their room that night, Lucy watched her mother rub scented cream into her hands from a little jar that had recently appeared on the dresser without explanation. Her outline was hidden under her shapeless nightgown, but even so,

Lucy could see that Miyako had wilted and withered. Recently, it seemed as though her anxiety was starting to make her body sick in addition to her mind. She was more haggard than ever, and some nights she lay down for a nap the minute she came home from work.

Lucy had tried to stay silent about what had happened with Jessie, but the pain of his rejection combined with her fears about Reg were too much to bear alone. Lucy knew that what was happening to Jessie was wrong, and it seemed to be breaking him inside, but she also knew he was right to fear Forrest. The image of him cowering at the end of Reg's bed combined with her memory of Rickenbocker's crushing grip on her leg: they might both be evil, but they were also powerful and used to getting what they wanted.

Lucy had no illusions that Miyako could make Reg stop. He was a staff member, and a man; she was a woman, utterly powerless. But maybe she would know what Lucy should do, how to help her friend.

"Jessie pushed me at lunch today," she said carefully, and Miyako looked up sharply, cream shiny on her fingers.

"What would make him do such a thing?"

"I don't know. He's—he's mad at me."

"Did you two have a fight?"

"No. I—" Lucy swallowed; the words were hard to get out. "I went to see Reg Saturday morning and Jessie was there and he was sitting on the bed."

"You went to Reg's *room?*" Miyako looked taken aback. "Why would you go see him?"

"No. I only wanted…" Lucy bit her lip. "I had a letter to deliver to him."

"On a Saturday?"

"I was supposed to deliver it the day before. I tried, but

he wasn't there," Lucy said, unwilling to mention the motor pool office, the party she'd interrupted.

"*Lucy.*" Her mother sat very close to her on the bed and gripped her wrists. "How could you? After what happened? We talked about this. You must never go to see any of those men alone. Not any of the staff, even if you think they're trying to be nice to you. Do you understand me?"

Miyako's grip was surprisingly strong. Lucy breathed in her mother's smell. Miyako had stopped wearing perfume, and in recent weeks she had often skipped her late-night bath. Her odor was unpleasant to Lucy, earthy and ripe.

"How could I say no?" Lucy protested. "It's my job. I have to do whatever they tell me. You do whatever Mr. Rickenbocker tells you."

Her mother slapped her so fast she didn't see it coming, but the impact of her palm on Lucy's cheek was stunning. Tears immediately stung her cheeks.

"Oh, Lucy," Miyako cried, horrified. She cradled Lucy's face in the hand she'd slapped her with. Lucy tried to pull away, but her mother held tighter, mashing her cheeks. Lucy turned her face from Miyako's stale breath, but she couldn't twist out of her strong grip.

"Mama—let me go—"

"I can't always be with you! Don't you understand that? Don't you *see?*" She shook Lucy by the shoulders, making her teeth knock together. "They do whatever they want. Whatever they can get away with. We have no power here, none. We are prisoners and your only hope is to *stay away* from them."

Lucy's defiance vanished at the pain in her mother's ragged, broken voice. "I can get a different assignment," she offered, wanting to reassure her mother. "I can ask Mrs. Kadonada if I can file, or—"

"No, don't you see? It will never be enough, not if they decide to go after you. You'll never get away from them."

"Why would they go after *me*?"

"Lucy." Finally, her mother relaxed her grip, but she did not let go. Her eyes were glassy, her hair wild. "Do you know why I married your father?"

Renjiro Takeda had receded to the background of Lucy's thoughts lately. In her memory he was always dressed in fine clothes and scholarly spectacles, always with a pocketful of treats. The men at Manzanar dressed in rough clothes and dug ditches or washed dishes, or crouched outside the barracks playing dice games and smoking. It was unimaginable to Lucy that her father should ever be in a place such as this, squatting in the dirt with farmers, eating beans from a tin plate. Perhaps, somehow, he had known what the future held, and had wisely died before he could be dragged into this place of shame and suffering.

"No, Mama," Lucy whispered.

Miyako pursed her lips, seeking the right words. "Your father was a gentle man. He protected us. I thought… But you see, no one can protect you forever. Not even me."

Lucy didn't dare disagree, but as she thought of the girls in the motor pool office, Jessie sitting at the edge of the bed, even her own absent and much-missed father, she felt the stirring of rebellion. Lucy was not like those others.

She might not be able to protect her mother. She might not be able to help Jessie. But her mother was wrong about one thing: Lucy would find a way to protect herself. The night in the frozen garden, when Reg had dug his fingers into her flesh, she had still been a child. But something had changed. She could feel her strength coiled inside her, tense and ready to spring. She was tough and she was clever. She could be stronger than her fears. All this was true even if none of it was apparent on the outside yet. With Jessie she had taken the first steps toward womanhood, but now it loomed like a branch of a tree that for the first time she found herself tall enough to touch as she walked by.

She would not make the same mistakes again. She would not walk alone at night, would not go with strangers. If Rickenbocker or Reg or any of the others tried to talk to her, she would ignore them, and show them that she wasn't afraid. Someday, the war would be over and George Rickenbocker and Reg Forrest would be gone, and then nothing could stop her.

"Don't worry about me, Mother," she said.

Miyako's bitter, crazy laughter filled the room. "Worry is all I have left, *suzume*."

That night Lucy dreamed of a dress Miyako had once owned, long ago in Los Angeles. It was blue rayon with a tiny flowered print and puffed short sleeves. In the dream, Miyako's face and limbs were so thin that her bones protruded. Only her torso remained plump and full, the silky fabric stretched tight across her belly, her breasts. *Worry.* She was made of worry, her skin stretched with it, her body stuffed with it, like one of those olives stuffed with bright red pimento.

In the morning, Lucy heard her mother moan softly and then get out of bed and hurriedly dress, and she knew Miyako was about to be sick. It had happened twice before. Once she hadn't made it to the latrine, and even after Lucy scrubbed the floorboards, the smell lingered.

Mrs. Miatake, the mother of a girl in the third grade, had declined this way, spending several months in agony in her family's cramped quarters before being finally transferred to a hospital in the town of Independence, fifteen miles to the north, to be treated. But her stomach cancer was too advanced, and her family had not even been allowed to go see her before she died a week later. Now she was buried in the Manzanar cemetery, under an arrangement of rocks and a thin white wooden cross. Lucy could not stop thinking of her.

When she finally gathered the courage to ask her mother if she was going to die, Miyako only laughed bitterly and turned over in her bed, muttering that dying might be better. Lucy lay awake for a long time, trying to guess how much pain it would take before you would prefer death. She pinched her skin as hard as she could, first her thigh, then the sensitive skin under her arm, which brought tears to her eyes, and finally the soft flesh under her chin. That hurt terribly, but Lucy could still not imagine longing for death.

But maybe her mother knew things that Lucy didn't. It was clear that Miyako was not going to part with any of her secrets. Lucy could think of nothing else; she stopped doing her homework at night, and told Mrs. Kadonada she couldn't work because she was so far behind on her schoolwork. But the extra hours meant only that she watched and worried and came no closer to understanding the dark cloud that had lodged over her and Miyako.

One morning a few days later, her mother got up only long enough to go to the latrine. When she returned, her skin was ashen and she had vomit in her hair, but she went back to bed without attempting to clean herself.

"Go by the factory on your way to school, please, *suzume*," she murmured, already half asleep again. "Tell them I'm too sick to work today."

Something had to change. Lucy would go to the factory as her mother asked—but then, instead of going to school, she would find someone who could help.

20

THERE WAS FAR MORE COMMOTION AT THE net-making operation than there had been at the dress factory. Dozens of workers streamed into each of the three long buildings, the women's hair tied in kerchiefs, some of them wearing trousers. Lucy could see the huge nets hanging from the ceiling, waiting for camouflage material to be woven through the knotted hemp before the nets were shipped to the front lines.

"Excuse me," she said to a pair of middle-aged women walking up to the entrance together. "I am looking for Aiko Narita. She works here... Can you help me?"

The pair conferred a moment before deciding that they might know Aiko, and when Lucy followed them inside, she could see the reason for their confusion: there had to be more than a hundred workers on the line already, many of whose faces were obscured by the masks they wore to keep the hemp fibers out of their lungs.

"Wait here," they told Lucy, and she watched the workers while she waited, trying to imagine the faraway regiments of American soldiers who the nets would help to protect.

"Lucy!" Aiko rushed toward her, her mask hanging from the elastic around her neck. "Is everything all right?"

Lucy nodded, but when Aiko put her hands on Lucy's shoulders, she realized she was crying. "I'm sorry." She sniffled, ashamed.

Aiko put her arm around Lucy's shoulder and led her outside, away from the din and the crowds. Across the street were the warehouses, and at this hour of the morning they buzzed with activity, trucks making deliveries and carrying away finished goods.

"Not here," Aiko said. "We won't be able to hear ourselves think."

They walked down D Street to Block Three, where the residents had built a pair of benches facing each other over a tiny gazing pond. A young mother dandled a baby on one bench, but the other was empty, and Aiko led Lucy there and patted the seat.

"Now sit and tell me what's wrong."

"It's my mother," Lucy said miserably. She managed to stay dry-eyed as she confessed her fears, describing Miyako's strange behavior, the sickness, her refusal to get up that morning.

"Oh, Lucy, your mother is going to be fine," Aiko said when Lucy finished speaking, brushing the hair off her brow.

"No, she isn't." Lucy couldn't bear to be lied to. "Please, Auntie, tell me what's wrong."

"Your mother…" Aiko began, and then she stalled, searching for the right words. "She has not had a lucky life. She tries hard, though, Lucy. You know that, right? There is nothing in this world that she loves more than you."

Lucy tried to control her impatience. Of course she knew these things already, but they did nothing to clarify what was wrong with Miyako. "She is sick a lot, Auntie. She doesn't eat. She sleeps all the time. Does she have what Mrs. Miatake had? Is she going to die?"

It was only because Aiko looked genuinely startled that Lucy believed her. "Your mother is dealing with some things, but she is going to be all right. I'll talk to her, Lucy. I'll come see her tomorrow. Okay?"

Lucy was reassured, but it wasn't enough. "You have to tell me what's wrong with her," she pleaded.

Aiko sighed and squeezed Lucy's hand harder. Up close like this, Lucy saw that Aiko's face was lined with a web of fine wrinkles that she didn't remember from before. Her lipstick was smudged and there were flakes of dust in her hair.

"There is nothing wrong with your mother that she won't recover from," Aiko finally said. "The important thing is that it isn't her fault. Nothing is her fault."

"I don't understand."

"Lucy, I can't tell you everything. You just have to trust me. I'm going to do what I can. There are good people here. All you need to do is look after yourself. That's your job right now, Lucy, to take care of yourself. And let us do the rest."

"But, Auntie Aiko, what's going to happen?" Lucy asked in a very small voice.

Though Aiko said all the right things, Lucy knew that she was lying. There was nothing Aiko could do. In the end, Miyako would continue to wither.

Eventually they got up from the bench, and Aiko patted Lucy's hands. "I will come visit tomorrow. It will all be okay."

Lucy walked slowly back through camp toward Block Fourteen, not realizing until she was nearly there that her feet had carried her by force of habit. She had already missed the start of the school day, and for a moment she considered going into her barrack and checking on her mother.

But in the end, she didn't go inside. She turned around and walked in the direction of the school, too afraid of what she might find.

The next day brought record cold, the windows laced with frost on the inside. Miyako seemed to be feeling better. She came back from the shower with color in her cheeks, and ate the toast Lucy brought her.

"I'm still so tired," she said. "I think I'll stay home from work one more day."

Before Lucy left for school, she piled all the extra blankets on her mother's lap and around her shoulders. The oil stove burned day and night, but it couldn't heat the entire barrack, and Miyako only stopped shivering when she was bundled up.

Lucy stayed late at school to make up for being late the day before. When she got back to Block Fourteen, it was already dinnertime, so she ate quickly and went through the line again to get a plate for her mother.

But when she got to the room, Aiko was visiting. She was still dressed for work, her hair tied in a scarf, an old blouse covering her clothes. Miyako was wearing a clean dress and a bit of makeup. She had made tea and set it out on the little table between the beds, but it looked untouched.

"Lucy, why don't you run along now," Aiko said, after greeting her. "Your mother and I need to talk. Just for a little while."

The last thing Lucy wanted was to go out into the cold again, especially since night had fallen fast and it was already dark. But Aiko had kept her promise, and Lucy was grateful. She made a show of stomping back out of the room, open-

ing the barracks door and letting it slam shut. Then she tiptoed back to eavesdrop.

"We can't talk here," Lucy heard Aiko saying softly. "But
I know a place. We'll need to bundle up."

Lucy had to hurry to get outside into the frigid night before they spotted her, holding the latch of the door with her
index finger as it closed, slipping it slowly into place without a
sound. She waited around the corner, out of view; after a few
minutes the door opened and her mother and Aiko came out.

It wasn't difficult to follow them. They walked slowly,
Aiko's arm around Miyako, supporting her thin frame. The
cold had kept everyone inside, so Lucy waited until Aiko
and Miyako had gone a block down D Street before setting
out after them. On either side, the lights inside the barracks
made little yellow squares in the inky night; up above, the
lights in the guard towers competed with the starlight.

It didn't take Lucy long to figure out her mother and Aiko
were headed for the net factory. Tomorrow it would be teem-
ing with extra shifts again, but for the moment it was dark
and shuttered. Lucy wondered if Aiko had been given her
own key—she had been promoted to supervisor—but she
and Miyako bypassed the front door and continued around
to the back.

There, between the first and second buildings, a shelter had
been constructed for workers to take smoke breaks. The small
wooden hut had tar-paper-covered walls for wind protec-
tion, and gaps at the base and roofline for circulation; someone had dragged chairs inside. Lucy cautiously approached,
and she could hear the scrape of the chairs against the plank
floors as her mother and Aiko settled in for their talk.

The cold was a small price to pay for precious privacy,
but for Lucy it was another matter, since she'd left the barrack with no hat or scarf. She huddled close to the hut, shel-

tered from the wind, but already her fingers and ears ached. When she pressed her cheek against the wall, she could hear their voices clearly.

"We'll find a way." Aiko's voice was soothing. "We have a little time. We will make our case."

"There is no case to make," Miyako protested. "Not if what you say is true. When will the charges be filed?"

"Not until Monday, and they won't meet to rule on them until later in the week. It will have to go in front of the judicial commission."

"But if they decide to prosecute, I'll be taken to Independence. And if it really was George who accused me—"

"It was him, Miyako. I am so sorry." In Aiko's voice Lucy heard echoes of the afternoons the two women had spent together back in Los Angeles, in their kitchens, two wealthy widows whose lives spun out before them with no greater hardships than monotony and loneliness. For a second Lucy allowed herself to wish that things had never changed, that she could close her eyes and return to the kitchen on Clement Street, her mother pouring tea from her great-grandmother's porcelain pot, serving the little dumplings they bought at Paris Bakery.

But then Miyako's voice dragged Lucy back to the present. "If it was George, then there is no hope."

"Miyako...there is something you should know. He apparently has witnesses tying you to the theft."

"But I've never even been in the warehouse!"

"I know, but he has people who will testify that they saw you there."

"Oh, Aiko..."

"Don't think about it now," Aiko said soothingly.

"I'll be found guilty for sure. No one will come to my

defense. And when I'm found guilty, they will separate me and Lucy."

Her mother's words stunned Lucy. Why would Rickenbocker accuse Miyako of stealing? And how could they take her away when she had done nothing wrong?

It had never occurred to Lucy that they might be separated. How would she survive without her mother? How would Miyako manage to take care of herself?

"Listen, Miyako," Aiko said hesitantly. "There is one thing we haven't tried. If someone could go to George and speak to him about the baby. Appeal to his sense of responsibility, of—"

"No," her mother interrupted, her voice breaking. *"No."*

But Lucy barely heard her mother, caught up short by Aiko's words. *Baby.* Lucy turned the word in her mind, and as she did, a dozen other pieces shifted and slid into place, and the mystery of her mother's illness faded. The dream she'd had of her mother suddenly made sense, her body shriveling to a skeleton, the life leeching from her, only her stomach growing, grotesque and distended. The smell of vomit and despair, faint blue lines in her mother's skin, tea growing cold in the cup.

Her mother was pregnant, and George Rickenbocker had made her that way—and now he was trying to send her away, to get rid of the evidence of their sins. No wonder her mother's behavior had changed. It wasn't that Miyako had refused him, as Lucy had assumed—but Rickenbocker, once he found out about the baby, no longer wanted her.

Lucy pressed her hands against the cold, splintered wood of the building, the bile roiling in her gut. Her mother was pregnant with a child who would be half Lucy's brother or sister and half the tainted, poisonous issue of George Rickenbocker. And now he had turned away from Miyako and his hungry, foul eyes had found Lucy.

"After everything I did, I tried so hard to protect her," Miyako mumbled. "I thought that if I just went along, I could outlast him. That the war would end, and if he had me, he would never go after her."

"Miyako, no one is going to hurt Lucy," Aiko said. "She's just a child."

"*I* was only a child!" Miyako whispered fiercely. "That didn't stop them."

"That was different, you have to see that. You were alone—there was no one around to help. Here, there are people everywhere you turn."

"But George—"

"Hush," Aiko said. "You have to stop thinking this way. George won't go after her. I hear he's already found someone new, a girl from steno."

Lucy felt frozen, remembering the way Rickenbocker had looked at her, how strong his hands had been when he squeezed her flesh. *I'm sure we'll be seeing each other again soon,* he had said.

"You don't know him the way I do. Those other girls are nothing to him. He was only happy when he was hurting me. The ones who let him—he doesn't care about them. He'll go after her to hurt me, don't you see?"

"That's crazy," Aiko exclaimed, but Lucy heard the tiny note of doubt in her voice.

"*Look* at her, Aiko, see what I see," Miyako implored. "She is ripe now. And when I'm gone—"

"If you are gone, then I will watch over her."

"You're at the net factory all day long!"

"And she is at school. This war is going to end, you must

never forget that. We just have to endure. A little longer, Miyako, for both of you."

"I have no more time." Miyako's words turned to sobs, choked syllables of grief, of despair. "I am cursed. We are both cursed. I should never have had her."

Aiko shushed her, soothing, denying—but Lucy was savaged by her mother's words. "Mama," she whimpered, but her voice was stolen away by the wind.

21

WITH DAWN CAME SHOUTING. AT FIRST IT WAS distant, maybe one or two streets over, and then people were running outside the thin walls of their barrack.

"It's George Rickenbocker! He's been killed!"

Lucy pushed at her blankets, struggling to sit up. Her mother was already out of bed, standing motionless in the center of the room. Her hair fell around her face in mussed waves, and her skin was as pale as a paper parasol.

Miyako turned slowly and gave Lucy a look she would never forget, and she knew her life had changed forever.

The building resounded with the clatter of feet hitting the floor and people talking over one another. Shouts echoed up and down the building as they pulled on jackets and shoes or, in some cases, bolted outside barefoot to find out what was going on. The door slammed over and over again as everyone raced out into the streets, and in almost no time at all the building was silent save for the wheezing of an old asthmatic woman and the whimpering of an infant.

"Mama…" Lucy whispered, her heart pounding.

"Get up now." Miyako's voice was calm.

She pulled back the curtain and headed into the hallway, where she opened the door a few inches and peered through for a moment. When she returned, tears glistened in her eyes, but she didn't bother to wipe them away.

Lucy had managed to sit up and was pulling up her socks, which had gotten twisted during the night. Miyako crouched down in front of her at the edge of her bed, and placed her hands gently on either side of her face. Lucy closed her eyes and concentrated on her mother's hands and pretended for a second that everything in the world was different.

After a moment, Miyako released her. "Someday you will understand. Everything I do, I do for you, *suzume*."

She walked into the corridor, and Lucy touched her face where her mother's hands had been. There was a humming inside her head, a cottony thrum. There had to be a way to undo all the things that had happened, all the grief that had settled in like veins of ore in stone. The baby her mother carried. The memory of Rickenbocker's hands on her flesh. The jagged place in her heart where memories of her father were secreted away.

There was a clanking sound from the hallway, the sound of metal on metal, a jagged scrape. After a moment Miyako returned, rubbing her hands on her skirt. Her shoulders were stooped, her face drawn and hopeless. She took Lucy's hand and tugged it, no longer looking at her. "Come with me," she murmured.

"What? Where are we going?"

"Nowhere." Miyako sighed wearily and added, "Somewhere safe."

Lucy allowed her mother to lead her out of the room, and the two of them walked barefoot into the empty corridor. The rough planks were cold and dusted with grit under Lucy's feet. Outside, the shouts of the crowd escalated and a truck rolled by. Miyako pulled her along, her grip tightening. Lucy wondered if they were going to look after the crying baby, but her mother passed by their neighbors' room without a glance.

Miyako finally stopped in front of the oil heater at the end of the hall. She murmured something Lucy could not hear and bent down behind the hulking metal box, and when she stood up again, she was holding a black dish in her hand. She flung her arm and liquid arced from the dish, flashing rainbows in the air, like spray sent up from a wave off Ocean Beach on a hot day.

Lucy had time to put out her hand, as if she were trying to catch raindrops. In the next second, her face exploded with pain so fierce she thought it had been cleaved in two.

22

SHE COULD NOT LATER SAY WHO PICKED HER up and carried her to the hospital. A man—someone with a broad, bony chest against which she remembered bumping as he ran.

Lucy eventually pieced together what had happened from fragments she heard from her hospital bed. They said that she never stopped screaming, that her eyes were open while the right half of her face cracked and blackened. Lucy did not remember seeing anything at all.

She had many weeks to imagine what the dawn sky must have looked like that morning, the path her rescuer would have taken to the hospital. She would have seen guard towers, the spindly branches of elms, electric poles, perhaps a few birds circling over the commotion. The last thing she would have seen would have been the overhang of the hospital entrance, then Dr. Ambrose's face as he bent over her. It was a stroke of luck that he was there at all—he'd been in Rickenbocker's apartment moments earlier, pronouncing him dead, and had just returned to the hospital.

Lucy did not know any of these things at first. What she knew was the pain, which consumed her.

Lucy forced her eyes open—the left first, and then, with a mighty effort, the right, though it took several tries and light flickered before she was able to keep them open. But it was bright, so bright, and the shapes and patterns made no sense. Lucy tried to lift her hands but she couldn't.

"Mama," she cried, but her voice came out a broken whisper and the effort of speaking hurt. Her mouth—her mouth was wrong, it was a searing, jagged tear. But it didn't matter. "Mama—" she tried again.

There was a whoosh of movement and then a shadow over her. Something touched her hair, softly. A face blurred and then slowly resolved, the soft and wrinkled face of an old woman floating above her, her head surrounded by the fabric of a wimple. It must be one of the nuns.

"Lucy," the woman said gently. Lucy focused on the woman's lips. She had uneven teeth, a bit yellow, but her smile was kind. Lucy tried to speak but evidently she wasn't up to the task.

Lucy hurt and she wanted her mother. She tried to sit up to look for Miyako, but she could not move.

"No, no, these are for your own good, these are to keep you from hurting yourself," the nun said.

It took a moment for Lucy to understand that the nun meant her hands, her wrists. Something was keeping them fastened down. Lucy thought she might ask, but it suddenly seemed like a very good time to take a rest, and her eyes fluttered closed.

The next time she woke up, Lucy found that her voice came to her more easily, though it was no less agonizing and her mouth was dry and sticky. On one side of her bed a curtain hung from a pole, but on the other the curtain had been pushed back and she could see another bed—in fact, an entire row of them.

"Hello," she croaked. She realized she didn't know the name of the nun. "Are you there?"

"I'll get her for you," a voice said somewhere down the row, a boy's voice. "Nurse!" he called, and a moment later a woman arrived, a stranger. She was dressed in a nurse's white dress and cap.

It was dizzying, trying to follow the nurse's face as she moved in and out of Lucy's vision. "Please don't move," the nurse said as her hands adjusted something near Lucy's face, sending sharp blades of pain through her. Lucy could feel layers of bandages covering her face; they shifted slightly at her smallest movement, adding to the pain. "I will get the doctor for you."

"No." The word dredged more pain, but Lucy pushed at her teeth with her tongue and managed one more scorched syllable: "Nun." She didn't want yet another stranger touching her. The nun's hands had been soft when she touched Lucy's hair, her voice gentle, her smile kind and unafraid.

"You mean Sister Jeanne? She's not here right now, but she might come by again later. Now you'll see the doctor."

Lucy breathed shallowly as she waited. Speaking had loosed a sharp new pain around her lips, and by the time Dr. Ambrose pulled a chair over to Lucy's cot and sat down, tears had pooled in her eyes. She was afraid that if they spilled onto her skin they would hurt, but she couldn't lift her hands to dab them away.

Lucy knew who Dr. Ambrose was. He'd been in charge the day she got her vaccinations. It seemed so long ago, but he looked exactly the same, an old man with a rounded back and white eyebrows that seemed to go in whatever direction they pleased. He pressed his hands together and regarded her with milky-blue eyes.

"Lucille," he said gravely, "you have suffered severe burns on your face, which we are treating to the best of our ability. These restraints are temporary, to assure that you don't injure yourself, but you may expect a full recovery in time."

He stopped and sighed, allowing his gaze to drift to the corner of the room for a moment. He seemed nervous or uncomfortable, patting his knees with his palms and clearing his throat. "There will be pain as you heal, but we will do our best to keep it under control. How does that sound?"

Lucy tried to speak but was hampered by the pain. The challenge of forming the sounds she needed—the "p" in *please,* the "m" in *Mama*—seemed insurmountable.

The doctor seemed to shrink back from her broken sounds, and Lucy was afraid he was leaving.

"Mother." She forced it out using all her stores of endurance, though it escaped as barely a whisper.

"Lucy, I am afraid I have some very sad news for you." He took off his glasses, cleared his throat again and put them back on. "You see, your mother, she… It's just that, after… well… We are all so very sorry, Lucy, but your mother… I'm afraid that she has taken her own life."

23

San Francisco
Friday, June 9, 1978

PATTY SLEPT POORLY, PLAGUED BY FITFUL
dreams of which she could only remember bits and pieces—
walking beside a razor-wire fence that never ended, searching
for her mother, a stack of torn photos in her hands.

Yesterday's talk with her mother had exhausted her. She
had been moved to tears as Lucy talked about her time in
Manzanar, especially when she spoke of her friend Jessie,
her first love, and the abuse he had suffered at the hands of
Reg Forrest.

Patty was stunned by this revelation, and by her mother's
display of emotion as she recounted the story. She couldn't
remember the last time she had seen her mother cry, and
she realized how deeply her time in the camp had wounded
her. Here was reason for her mother to resent Reg Forrest—

enough to wish him dead. But why now? Why wait all these years?

"I hated him," her mother said quietly, as if reading her thoughts. "Sometimes I'd think of him, getting to live out his life like he hadn't done anything, like he was innocent. You asked me if I knew he lived in the neighborhood, Lucy, and I admit I didn't tell you the truth. I did know, probably for the last eight or ten years, since he was listed in the newsletter. I can't even stand to walk by that place."

She shuddered—convincingly, Patty had to admit. "But you never told Jessie?"

"Of course not. We lost touch."

"And the newsletter…"

"It doesn't list everyone, Patty. How could it? There were ten thousand of us, scattered everywhere now."

She returned to the story of her camp years, talking about the teasing she suffered at the hands of the Caucasian girls, the academic prizes she won despite a textbook shortage. Patty was having trouble reconciling the solitary, taciturn woman she knew now with the spirited girl in the school photos. It was as though her mother had once been an entirely different person, and Patty faulted herself for never having seen far enough into her depths, for not being curious enough to coax out the story until now.

But once Lucy started, she didn't stop.

When evening came, and neither of them had touched the lunch they brought home, Patty threw out the ruined meal and offered to make dinner. As she boiled spaghetti and opened a jar of sauce, she made a mental list of questions and wondered how she might apologize to her mother for not asking them sooner. But by the time she had the food on the table, her mother had fallen asleep on the living room couch.

Patty covered her up, ate a few bites of spaghetti, scraped the rest down the drain and was in bed herself by ten.

By the time she woke up, her mother had already left for work. After her shower, Patty put on the silky robe that Jay had given her for Valentine's Day and dried her hair with her new round brush, the one that was supposed to give her waves like Jaclyn Smith's. She'd been planning to work on the wedding favors, but she couldn't stop thinking about the box of photos her mother had managed to keep secret all these years. She checked on the coffee table where she'd last seen it, but her mother must have put it away when she woke on the couch in the middle of the night and went to bed.

Patty hesitated only for a moment before deciding to search for the box. She had a pretty good idea where to start looking. Lucy wasn't sentimental, but she did keep a shelf full of things from the past in her bedroom closet, mostly her old taxidermy equipment, the tools of a trade Lucy had practiced when Patty was still a baby. Patty had always found it gruesome—embarrassing, even, during her adolescence—and she hadn't looked in that closet in years.

She padded barefoot to her mother's room and opened the door carefully, though she was alone in the house. The closet door squeaked when she opened it, startling her. The wooden and metal implements from her mother's long-ago taxidermy practice shared shelf space with boxes bearing incomprehensible labels like "Stuffers" and "Merlins wheels."

Lucy found the soap tin behind a cardboard box of paints and glues. For a moment she stared at the dark, dusty corner of the closet, thinking about her mother moving the little cache of memories from one cramped apartment to another. She pushed the box of paints back into place and shut the closet door, then took the tin to her own room. She crawled back into bed, pulling the sheet up over her lap, then set the tin in her lap and looked at it for a moment. Finally she took a deep breath and pried off the lid. She took out the first few photos, the ones she'd already seen, and laid them face-down. Her plan was to view everything in order, so that if her mother checked, she wouldn't know the contents had been disturbed.

The next item was a letter, written in a blocky hand on unlined paper, folded in thirds. It was worn along the creases and edges, as though it had been read many times. Patty unfolded it carefully, barely breathing, and read it through. Then she read it a second time.

Lucy:
It is almost three o'clock in the morning, and I think you are asleep. You are only ten or fifteen feet away from me, but it might as well be a thousand miles. Now that you know ev-erything I can teach you, I have nothing more to give. I wish for so many things, but most of all I wish for your happiness. I have had so many long nights to wonder why things happen the way they do, why people get hurt and dreams and plans disappear in a single second, and I am no closer to understand-ing now than I have ever been. But one thing has changed. I used to believe I could never be happy again, but then you taught me that life continues, even after it seems that every-thing has ended.
May angels watch over you as you sleep.
Your G., always

Patty read the letter again, and then once more before setting it gently on the stack. Who was G.? Was it possible it was the boy from the picture, the boy who helped out at the motel? But this letter didn't sound like it had been writ-ten by a boy at all. What did Lucy mean to him? Could the letter have been written by Patty's father? If so, who had he been and what had he taught Lucy?

The doorbell rang, making Patty jump. She set the letter down carefully and raced to the front door, pulling the robe tighter and adjusting the sash. She opened the door without undoing the safety chain, just far enough to see that Inspector Torre waited on the porch, accompanied by a uniformed police officer.

"Miss Takeda," he said, nodding.

"My mother isn't here."

"Yes, we know. She's at the police station."

"What? Why is she there? Did you arrest her?"

"No, we asked her to come in and answer some questions. We can call her in a few minutes if you like. But first, Officer Grieg and I would like to come in and take a look around."

"In—in here? My mother's house?"

"Yes, Miss Takeda. We have a warrant." Torre pulled a piece of paper from his pocket, and handed it to her through the narrow opening.

Patty scanned the single page quickly, then forced herself to slow down and read. There—her mother's address. The date. A bunch of legalese.

She fumbled with the chain, her fingers shaking, then stepped back from the door. The men walked past her, Torre murmuring a polite thank-you as he passed, Grieg already pulling a pair of disposable gloves out of a bag. The situation felt like it was getting away from her, as though she had made a fundamental error from which it would be impossible to recover.

"I think I should talk to my mother. And I wasn't... I just got out of the shower." Her more pressing concern was the box of papers sitting on her bed. She winced as she realized she was doubting her mother's innocence—but it wasn't that, not really, was it? She just wanted to have a chance to make sure there wasn't anything in the box that could be misconstrued, that could give a wrong impression.

"Don't worry, Miss Takeda. Why don't you go take a minute for yourself and I'll call the station. May I use your phone?"

Patty showed him where the phone was, then hurried to her bedroom and shut the door behind her. She scooped up the letter and photos and jammed them back into the tin box and mashed the lid back on. But where to put it? Patty looked frantically around the room for a hiding place. She yanked open the nightstand drawer and shoved aside a stack of old *Reader's Digests*, a tube of hand lotion and a wadded Kleenex. The tin barely fit, and she had to shove hard to get the drawer to close again.

She had a better hiding place for the albums. She swung open the closet door, unzipped the garment bag that held her wedding dress, and slipped the albums under the square piece of satin-covered cardboard that formed the base of the bag. Their weight made the bag droop a little, but that was all.

Patty grabbed a few things out of her suitcase—a pair of slacks and a work blouse. The floor around the suitcase was covered in laundry, and after quickly changing, she gathered up all the clothes and her robe and tossed them into the case and closed it. It seemed like ages since she'd moved out of her old apartment, but it had only been a week.

By the time she returned to the kitchen, she was perspiring. Down the hall, she could hear Officer Grieg moving things around.

Torre was talking on the phone. "Oh, here she is. Go ahead and put Mrs. Takeda on."

Patty grabbed the phone. "Hello? Mom?"

"Patty, it's me. I'm at the police station." There was talking behind her, men's voices, their words indistinguishable.

"Mom, the police are here. They're searching the house."

She waited, certain that now her mother would tell her something that would explain it all, why she was in the DeSoto the other day, a coincidence, an explanation, *something*. But Lucy said nothing.

"Mom? Are you there?" Panic rose up in Patty's voice and she squeezed the receiver with both hands.

"I'm here, I'm fine. But I think it's time I get a lawyer."

"What? Why? When are you coming home?"

"I might be here a little while longer. I'm sure it'll be fine."

"When can I see you?"

"I don't think they'll let you see me here, Patty. Listen… I'll call you as soon as I can." There was a hesitation, and Lucy thought her mother had already hung up. "I love you, Patty," she said, very quietly, and the words echoed in Patty's mind long after the phone went dead.

24

Manzanar
April 1943

DAYS WENT BY—THREE, FOUR, LUCY COULDN'T keep track—and gradually the haze began to lift. She was becoming aware of the people around her. The boy who had called for the nurse that first day was gone, and other patients came and went before she could learn their names. The nurses, all of whom had worked in Los Angeles before being interned, spoke in soft voices as they moved efficiently around Lucy's bed, whisking away her linens and replacing the water in the pitcher next to her bed.

Sister Jeanne came to visit most days, often sitting quietly by Lucy's bedside, reading or marking papers. Sister Jeanne was not a big talker, but she was a comfort nonetheless. Behind her thick glasses, her eyes were large and curious. When Lucy moaned or winced with pain, Sister Jeanne held her hand and soothed her with idle conversation about the pets her family had owned when she was little, or about the trips she took to visit her sister in San Diego, where her sister made ice cream on the back porch.

One afternoon she brought Lucy a bouquet of flowers in a glass pickle jar, orange poppies and pastel snapdragons and a burst of tiny white daisies.

"These are from Block Twenty-nine," she said. "With their best wishes for you to get well soon."

As Sister Jeanne fussed with the blooms, Lucy tried to re-member if she knew any residents of Block Twenty-nine, and couldn't come up with anyone. Lucy knew she wasn't allowed visitors yet, but now she wished someone from her own block had sent the flowers, or one of the kids from school. Jessie—how she would have loved a note from him, a flower, even one of the flat stones he loved to skip in the creek. Maybe, once she was better, she could ask Sister Jeanne to take him a letter.

As soon as she had the thought, Lucy dismissed it. She had yet to see her face in a mirror, but she knew from the pain and from the way the nurses looked at her that it was bad. Jessie wouldn't want her anymore, even if he wasn't so angry all the time.

"Sister Jeanne," she said. Nearly a week had passed, and talking came more easily now. "Tell me what really hap-pened."

Jeanne's hands stilled on the bouquet. Lucy could tell that she had pains of her own, from the way she moved her thick legs and freckled arms so carefully. She knew Jeanne didn't want to tell what she knew, but Lucy had no one else to ask.

The only other patient in the ward, a little girl with the measles, was sleeping, but Jeanne still spoke softly, as though what she had to say was a secret.

"People heard your screams and came running," she said,

tucking a loose strand of Lucy's hair behind her ear. She liked to keep her hands busy when she sat with Lucy, and she was always adjusting the sheets and pillow, smoothing her blankets, patting her arms. "They found you on the floor in the hall of your building."

"Was I alone?"

"Yes, of course you were," Jeanne said. "This was just a terrible accident, Lucy. They say the heating pan had somehow come loose from the brace inside the stove, they don't know how. You don't remember that? You didn't touch the stove, maybe try to adjust it yourself?"

Lucy had been asked the question so many times—by Dr. Ambrose and, later, by a man from the maintenance staff— that she lied with ease. "I don't even remember going into the hall."

"Well. It's no matter now, no sense focusing on that. They think it might have ignited and flared up, or there was maybe even a bit of an explosion that made the oil go through the air like that. But that's not what you want to know, I don't think." She picked up one of Lucy's hands in her own. They were old and wrinkled but warm. "I am guessing you want to talk about your mother."

Lucy nodded, not daring to look into Jeanne's kind eyes. She had replayed that morning dozens of times in her mind: Miyako, taking her hand and leading her into the hall. Their bare feet on the rough, cold wood. The shouting outside the building. The stove, hissing and smoking, her mother, reaching for something behind its iron hulk…

Her memories really did stop there, but she knew the truth: Miyako had done this to her. Deliberately. She would never tell a soul, but she still longed to know about her mother's last moments, the time between when she let Lucy go and when she died. "I just wondered if anyone saw her after."

"She wasn't at the barrack," Jeanne said. "You already know that after they found you, some people brought you here to the hospital. Everyone was terribly worried about you. They didn't know the extent of your injuries."

"You mean people thought I was going to die?"

"I think some people were afraid that was a possibility," Jeanne said quietly. "So you can understand that people were searching everywhere for your mother. It wasn't until later in the day that some kids playing near the net factory found her."

"And she hanged herself." Lucy said it herself to spare Sister Jeanne, a fact she had pieced together from the bits she'd heard the nurses saying when they thought she was asleep. "In the smoking hut."

Jeanne blinked. "Yes, Lucy, I am afraid that is true, although—"

"Was there a note?"

Surprise and dismay flashed across the nun's face. "Please, Sister Jeanne, please just tell me. I have to know."

Sister Jeanne sighed and she looked even older, her wrinkled skin sagging. But she didn't let go of Lucy's hand, and Lucy held on tight. "You must understand, Lucy, the MPs took the note. I never actually saw it."

"But they told you what it said. Right? When you started coming to see me."

"In general terms, yes, but I can't tell you exactly—"

"I don't need to know exactly, just tell me what you know."

For a long moment Jeanne said nothing, biting her lip. "Your mother confessed to killing George Rickenbocker."

Lucy felt as though the air was sucked out of her. "Does... does everyone know?"

"The case is closed, Lucy, and since your mother has

passed, there is nothing more to be done. But people talk. There are rumors…all kinds of rumors. The note didn't give any reasons, just your mother's confession, and her body was laid to rest without any further investigation."

Lucy wondered if Sister Jeanne was alluding to the baby inside her mother. But no one knew about the baby, no one but Auntie Aiko and her. And Rickenbocker, but he was dead too. And now the baby was buried inside her mother, and they would always be together, in the little cemetery at the edge of the camp.

"He was so mean to her," Lucy whispered.

"I'm sorry," Jeanne said. "So very sorry, for everything. For your mother's suffering."

Lucy saw how it would be; people would learn that Mi-yako had been hurt, and maybe they would forgive her, at least a little. The story would swell up with all their guessing and gossiping, but eventually it would fade away, and people would remember how beautiful she was, and be glad that she died without ever having to know what happened to her daughter. Maybe they would curse Rickenbocker and be glad he was dead. Maybe the pretty girls would stop going to the parties in the motor pool. Maybe the soldiers and the staff would be more careful now, even a little bit afraid.

Maybe Reg would leave Jessie alone.

"Lucy, I want you to know something else," Jeanne said. "In a case like this, where someone has suffered, as your mother suffered, God can be…compassionate. I believe for-giveness is possible, even for the gravest of sins. Even for taking a life."

It took Lucy a second to understand that Jeanne meant God's forgiveness, not her own.

"You mean she won't have to go to hell."

Jeanne nodded. "I have been praying for her soul, Lucy, and for the intervention of the Holy Spirit."

Sister Jeanne was kind, but Lucy knew, without even a hint of doubt, that her mother was finally at peace, that all she ever wanted was to be safe. In death, no one could ever hurt Miyako again. Lucy wasn't sure she even believed in hell, at least not for someone like her mother. Someone who'd done her best all her life, whose failures were never for a lack of trying.

Before she died, Miyako had made sure no one would ever try to hurt Lucy either. If her mother's gift had been bound up with suffering, Lucy knew it was also a gift of mercy.

She would never tell anyone what her mother had done to her. Miyako was past suffering, but people would never understand. Lucy couldn't even tell Jeanne, which made her sad: already, she was learning how lonely it was to be a keeper of secrets.

But she would manage. That would be her gift to Miyako.

25

WEEKS PASSED, AND THE PAIN RECEDED. THE bandages were gone now, and sometimes in the dark Lucy snuck her fingertips over the landscape of her scars. She begged the nurses to give her a mirror, but they said it was too soon. "Just a little while longer," they always promised. "So you can see how you are healing."

So you don't see how ugly you are now, Lucy imagined them thinking. It was disturbing to think that next time she saw her reflection, it would be a new face, a stranger's face. But she still wanted to know.

In a few weeks the risk of infection had passed and Lucy was allowed to have guests. Auntie Aiko and Mr. Hamaguchi were the first to come visit her, and Lucy was sitting up in bed when the nurse led them into the room one Saturday, her breakfast tray barely touched at her bedside. Mr. Hamaguchi was wearing a suit that was too large for him, the cuffs overhanging his wrists and the shoulders sitting awkwardly on his thin frame. Lucy thought that if Miyako were alive, she would have insisted on helping Aiko tailor his suit. She would never have allowed Lucy's father out of the house in such badly fitting clothes.

Aiko was dressed up as well, like the privileged woman she once was. The dress she wore was one Lucy remembered from before—a green bouclé with three-quarter sleeves—but the privations of camp life showed in the way the dress hung on her. She and Mr. Hamaguchi were like a matching pair of scarecrows.

Aiko clutched her purse and a neatly folded paper bag tightly at her abdomen, smiling stiffly. "Lucy…it is so good to see you." She held out the paper bag. "We brought you some things from the store. Magazines—*Movie Life,* and *Movie Story Year Book*. And candy."

"Thank you, Auntie." Lucy swallowed the lump that had suddenly formed in her throat.

Aiko's smile faltered. "Oh, Lucy," she said softly, her voice catching.

"You can sit in that chair," Lucy said politely, pointing at the chair Sister Jeanne used when she visited. Aiko dragged the chair so close to the bed that her knees touched the mattress, and took Lucy's hand in hers.

"I'm sorry," she murmured. "With everything that's happened… Oh, Lucy, I don't even know what to say."

Lucy held on tight, not trusting her voice. She remembered how Aiko used to come over with shiny pennies for her when she was little, slipping them solemnly into Lucy's little white patent-leather purse, whispering that one day she would be rich and famous.

"The nurses say you are healing very well," Aiko continued gamely. Mr Hamaguchi nodded encouragingly.

Lucy tried for a smile, grateful for once for the pain, since it took her breath away, along with the urge to cry. "They treat me very well."

"This will help you to pass the time." Aiko tapped the bag of gifts, the paper crinkling. "Before you know it, you'll be out of the hospital."

"Thank you," Lucy repeated.

"Lucy, I thought you'd like to know that Mr. Hamaguchi's friend has made a marker for your mother's grave."

"Mr. Kado, he is very skilled. He made the cemetery monument." Mr. Hamaguchi clasped his hands behind his back and rocked on his heels. Lucy knew the monument he was talking about—it loomed large and impressive in the center of the graveyard, which had been cleared and ringed with smooth stones by volunteers. "Maybe you would like to go see it, when you are feeling a little better."

Lucy had not allowed herself to think of her mother's body buried under the earth. It was simply too painful. "Auntie Aiko," she said, changing the subject, "do you have a compact in your purse?"

Aiko froze. She loosened her grip on Lucy's hand and shifted her gaze to the starched hem of the bedsheets. "I am sorry, I don't."

Lucy knew it wasn't true: Aiko carried a compact with her everywhere. "Please, Auntie, I need to see," she whispered.

"I don't think it's a good idea," Aiko said. Lucy's hand slipped from hers. "Give it time—you have more healing to do. The doctor will say when you are ready."

"Please. It's my face, I need to know."

The look that passed between Aiko and Mr. Hamaguchi was full of regret. Years later, it would occur to Lucy that they had been considering taking her with them. They would be married by the end of the war; they could have adopted her, given her a home. And she would wonder if it was in this instant that the decision was made: looking upon her face, calculating the damage, the strain such a responsibility would place on their new life.

"My mother would want me to see," she pleaded. "She always said you must do the things you're afraid to do."

This was, in fact, not something Miyako ever would have said, but rather an approximation of an Eleanor Roosevelt quotation. But in this moment, Lucy was not above lying to get what she wanted. What she needed.

"I still don't think…" Aiko sighed, but she reached for her purse and withdrew the compact. She opened it and swiped at a speck on the mirrored surface. "Just promise me that you'll remember that you'll keep getting better and better, and—"

Lucy snatched the thing from her hands, too impatient for manners. The mirror flashed brightly in her eyes, making her blink. Then: a glimpse of red-washed dunes, fissures and valleys of shiny stretched flesh, half her face twisted beyond recognition.

She caught her breath. Tilted the mirror and slowly moved it down to reveal her chin, her…

Her mouth. She knew it was wrecked from the agony she felt the first few times she tried to speak. But she couldn't form a picture in her mind of what it must have looked like. The oddest thing was…one side was perfect, her lips rosebud-pink and tipped up at the corner. But the other side dove down in a grotesque leer, the damaged flesh reknitting itself in a new order.

She couldn't bear it; she tilted the mirror away. She followed the path of the scar up the side of her face to her eye, where the tissue was thick and shiny, pulling cruelly at the part of her face that had escaped. Her lower lid canted down, the scar's northern reaches stopping just short of the outer arc of her brow (how many times would Lucy have to endure Dr. Ambrose reminding her of her good fortune at not losing the eye?); sometimes she felt that eye water when the other did not.

Finally Lucy held the compact away from her, trying to see her entire face, but the surface of the glass was too small and she managed only about two thirds. Regarding herself this way, it was difficult to believe it was truly her. She switched to her good side, and there she found herself. Her expression was unfamiliar, true, but it was *her* eye, lip, nose, chin. Moreover, it was also her *mother,* captured there in the glass, her spirit, her memory.

"Thank you," she said, snapping the compact shut and handing it back to Aiko, trying to keep her voice steady.

"Oh, Lucy, please don't be sad, please don't—"

"I'm not," Lucy lied. "I'm fine. It's what I expected." Also a lie. Because hadn't she endured these painful weeks by tricking herself, convincing herself that maybe it wouldn't be so bad?

Pathetic, Lucy now realized, and weak. She wanted to throw something, throw the mirror and watch it break into a million sharp pieces.

"I'm just so tired," she said instead. "I think I need to rest now."

Aiko looked as though she was going to cry herself. "We'll visit again soon. You'll be moving to the Children's Village, the nurses say, and we can come every weekend."

"That would be nice," Lucy said, pushing her hands under her blankets so Aiko couldn't see the way she squeezed them into fists, turning her knuckles white and leaving half-moon marks on the tender flesh of her palm with her nails.

Mr. Hamaguchi made a sound in his throat as Aiko bent over Lucy's bed and kissed her gently on the forehead. Lucy suddenly realized that no one was likely to ever kiss her cheek again, not even when it was healed and didn't hurt anymore. She reached her arms up and circled Aiko's neck, pulling her closer, pressing the good side of her face against hers. She knew she was giving in to weakness she couldn't afford, but she closed her eyes and tried to pretend everything was the way it used to be, even if just for a moment.

"We'll be back again soon," Aiko said as they turned to go, but her embrace had felt a lot like goodbye.

The day dragged slowly on. Lucy hoped Sister Jeanne might make an exception to her usual schedule and visit early. Lucy had no intention of confessing to having borrowed the mirror, because she wasn't sure she could take much more overt kindness today, but it would be a comfort just to have Jeanne's company. The ward felt even lonelier than usual, the little girl with the measles sleeping fitfully and the weekend nurses scarce.

Late in the afternoon, Lucy was dozing when the feeling of being watched tugged her out of some instantly forgotten dream. She opened her eyes and discovered Jessie standing over her.

For a moment she wondered if he was part of the dream, invoked by her longing. His hair had been cut since the last time she saw him, and he stood with both hands in his pockets, the way he often did when he waited for her after school. "Jessie?" she whispered tentatively. "Is it really you?"

"Hi." He spoke quietly, as if he was in a church.

"How long have you been standing there?"

"Awhile." The smile he gave her was tentative, almost a little afraid. He was wearing a shirt she recognized, blue with white stitching. She had once put her hand on that shirt and felt his heart beating underneath. "My mom thinks I'm at dinner... She thinks it's too soon for me to come see you. But I didn't want to wait."

Lucy's joy at seeing him was tempered by the knowledge of what she looked like. She lifted a hand to her face, pressing it against the worst of the scars. "I don't want you to see me like this," she said, eyes downcast.

"It's all right." He thought for a moment and added, "It's not like I thought it would be. It's still you, but different."

"I'm not pretty anymore." It was the first time she'd said it out loud, the first time she'd acknowledged it completely. "I'm... I'm going to be a freak."

"That's not true." Very gently, he put his hand over hers. "Does it hurt?"

"Sometimes. Not like before. It's getting better."

He pulled her hand away from her face, and she could feel him looking at her and it was almost all right.

"Can I sit with you?" Jessie asked. "I mean, in the bed? Is there room?"

Lucy blushed, the sensation of warmth stealing over her scars unfamiliar and prickly. "Okay." She wiggled over in her bed and patted the space she had made.

Jessie got under the blankets with great care, as though he was afraid of hurting her. He kicked off his shoes before sliding his legs under the covers, and they echoed on the wooden floor. The last of the sun lit his face softly as he pulled the blankets back up, his body touching hers at the shoulders and hips.

"Will I get in trouble?" he asked, staring at the ceiling.

"I don't know. Probably, if they see you." After a moment, she added, "Thank you for coming."

He nodded. Under the sheet his hand found hers, holding it lightly at first, and then weaving his fingers through hers and hanging on hard. "I just wanted to tell you—he quit, Lucy. He quit coming for me. They say he's getting transferred."

For a moment she thought about telling him the truth, about how her mother had led her into the hall, the way she had looked at her one last time before she reached behind the stove. But she couldn't bring herself to say it.

Once, not that long ago, she and Jessie had spoken of the future as though they might share it. "When the war's over," they would say, or "When we're in college." Now that future was lost. Jessie might not even realize it yet, but the truth lodged in Lucy's heart like a pebble in a shoe, impossible to ignore.

If she was lucky, he would remember her the way she had been before, when all the girls in their class envied her and all the boys wished they were the one walking with her after school. Someday, when Jessie had a wife and children of his own, he might think of her sometimes when he was alone. Lucy hoped he would think of the first time he kissed her, the way their hearts pounded as they ran, laughing, from the creek that day, too fast and too clever ever to be caught.

Jessie put his arms around her and pulled her close. She pressed her face into his shoulder and breathed his smell. She whispered his name and he whispered hers and she cried a little and he didn't say anything when her tears dampened her shirt. *I love you,* she thought, and though she had lost the right to say it out loud, though that privilege was reserved now for some other girl, some girl with smooth skin and a beautiful smile, Lucy thought the words with all her might and hoped that somehow he understood.

Later, when she woke up, it was dark and he was gone.

26

ON THE FIRST DAY LUCY WAS ALLOWED TO BE up and out of bed, she spent all morning pacing back and forth, looking out each window at the Children's Village across the road. She felt weak and her scars throbbed at the slightest exertion, but it felt good to be on her feet.

Lucy knew that soon they would be sending her to the village to be with the orphans. The *other* orphans. What was worse, there were rumors that the orphans were to be sent to the social services department in Los Angeles, that the Japanese orphanages that had been closed before the war would not be reopening. Lucy was terrified she would end up in a sanitarium like the Mercy Home for the Crippled and Deranged, not far from her old neighborhood. She suspected that Sister Jeanne was worried too; she had caught Jeanne staring at her with anxious speculation during her visits.

Sister Jeanne came to see Lucy one night after dinner, bringing a thick novel that had come in a donations box.

Lucy thanked her and set the book carefully on top of the others on her nightstand. "Sister Jeanne, I need your help. Dr. Ambrose says I'm almost ready to leave the hospital. I can do the salve myself—I don't need the nurses to do it."

The familiar worried expression settled on Jeanne's face. "Let's not rush things. Everyone wants to be sure you're fully recovered. There's plenty of time."

"But I have an idea," Lucy said. "I was thinking that I could go work on the sugar-beet harvest in Idaho."

Sister Jeanne's eyes widened.

"Wait, don't say no yet," Lucy said quickly. "I've got it all figured out. We can change the papers so they say I'm eighteen. No one will ever know. I heard the nurses talking, they're taking almost anyone who will go. They're going to lose the crop if they don't get enough volunteers. And I work hard, they wouldn't regret it. I'm well, I hardly have any pain at all." This was a lie, but Lucy told it gamely. "In the field, no one will have to look at me, no one except the other workers. And everyone keeps saying that I'll heal more as time goes on, so when everyone comes back after the harvest I'll look better."

"Lucy, that's preposterous, you can't possibly—"

"*Please.*" Lucy looked directly into Sister Jeanne's kind eyes and willed her to understand. "There is nothing for me here. I can't— My mother is gone, and every day here is a reminder. Let me go and do something useful. Let me start over."

For a long moment, Sister Jeanne regarded her thoughtfully. Then she shook her head and sighed.

"Lucy, I need to think about this. I cannot promise you anything. I will absolutely not be a part of a plan to send you a thousand miles away to do hard labor after you've suffered so much. But let me see what I can come up with."

"Oh, Sister, thank you!"

"Don't thank me yet," Jeanne said crisply, standing to leave, "because it's entirely likely that I won't be able to help."

Sister Jeanne did not return for two days. Lucy tried to pass the time with reading and walking laps in the ward, trying to restore some strength to her muscles, but as time went by with no word, she began to lose hope. She struggled not to think about what waited for her in Los Angeles if she couldn't escape her fate, but at night she tossed and turned, unable to shut off the memories of vacant-eyed patients staring out from inside the sanitarium's fence back home.

After dinner the second night, Sister Jeanne arrived, her face full of misgivings.

"I am afraid I am going to regret this," she said in lieu of a greeting, "but there is…an opportunity which has come to my attention. One with a lot of problems, I must be honest."

"What is it?" Lucy demanded. "What kind of opportunity?"

"Certainly better than working in the fields," Jeanne said. "And not far from here either. I might even be able to look in on you now and then."

"Is it working for a family?" Lucy asked. She'd heard that men out east were working as houseboys for wealthy families—maybe there were opportunities for young women too. "Is it taking care of children?"

"Hush, before I change my mind," Jeanne said. "This is far from a sure thing, and I'm not even sure it's legal."

"But there've been dozens of people who've left for jobs," Lucy protested. "Hundreds. They say the camps will be half-empty by fall."

This was only a slight exaggeration. Public outcry against internment had increased, especially after Roosevelt reversed himself and started letting Japanese Americans enlist. What began as a slow trickle of people leaving the camps was turning into a steady stream. Young men and couples who could prove they had a job and a place to live were heading for Chicago and New York.

"That's enough, Lucy. You know as well as I do that nothing's a sure thing until the WRA says it is." Jeanne sighed. "Give me a little time, and I will see what I can do. All right?"

"Yes," Lucy said, and for the first time in a long time a tiny ray of hope pierced the dark specter of her future.

Two weeks later, Lucy was sitting in the dusty parlor of the Mountainview Motel in Lone Pine, wearing a dress Sister Jeanne had found for her and a thick layer of foundation that made her scars itch. One of the younger nurses had applied the makeup with a soft brush, adding more and more until the sheen and redness almost disappeared. Unfortunately, nothing could be done about the pocked and bumpy landscape of the scars, or the malformation of her eye and mouth, which continued to worsen as the scars matured and tightened.

"She's eighteen," Mrs. Sloat said, scrutinizing Lucy. "If Sister Jeanne says she's eighteen, then she's eighteen. I would think you'd trust a nun to give it to you straight."

Mary Sloat took a sip of the tea she had set out for the three of them. She was a stern but handsome woman built on a sturdy frame. Her arms were finely shaped, browned by the sun with faint freckling and pale undersides like dough on a second rising. Lucy guessed she was somewhere in her late thirties, though the lines etched in her face made her look older. Brackets around her mouth might have passed for dimples on another woman, one who smiled. Under her eyes the flesh pleated, and she seemed to recede behind her gaze, the bright embers of her eyes deep set and guarded.

Lucy was aware that she was staring openly, but one of the advantages of being a freak was that no one noticed if you stared, because they were too busy trying not to stare themselves. Her scars throbbed today. Sometimes now she could go an hour or two without pain. Today was not such a day.

Outside the picture window, separating the street from the front lawn, was a crumbling stone wall that reminded Lucy of the Robert Frost poem they'd read in class. Of course, there was no need for such a wall here. There would be no frozen-ground-swell, no spring mending-time. There was only the dusty, flat earth, the chaparral and scrub, the mountain views she already knew by heart.

Behind the parlor were the registration desk and dining room. The Sloats' living quarters were upstairs. The old house loomed over the motel court next to it like a staggering old drunk about to collapse on a bench. The walls peeled and the porch sagged. A potted geranium sprouted small green leaves from among the winter-dead stalks. When Sister Jeanne described the Mountainview Motel, she had neglected to mention it was in complete disrepair, and Lucy wondered what other omissions she had made.

"She's not eighteen," Mr. Sloat said, regarding Lucy. His face was weathered, and he patted the pocket in the bib of his overalls as if he wanted to reassure himself its contents were still there. Tobacco, probably.

Mrs. Sloat squinted harder. "How old are you, dear?"

"Eighteen."

She was still sixteen and there were plenty of records to say so, if anyone cared to look. That Sister Jeanne had lied on her behalf, Lucy appreciated; that the Sloats had not made careful inquiries was useful information too. They didn't want to know.

"See?" Mrs. Sloat said, nodding. "And you're caught up on your lessons?"

"Yes, ma'am."

"She speaks good, I'll give her that," Mr. Sloat said. "No Jap accent at all. Girl, say something for us."

"What do you want me to say?"

"I don't know, don't matter."

Lucy was silent. She could recite all of the Frost poem, or her algebra theorems, or she could list the capitals. She doubted that was what Mr. Sloat had in mind. The challenge was to win them over, and she knew she had only this one chance. Mr. Sloat seemed dull, perhaps a bit slow, not especially kind. But Mrs. Sloat was a more difficult read.

"Sister Jeanne was not clear about your experience," the woman said, her gaze roving across Lucy's face, seemingly unembarrassed. "We were very specific with her that we wanted someone with experience."

Lucy resisted the temptation to roll her eyes. Sister Jeanne had said the Sloats were having trouble keeping help; with the war on, there were other opportunities for young women, opportunities that paid better. An ambitious young woman with a lick of sense would not have to settle for a job as a maid at a run-down motel. But Mrs. Sloat seemed to be having trouble accepting the fact that she would be stuck with someone like Lucy, that she too would have to settle for life's leftovers.

"I worked as a maid in Manzanar," Lucy said, a lie that had just occurred to her. Why not—if the Sloats checked out any part of her story, all of it would collapse. "I cleaned for the staff."

Mr. Sloat burst out with a loud bellow of laughter. "Hear

that, Mary? She's been cleaning for the WRA. If that ain't good enough for you, I don't know what is."

Mrs. Sloat pursed her lips and refused to look at Mr. Sloat. Instead, she fixed her gaze firmly on Lucy. "This is not an easy job."

"I don't expect it to be, ma'am."

"You'll start at five because the guests will want their breakfast. You'll take your meals in the kitchen with us and Garvey. You'll start on the rooms as soon as the morning dishes are done. We have a girl in to serve on weekends, but you can help prepare meals for the family the rest of the time. Evenings, you can read to Garvey, maybe, since you've completed your primary studies."

Mr. Sloat made a harrumphing sound, which, like his laughter, was unexpected. "Garvey don't need anyone to read to him. Ain't his eyes that's wrecked."

Lucy had no idea who Garvey was, but it didn't seem like the time to ask. And it wouldn't make any difference, anyway. The duties outlined by Mrs. Sloat were what she expected; the only things she wasn't sure of were how hard it would be to meet their standards and how harshly they would punish her when she failed. There'd been stories circulating in the camp; internees returning to the cities wrote of poor treatment by their employers. Anti-Japanese sentiment was as strong as ever in some places.

"So...does that mean I have the job?"

"You'll have the room off the kitchen. It's small but it does have a nice bed. You'll receive eight dollars per week. Mind, you're getting your room and board. Mr. Sloat will keep your account for you."

"All right." Lucy doubted she would ever see any of the money, but this was a start.

"Is that all your things?"

They all turned to look at Lucy's battered suitcase. She didn't have enough to fill it, small as it was. After her mother's death, their room was reassigned and she never found out what happened to their belongings, which were long gone by the time she was well enough to ask about them. She owned two donated dresses besides the one she wore. A strange little book given to her by Jeanne as a going-away present: *The Little Prince,* written by a Frenchman. It was about a little boy in a desert but apparently it was supposed to be about the war. Two textbooks—science and math—that Jeanne said she could keep.

Mr. Sloat pushed himself away from the table and got up in stages, his knees making a popping sound loud enough to hear across the parlor. He cleared his throat as he went out the front door. He was a man of ungainly sounds and coarse habits; Lucy wondered how Mrs. Sloat had ended up marrying so far beneath her. Well, she'd have plenty of time to figure that out.

For a moment neither Lucy nor Mrs. Sloat spoke, and Lucy could feel the tension in the room.

"I don't know if you'll enjoy this job."

"I don't expect to enjoy it."

"I won't tolerate laziness."

"I'm not lazy." Lucy suspected that Sister Jeanne had exaggerated her industry, but she'd work as hard as was required here.

Mrs. Sloat nodded. "You've been told, I expect, that Mr. Sloat and I have no children."

Lucy had been told, more precisely, that Mrs. Sloat could not bear children, gossip that Sister Jeanne had managed to pick up somewhere. She suggested to Lucy that Mrs. Sloat might be sympathetic toward a young girl—might even, in time, become a surrogate mother figure. Half an hour with the woman convinced Lucy that would never happen.

"It's good that you're nearly grown," Mrs. Sloat went on. "Eighteen—well, that's more of a woman than a girl, isn't it? I don't care for children."

She lifted the delicate teacup to her lips and took a dainty sip, closing her eyes and inhaling the tepid brew. In that moment Lucy realized that she might have underestimated Mrs. Sloat's capacity for cruelty.

When she rose from her chair to take Lucy on a tour of the premises, Lucy saw that there was something wrong with her legs. Mrs. Sloat walked with a distinct limp, though Lucy could tell that she was attempting to hide it. Her hips made a sort of rolling swivel with each step, the foot coming down as though she was about to turn an ankle. Was one foot smaller than the other? One leg shorter? She touched the chair rail lightly with her fingertips as Lucy followed her down the hall. Her left foot made a percussive clack on the wood floors, followed by a much softer landing of the right foot. *Clack* drag, *clack* drag.

Lucy was reminded of a lame duck she'd seen at her father's warehouse one day. One of his distributors kept the poor thing as a pet. It rode on the bed of the truck that was being loaded with crates of apricots, and it had a small dish of corn from which to peck. As her father and the merchant talked, the men loading crate after crate onto the truck, the duck jumped down and walked about in circles. Her wing had been damaged, practically sheared off, its quills broken and jagged at the ends. Without use of the wing, she seemed unable to walk a straight line. The workmen had laughed at the spectacle, but Lucy had cried.

Perhaps Mrs. Sloat was like that duck—trapped, helpless. Lucy wondered if she felt condemned here, in the small life of a motel keeper in a tiny town far from anything except cracked earth and harsh winds and dirt-brown weeds. She had no children to distract her from the monotony of her days. There seemed to be little affection between her and Mr. Sloat; perhaps he had a roving eye, grasping hands, and he was the one who drove the former maids away.

Out the back door, a clothesline stretched between aluminum poles in the middle of an enormous, weed-choked yard. From the line hung a limp pair of men's long underwear, several billowing white sheets, three or four undershirts.

Mrs. Sloat followed Lucy's gaze, and her lips turned up slightly at the corners. "Those are Garvey's, of course."

Now that Lucy knew her employment was secure, she asked the question. "Who is Garvey?"

Mrs. Sloat tilted her head in mock surprise. "Sister Jeanne didn't tell you about him? About my brother?"

"No, ma'am."

"Oh, I see. I'm so sorry, I thought you knew. Garvey is my younger brother. He's a war hero. He was wounded in Guadalcanal, in the Battle of Edson's Ridge. Do you know it?"

"No, ma'am," Lucy muttered, even though the name was lodged deep in her mind along with so many others: battlefields in which Japanese and American blood was spilled, names she'd heard the men talking about as they clustered around the radios for news of the war. *Tulagi. Savo Island. Henderson Field.*

"I just thought—well, you being Japanese and all."

"I'm not Japanese. I'm American." Lucy forced herself to maintain eye contact. What she knew about Edson's Ridge was that the Japanese were defeated, losing many soldiers for every American loss. Cheers went up around Manzanar when the news came in.

It was impossible not to know some things.

Mrs. Sloat raised an eyebrow. "Indeed. Anyway, don't pay Garvey any mind. Sometimes he lets off a little steam, but it's all just talk. You two are going to get on fine."

"Yes, ma'am."

"There's nothing wrong with his mind," Mrs. Sloat continued. "He was lucky, as these things go. It was a lower vertebra that was damaged. He retains some sensation. He's continent. He gets tired, but don't worry, he takes care of himself. You'll do the washing and cleaning, of course, but he can…"

Mrs. Sloat made a gesture with her hand that seemed like she was tying a knot; Lucy was bewildered. Dress? Fold his clothes? Brush his teeth? Here was the reason the Sloats had been willing to hire her, the reason the position must have been difficult to keep staffed. She supposed she ought to be grateful.

Well, so be it. Lucy had been prepared for worse.

"You'll meet him later.… He's in his workshop now. He doesn't care to be disturbed in the afternoons. It's when he gets the most work done."

Mrs. Sloat limped briskly across the yard—it had been carelessly mowed, with missed patches sending up long spurs of weeds and sawgrass—toward the motel. It couldn't have been more than eight or ten years old, but a certain shabbiness had set in. The stucco was dingy along the bottom, a few of the screens were torn, and the weeds had made inroads along the brick edging sunken into the earth. Geraniums grew valiantly in the flower beds, but they could have done with some fertilizer, some compost. There were metal chairs with shell-shaped backs that stood in front of each room next to the door, where Lucy imagined a traveler might rest after driving all day, enjoying a sunset or reading a book.

The nicest feature of the motel was the breathtaking view of the ice-topped mountains in the distance.

The motel was shaped like an L, with the long leg fronting the road, and the short end opposite the big house. In a way, the motel resembled the camp barracks: a row of boxy rooms. But these rooms were larger than any in the camp, and they each had their own bathroom. There would be no cracks or chips in the walls or floors, and though the walls might not be thick, a whispered conversation in one room would not be overheard in the next.

On each door a shiny metal numeral was held in place by a pair of tiny nails. In most of the windows, the drapes were drawn. Each window was flanked by a pair of green shutters. At each door, a mat of plain rubber waited for travelers to wipe their feet before entering.

Mrs. Sloat took a ring of keys from her pocket. "Leo'll be getting you your own set. Just the rooms, mind you—no reason for you to have any of the others."

She slipped a key into the lock and the door swung open. Inside, the room was dim and smelled of mothballs and ammonia. Mrs. Sloat stood aside to let Lucy enter.

"This is very nice," Lucy said.

Mrs. Sloat pushed open the drapes. There was a bed with a plain brown coverlet. The carpet was mossy-green, worn in places. A desk held only a gooseneck lamp. Next to the sink was a cake of soap wrapped in paper. Lucy wanted to break open the seal, peel away the paper, press it to her nose. She wanted to caress the satiny cake before running water over it, lathering and lathering for hours. She had not touched a fresh cake of soap since before they left Los Angeles. Her mother had favored a brand called Cadum, with French writing on the wrapper.

"It's clean." Mrs. Sloat ran a fingertip along the desk, held it up to show Lucy. "See? No dust. Not a speck. That's what I'll expect from you. If I receive a complaint, I'll dock your pay for that day."

"Yes, ma'am."

A scratching sound outside the open door was followed by a thud that shook the building. A man in a wheelchair appeared in the door frame, his large hands gripping the wheels. His indisputably handsome face was angled with sharp edges and flat plains, and his eyes flashed with fury. Light brown hair, allowed to grow too long, fell across his brow. His feet were held in place by metal stirrups, and he wore only socks on his feet, no shoes. One of them had bunched around his ankle and seemed in danger of falling off, a detail utterly at odds with the tensed strength in his muscular, veined forearms.

"You the girl?" he said gruffly. His voice was raw and hoarse, as though he did not often use it. "Let me look at you."

Beside her, Mrs. Sloat stiffened.

"Go ahead," she said, shoving Lucy forward. "Let him see."

Lucy took a step toward the door, which was too narrow for the wheelchair to pass through. Mrs. Sloat stood directly behind her with her strong fingers pushing at her spine.

"Well, you're not much to look at, are you," he said softly. "Ugly as original sin."

Something inside Lucy twitched, a snag in the stoic façade behind which she had been determined to hide. She would endure whatever the Sloats dished out, but she would not allow this man to shame her.

"Yes, sir, I am ugly," she said. "I guess that makes two of us."

The smug expression froze on his face, his icy-gray eyes callous and cold.

He pressed his lips together and suddenly a gobbet of spit came hurtling from his mouth, landing on the front of Lucy's dress.

"You can go to hell," he said, backing up his wheelchair and turning with surprising agility. "You and every other Nip left on this planet."

27

IN THE KITCHEN, MRS. SLOAT FETCHED A RAG for Lucy, and watched silently as she wiped away Garvey's spit.

"Throw it in there," Mrs. Sloat said, pointing to a bucket in the corner of the kitchen. "You can start the wash this afternoon."

Several hours later, Lucy was alone in the backyard with a huge basket of wet laundry and her first moment of solitude since arriving at the Mountainview Motel. As she hung the sheets and towels from the clothesline, she stole glances at the house, wondering if anyone inside was watching her work.

From the yard, she could see that the main house had suffered several shoddy additions. A screened porch was crowded with furniture and junk, spiderwebs and wasp nests lodged in every corner. To the right, a boxy extension jutted out toward the motel. An angled ramp clinging to the side suggested that the addition was where Garvey lived.

Was it her imagination, or did the curtains in Garvey's window move slightly now and then? Lucy worked steadily, going through nearly all the clothespins from the cloth bag around her neck, but every time she bent over the basket she could sense Garvey watching her.

She pictured his face, how it contorted with anger, and wondered what had happened to him. A bullet to the spine seemed most likely. Was it a stroke of luck to return from the war with an injury like that? Or would it be better to be dead? Lucy was quite sure that it would have been better for her to have died than survive her burns. Even better would have been if she and her mother had both died on the same day as her father. A car accident, perhaps—something quick and tragic.

Lucy imagined her father in his grave in the cemetery behind Christ Community Church back in Los Angeles. The Presbyterians preached that the immortal soul would spend eternity in heaven, and that all of life was a journey to that end. Sister Jeanne had assured Lucy that her own beliefs were pretty much in line with the Presbyterians on the matter. Lucy had her doubts.

When Lucy had pinned the final sheet to the line, shaking out the fabric to minimize the wrinkles, Mrs. Sloat materialized at her side. Perhaps it was her gaze, not Garvey's, that Lucy had sensed while she worked.

"These are too close together," Mrs. Sloat said, unpinning several towels. "They'll drag down the line." Lucy didn't point out that when they were repinned, the line sagged just as much.

"I suppose that will have to do for now," Mrs. Sloat said, her hands at her hips. "Now come with me. There is one more thing to see."

Lucy followed Mrs. Sloat to the wheelchair ramp leading up to the addition. Up close she could see that the boards were neatly swept and the glass panes set into the door were sparkling clean—except for the top row, which was thick with grime. The slope gave Mrs. Sloat some trouble: she had to hold the rail for balance, and the dragging of her right foot seemed worse. She opened the unlocked door without knocking and called her brother's name.

Once through the door, Lucy stopped in surprise. The addition seemed larger from the inside, with private quarters in between the spacious outer room and the main house. The walls of the large room were lined with shelves, and a long workbench took up much of the wall separating the addition from the main house. It had been built low, to accommodate Garvey's wheelchair. Hutches on either side of the desk held orderly rows of instruments and knives, clamps and jars, curious wooden forms in strange shapes, ranging from the size of a child's fist to several feet long.

But all of these details barely registered, because on the remaining shelves, dozens of animals stared out at Lucy with shining eyes.

Lucy gasped. There were just so many of them. Squirrels—a lot of squirrels—but also mice, raccoons, possums, coyotes. A fox occupied a double-height shelf, his plumed and brushed tail arcing out into the room. Birds were suspended from the ceiling, ranging from a red-tailed hawk with an astonishing wingspan, to tiny white birds, smaller than the palm of her hand. Above the shelves, near the ceiling, were fish mounted on boards, with pert fins and gaping mouths and eyes that seemed to look inward.

In Los Angeles, Lucy never had any pets. Other than Aiko's cats, she'd observed animals only from afar at the zoo. But these animals were different. They seemed intelligent, their poses cunning, their artificial eyes crafty. They were not arranged to appear as they were in their natural habitat, like the stuffed beasts that Lucy had seen in the Natural History Museum on a third-grade field trip. *These* animals were arranged in practically human poses.

Many, if not most, stood on their hind legs. Some reached beseechingly toward the viewer, paws outstretched. A beaver crossed his paws over his chest and sat back on his tail, looking for all the world like a businessman in a boardroom. An owl with a tiny vole hanging from its beak raised a claw in the air as though pumping a jubilant fist. A rat mounted on a stand kicked up its tiny feet, dancing several inches above the shelf.

"*This* is how my brother spends his time," Mrs. Sloat said triumphantly.

As if on cue, Garvey appeared in the doorway of his bedroom, glowering at his sister. If anything, his expression became even more hostile when he saw Lucy. He wheeled himself over to his worktable, where the skin of an animal was stretched over some sort of wooden support. Pink flesh dappled the thing nearly to the ruff of fine black-and-gray fur at the top edge. It took Lucy a moment to realize that the creature was inside out.

"I've asked you to knock," Garvey muttered.

Mrs. Sloat shrugged. "Well. You wouldn't have heard me." She turned to Lucy. "Garvey has his own bathroom. It's specially fitted for his needs. Cost a pretty penny, but what can you do? Hygiene can be quite time-consuming for him."

Lucy blushed, discomfited not just by the discussion of private matters, but by the tension that filled the room.

"I don't want that girl in here."

"She'll have to come in, to clean," Mrs. Sloat said blandly. She picked up a small muskrat from a nearby shelf, one of the more conventional ones. Three of its paws were attached to the board on which it was mounted; the fourth was raised as though in admonishment. Its mouth was open and its pink-and-black gums seemed to glisten. Lucy wondered how Garvey accomplished that. Far from being put off by the stuffed corpses, she wanted to examine each more closely, to search for evidence of seams or means of death, to understand how he had created such lifelike replicas of tissues which surely could not last, like tongues and gums and glistening lips and pearly-pink translucent ears.

"Hold it by the base," Garvey snapped, and Mrs. Sloat set the thing back on the shelf. "She doesn't have to come in to clean. *I* clean just fine."

"And look at what a splendid job you've done of that," Mrs. Sloat retorted, pointing at the walls. It was just like outside—anything that Garvey could reach from his chair was dusted, polished, arranged with care. But thick cobwebs hung in all the corners, and the upper third of the walls were grimy and streaked with dust. "If you don't want to get buried in dirt, you're going to have to let her help."

"I don't want people in here," Garvey protested, a note of panic coloring his petulance.

"And I don't want *you* here," Mrs. Sloat shot back, "but neither of us has ever got what we wanted, have we?" A moment later she added, in a calmer tone, "Garvey makes good money mounting trophies for other people."

"*Fish,*" he said, as though it were a curse word. "Deer."

Mrs. Sloat ignored his interruption. "Owens Lake is less than twenty miles down the road. There's a fellow, Mr. Dang, who runs a fishing camp there. We buy from him sometimes for Sunday dinners. He could give Garvey all the work he could handle. Gentlemen come for vacation, they want something to take home, to show off. And let me tell you, there's big money to be made from the tourist trade."

"Well, I'm not about to work for some goddamn Chink, that's for sure."

"Not if you can sit in here playing with your little glue pots while other people put bread on the table," Mrs. Sloat said. "God forbid you should contribute to this household."

Lucy wasn't sure of the source of the siblings' antagonism, and she sensed that her only power lay in alignment. But she would have to choose carefully.

"You Japs eat fish?" Garvey asked.

"Garvey."

"I know they turned up their noses at perfectly good food in that camp. When our boys were making do with K rations."

Lucy could have told him about the slop that passed for food, the scarcity of decent meat, the shortage of fresh produce. But instead she remained quiet and focused on the pelt stretched on the stand. She thought she could make out knobby fissures where the creature's eyes should have been. Seeing them from the inside was strangely fascinating.

"It's a burn, right?" Garvey prodded, when she didn't respond. "What happened to you? Grease fire? Electric?"

Lucy knew better than to let him rattle her that way—she'd had plenty of practice telling this particular lie. "It was an oil fire. A stove exploded."

"Who knows. Maybe getting burned improved you," Garvey said, but it was his sister he stared at as he spoke. "Nothing uglier than a Jap girl."

"Garvey!" This time Mrs. Sloat advanced on him, lurching as her bad leg came down too quickly, and she had to

grab the workbench to steady herself. Garvey's face flickered with victory.

"A pretty face is nothing you'll need here, anyway," he
muttered. "Now get the fuck out of my house."

28

THIS ROOM WAS AN INSULT, SMALLER AND filthier than the one she'd shared with her mother in the camp. Lucy found it hard to sleep with the dust and odor assaulting her nose and lungs. She experimented with leaving the door open a crack, but it didn't seem to help the ventilation. She lay awake, exhausted to the bone, staring out the tiny window at the stars sprinkled across the patch of night sky. Searching for sleep, she replayed moments she had spent with Jessie—the first time he held her hand, the way he would push her hair gently away from her face before he kissed her—but even these memories were not enough to take her away. Her heartbeat throbbed in the condensed and matted tissue of her scars. She imagined her blood moving, slow and thick, through her veins, the blood of her doomed family.

Lucy's room next to the kitchen had never been a maid's room, as Mrs. Sloat claimed; the moldering debris in the corners was proof that it had served as a larder. A single small, unglazed window was covered only with a rusting screen. The walls were marred with rows of holes where shelves had once hung, entire chunks of plaster missing. A meat hook in the ceiling was surrounded by a spreading stain. The only furniture was a stained mattress on a cot that looked even older than the one Lucy slept on at Manzanar.

Just once—the third morning or the fourth—she failed to get up right away when Mrs. Sloat rapped on her door. Moments later, it was flung open, banging into the wall and sending up a shower of plaster dust. Mrs. Sloat stood over Lucy, bristling with rage.

"Don't you forget—" she spat the words with cold fury as Lucy scrambled to cover herself with the thin sheet "—that you are here as an act of our mercy. The world does not want you, Lucy, no one wants you. And you have to earn your place here just like the rest of us."

Lucy cowered, and for a moment she thought the woman was going to strike her. She rolled as close to the wall as she could, sharp lath cutting into her back through her thin nightgown.

"Earn your place," Mrs. Sloat muttered and turned away to leave.

Seconds after her footsteps faded, Lucy finally breathed.

A small reprieve arrived unexpectedly on Saturday. Lucy was starting the day's laundry when an old Chevy High Boy pickup rattled to a stop in front of the house. Three people got out—a middle-aged woman and a boy and girl in their teens—and started unloading tin pails from the back. Lucy watched them through the laundry window, and didn't hear Mrs. Sloat come in.

"Got your eye on Hal McEvoy, I see," she said. "You and every other girl in town."

Lucy hastily got back to the laundry. "I was just wondering who was here," she said. She *had* noticed the boy—sun browned, hair cut to bleached-blond stubble, broad back of a hard worker—but not the way Mrs. Sloat was implying. She seemed to delight in even the smallest opportunities for meanness, and Lucy had learned that ignoring her slights was the best way to defuse her.

"That's the weekend girl, Sharon McEvoy, and her kids. Twins, they must be seventeen, eighteen by now. Ruby helps serve, and Hal helps Leo around the house."

Lucy picked up a pile of rags and started folding them, feigning indifference.

"You stay out of their way, hear? We'll have a couple dozen guests for lunch and who knows for dinner. I don't need you getting underfoot."

There were few restaurants in Lone Pine, and the Sloats picked up extra business serving family-style meals on Saturday and Sunday. Lucy had seen the menus: a dollar seventy-five bought coffee or tea, an entrée, vegetable and starch, and cake or pudding. Ten could be seated at the big walnut table, and Leo had dragged in two extra cloth-covered card tables that morning.

"Go make sure the kitchen's picked up," Mrs. Sloat said. "You can finish this later."

Sharon McEvoy was already at the sink, a ruddy, stocky ranch wife with brown teeth and a shapeless bosom. Ruby looked like a younger version of her mother. They clattered around the kitchen, making themselves at home at the cupboards and counters and glaring at Lucy, who raced to get the breakfast dishes dried and put away. She wasn't about to argue with her first opportunity for free time. She could have the six occupied rooms cleaned by one o'clock and the rest of the day to herself. And if her luck held, the same tomorrow. She had been collecting stones all week when she made the trek from the house to the burn barrel with the trash, or to dump wash water on the shrub roses along the back fence. She had in mind to start a rock garden of her own, a miniature version of the ones she remembered from Manzanar.

She had scouted the best location, the scarred and barren earth beyond the porch addition at the opposite end of the house from Garvey's apartment. From the looks of it, no one ever went there; an untended plot of land separated the motel from the street. The narrow strip was shielded from view on two sides: by a sagging trellis in the front, and an overgrown tangle of blackberry canes that sprawled into the neighboring lot. Her stones were piled next to the house, some as small as a robin's egg, others larger than her fist. She wanted to plunge her hands into the warm earth, to sift out the pebbles and twigs and create something orderly, something that was hers alone.

Lucy cleaned the first three rooms without incident, but when she got to room nine, she found the door slightly ajar. She knocked, not hard, hoping no one would answer. Lucy usually preferred to avoid the motel guests, with their lingering stares and awkward apologies upon seeing her scars.

From inside the room came the sound of a man hawking phlegm, and Lucy turned to go. But she'd gone only a few steps when he called out. "Hey! Girl! Come on in. You can clean around me, just pretend I'm not here."

Lucy came back, leaving her cart outside the door as she tentatively entered. The door swung shut behind her. Inside, the room looked much like any other: the bedcovers were mussed, half a dozen cigarette butts were crushed in the ashtray, a suitcase lay open on the bed.

The man at the sink didn't turn around. He was shaving the underside of his chin with a safety razor. "Start on the bed," he said, and his voice triggered something inside her, a warning, a memory. Lucy tugged at the handle of her cart and tried to ignore her sudden unease. "Don't mind my stuff, you can just throw it on the chair."

A crumpled pair of pants had been discarded across the bedspread, inside out. When Lucy reached for them, she saw that the man's underpants were twisted in the pant legs. She glanced back at the man, his muscular back and close-shorn, wheat-blond hair, and something snagged in her mind. Her hand hovered in the air as the memory took shape.

And then she knew, and it was too late.

"Well, what do you know." He turned around and smiled at her. "Little Lucy Takeda. With a face like that, I'd know you anywhere."

Lucy backed away, banging into the desk chair, but Reg Forrest was fast. He crossed the room in a few strides, standing much too close to her. He hadn't bothered to rinse away the flecks of soap on his face, but he was as handsome as ever, even in his undershirt and shorts. Another man's knees would be knobby and his gut flabby; another man would be self-conscious about his state of semi-undress. But Reg watched her like a cat with a mouse.

"I'll leave," she said quickly. "I can come back later, I can—"

"No, Lucy, stay and talk to me a minute." He maneuvered himself between her and the door. "Tell me what happened to you. How did you end up here?"

"I—I just—" *Act like nothing's wrong,* she thought, and maybe he would too. Maybe he wouldn't remember. But *she* remembered.

"Feeling shy, eh? Just like your mother. Oh, she was a quiet one all those nights—fellows breaking their backs trying to get her to look at them and she didn't give them anything. Except to George, of course." He laughed, a hard grating chuckle. "Old George. Rest his soul. As for me, I got promoted, you know. Well, you probably don't know, seeing as you were in the hospital. Sorry we didn't visit, by the way… me and the boys. Some of them, well, after what your mother did, you can understand."

Lucy's fear trickled through her body, immobilizing her. It was like the night in the gardens, when Reg gave her the message from George Rickenbocker: his voice was pleasant, his expression friendly. There was nothing to suggest he intended her harm. Neither had there been that night—even as his fingers deftly pinched the nerve in her neck, causing such terrible pain.

"Please, I just want to get my job done." Whispering now, giving away her fear.

"And you can in a minute. Hell, I'll even leave you a good tip, how's that?" He took his time looking at her, and she could feel his gaze traveling the surface of her face…then down across her dress and back up again.

"Why are you here?" she managed, swallowing.

"Gave up my apartment. I travel between the centers now. I'll be heading down to Poston tonight." There was a note of pride in his voice.

Reg reached out then, as though to offer his hand, and before Lucy could react he had rested it lightly on her waist. It hovered there for a moment and then slid down onto her hip, which he gripped more firmly. His hand was warm through the thin cotton of her dress.

"You want to know what the *real* tragedy is?" he said, his breathing going rapid and shallow. His fingers squeezed, kneading the flesh of her buttock, and Lucy laid her hand on his arm. She meant to push him away, but found she was shaking so hard that she could barely manage even a small shove.

"Please," she whispered.

"You could have been someone, with a face like that." His other hand settled on her shoulder, then quickly patted its way down her dress front, settling on her breast, which he squeezed. "You were a pretty girl, weren't you," he murmured, no longer looking at her face, but watching his hand squeezing. Lucy closed her eyes for a second and focused her fear, sucking in a breath, and then she released a sound like a balloon leaking air as she shoved him away with all her might.

"What's the matter, don't you like me?" Reg didn't look offended, merely amused, as he stumbled away. He wiped a bit of shaving cream from his chin and tugged at his belt loops. "Maybe you're like your mother—you don't even know what you want. She was crazy, though. Beautiful lady, but…" Reg looped his finger at his ear and mugged at her. "I mean, George *loved* her. In his way."

"He lied," Lucy said hoarsely. "He said she stole."

"*That.*" Reg chuckled. "Lovers' quarrel. You'll understand someday. When you're older… Once a man gets done showing you how to be a woman."

He reached for her again, this time sliding his hand inside the neck of her dress, deftly unbuttoning. His fingers found the edge of her camisole and slid inside before Lucy could react, but then she jerked backward, running into the chair for a second time and stumbling. Her hand closed on the chair back and then she went down, the chair tipping with her, and she was on her hands and knees crawling, so desperate was she to get away. She reached the door and grabbed the knob to pull herself up to her feet, her hands shaking.

"Aw, don't go away mad," Reg said, his voice full of merriment. "It was good to see you again, Lucy. Don't forget me, hear?"

Lucy finally got the door open. She pushed it open and stumbled outside, into the blinding sun. There was her cart, so familiar she wanted to cry, and she grabbed its handle as the door closed softly behind her. She pushed the cart down the sidewalk, dirty water sloshing over the side of the mop bucket. *Slow down,* she had to slow down, or the thing would upend—its wheels were sprung and its balance was tricky. Her heart pounded and she sucked in air, coughing from the pollen; spring had arrived and tiny white petals drifted down from blooming trees. In the parking lot, a man shouted a greeting to another; people were arriving for lunch.

Lucy forced herself to slow down to a normal pace. Reg couldn't do anything to her here. Not now, and she wouldn't make that mistake twice, would not go into a room until she knew who was inside. She'd been caught off guard, that was all, but she would not allow him to frighten her.

She pushed the cart down the walk to another room and unlocked the door with her key. Inside, there were sodden towels on the floor, an ashtray overflowing, the remains of a sandwich on the desk. Half the bed linens had been pulled clean away from the bed and lay on the floor.

Lucy bolted the door and then, after a moment's hesitation, pushed the chair under the knob. She pulled the drapes tight and turned on all the lights and got to work, listening for sounds through the thin wall, but there was nothing. While she sprinkled the tub with Old Dutch and got on her knees to scrub it, acrid steam stinging her eyes, she replayed what had happened with Reg. What she had done. What she wished she had done.

No one would protect Lucy here. Any guest could do anything he wanted, anytime. He could accuse her of stealing, as Rickenbocker had accused her mother. But if Lucy were accused, she would refuse to confess to anything, ever. If she were locked up for a crime she didn't commit, she wouldn't care. After all, she'd already traded one prison for another. What difference would a third make?

29

AFTER FINISHING THE LAST OF THE ROOMS, Lucy pushed her cart back along the walk toward the main house, the aroma of fried chicken making her stomach growl. She passed room nine and forced herself not to speed up or look back. She would not mention to Mrs. Sloat that she hadn't cleaned that room. With any luck Reg wouldn't either, and Lucy could take care of it tomorrow before it was rented again.

Resolve changed things. Lucy had no solutions, no alternatives, but she had a next step and a next. Do her work. Do not back down. There was one thing that belonged to her in this world. It wasn't the job, which could be taken away from her, or the suitcase full of clothes, which had belonged to other people first. It wasn't pride, which Lucy had only borrowed from her mother and which had been extinguished when her mother was gone.

No. What Lucy had was a tiny seed inside her, a hard thing

like a popcorn kernel. The first time she ever watched the boy behind the concession counter make popcorn at the Orpheum, she had been astonished that such a big, fluffy thing could explode out of such a little case. But Lucy's kernel—she didn't know where it was located exactly, in her heart perhaps, or more likely in her spirit, wherever that might be found—would explode large as well. She didn't want much—a place of her own someday, a job of her choosing. But she meant to have it. And when she finally exploded, no one would ever be able to take her future from her again.

In her pocket was the fifty-eight cents she'd found that week as she cleaned. She didn't trust Mrs. Sloat not to search her room while she was working, so she'd carried the money with her. It wasn't a lot. But it was a start. She would have to figure out how much she would need to set out on her own. How much did a room cost, a coat, a streetcar ride? A bus ticket to a city, the bigger the better? Only in a city could Lucy live without being seen, without being singled out, ogled, isolated.

In Los Angeles every year on her birthday, Lucy's parents took her to the Beverly Wilshire or Perino's. She and her mother wore new dresses, her father a dark suit, and people in the street paused to watch them arrive. But as the valet helped her mother out of the car, Lucy also saw the others, the ones in the back of the crowd, dressed in rags, begging for change. People ignored them, rushed around them, like a stream flowing around a stone lodged in the current.

Lucy would be that stone, and the city would flow around her, indifferent and preoccupied. But unlike the beggars with their hollow eyes and gaunt expressions, Lucy would not ask for help. She would work hard and learn a trade. She would depend on no one. Her mother had already closed one avenue for her: no man would ever choose her. So be it. Lucy would make her own way.

Inside the house, Sharon and Ruby worked in silence, washing and drying and stacking the dishes. Lucy scanned the bare sideboard hungrily.

"Excuse me," she said. "Is there... May I make myself a plate?"

Sharon turned and regarded her coldly. "Mary didn't say anything about that."

"Is she here? Did they already eat?"

"She went to see Mr. Dang."

"That's the fish man. He's a Chinaman," Ruby added shyly. She lacked her mother's hard edges; there was a sweetness to her, an innocence that made it all right that she was staring openly at Lucy's face. "But he's nice. He comes around here a lot. Mrs. Sloat always drives down there to get the Sunday fish."

"It's a long drive," Sharon muttered, her arms plunged into the suds in the sink. "She won't be back for a while, so I won't be able to ask her, if we ought to fix you something. She should have left instructions."

The door clattered and Hal came into the kitchen, rubbing at his face with the back of his hand, his palms coated with dirt and grime.

"Mercy!" Sharon exclaimed. "Get back outside, looking like that!"

Hal grinned and walked past her to the sink, where he ran the taps full blast. "Smells good in here."

"There's a perfectly good sink in the powder room," Ruby said.

"And walk on the carpet? Mom would kill me," Hal said.

"We've got a few legs left," Ruby said. "You want 'em?"

"Yes, please. Me and Leo been clearing barbed wire at the

back of the lot. He'll be along in a minute—he got snagged."
He patted his backside, and he and Ruby laughed. Even Sharon flashed a smile.

Sharon handed her son a glass of milk, then went to the back door where the tin pails were lined up and fetched a large bowl. She lifted the cloth draped across the top, revealing a pile of golden chicken that made Lucy salivate.

"Just fix me a plate to take with me," Hal said. He drained the milk and went to the refrigerator to get the jug. "I want to take a look at that mower Leo's been having trouble with. You want some?"

It took Lucy a second to realize he was talking to her, raising the milk jug in her direction.

"Um…yes? Please," she added hastily.

"I'll fix you something too," Sharon relented. "But take it outside. We have work to do."

Hal kissed his mother on the cheek and took his lunch out the back door, loping across the yard to the shed. Lucy carried her own plate and glass of milk onto the porch and sat on the top step. The chicken was delicious, better than anything she had eaten in years. She ate the skin first, then the tender meat, and then she sucked the bones. She licked the grease from her fingers and looked around for something to wipe her hands on. There was nothing. She wiped them on her bare legs, leaving shiny streaks.

"You were hungry." Ruby had come out onto the porch without Lucy hearing the door, and was watching her from the shadows. "Can I sit down with you?"

"Yes." Lucy scooted to the edge of the step, embarrassed, wondering how much Ruby had seen. All that was left on her plate was a neat pile of bones. "Thank you. It was really good."

"Mom's chicken's practically famous," Ruby said. "Don't

mind her. She only acts mean. She don't do it around Pop or Hal, only me. Guess 'cause she wants to teach me everything. I'm engaged," she added, blushing. "I mean, we haven't told anyone yet, but I'm going to marry this boy Paul."

Lucy relaxed, listening to Ruby's chatter. When Garvey's door opened and he wheeled down the ramp, Lucy stiffened and Ruby fell silent. They watched him wheel around the corner of the building, never looking their way.

"Have you seen pictures of Garvey from before?" Ruby asked. "He was something!"

"No."

"Wait here a minute, will you?" Ruby jumped to her feet. Then she bent down and took Lucy's plate. "I can get that. Just…don't go, okay?"

Ruby disappeared into the house. When she came back moments later, she plopped down on the step next to Lucy, a scrapbook in her hands.

"Mrs. Sloat's parents built this place for her after her accident," she said, opening the cover. The first page held a large photograph of the motel when it was new. A painted wooden sign sunk into a much more well-kept lawn read The Mountainview—Gateway to Whitney and Yosemite. The metal chairs in front of the door were the same, and the maples and magnolia trees lining the walk were freshly planted, not even the height of a man. A crowd of people posed on the porch of the big house, smiling. A caption read Grand Opening, 1935.

"What accident?"

"Oh…you don't know about that?" Ruby was obviously happy to have a secret to share. "Mrs. Sloat went to college down at Mount St. Mary's in Los Angeles, but she came home her senior year. They say she used to be real headstrong. Never even graduated, after they spent all that money—can you imagine? Anyway, this boy she knew at school came up for a visit, and she was with him when they had the accident. He drove his car right off Tuttle Creek Road, it spun twice and landed upside down and he was killed instantly. Mrs. Sloat's leg was crushed. She was in the hospital for ages, over in Independence. I mean, I was just a kid then, but it was all anyone talked about."

"Is that why she limps?"

"Yes, and she's lucky for that. She couldn't walk at all for a long time. Well, after that, her parents built the motel so she'd be set up for when they were gone." Ruby dropped her voice and added, "Lots of folks say that's why Mr. Sloat married her. Just to get his hands on the place."

Lucy thought about that possibility. She'd never noticed any affection between the two. They barely spoke, Leo spending his time puttering around doing chores or smoking his cigars and listening to the radio; he spent every morning in town at the diner with a handful of retired men.

In fact, the entire family seemed to try to avoid each other: Mrs. Sloat at her desk checking people in and going through the mail and reading her magazines, Leo as absent as he could manage to be, Garvey locked away in his apartment, working on his creatures. "Was Garvey supposed to work in the motel too?"

"Oh my, no, Garvey was supposed to marry this little trust fund girl he met at school. Here, look." She flipped a couple of pages and pointed to a photograph of a young man throwing a football on the lawn. "He'd just graduated from Cal. He came home before he started his new job up in Sacramento. He was going to be an engineer."

Lucy gawked. The man in the photo was beautiful, fair-haired and well built in a white shirt that set off a summer tan, laughing as he reached for the ball spiraling toward him.

The features were Garvey's, the fair hair the same, but the moment caught in the snapshot was infused with joy, with the energy of youth and optimism.

"Of course he got called up not too long after that," Ruby continued wistfully. "There's the car his parents bought him. He barely ever drove it."

The same young man leaned against the door of a convertible, hamming it up for the camera. Sitting in the passenger seat was a beautiful girl with a spill of blond curls. Even in the black-and-white photo, Lucy could tell that her lipstick was bright and her teeth perfectly straight and white.

"That's the same car Ford showed at the world's fair that year," Ruby said. "Garvey's father saw it in a picture and ordered it the same day. Oh, he was crazy about Garvey. Everyone in this town was…." She tapped the girl in the picture with her finger. "'Course, *she* broke up with him after he came home crippled."

"You know a lot about him," Lucy said.

Ruby blushed. "All the girls liked him so much. My cousins, they're all heartbroken, 'specially because he hardly ever goes into town anymore. He's still handsome, don't you think?"

What Lucy thought was that Ruby had spent a lot of time with the scrapbook. She wondered if Sharon knew. Or if Garvey knew, for that matter. Yes, he was still handsome, but he burned with such anger, it was hard to imagine him being the object of girls' crushes.

"I guess it's nice he has a place to live here."

"Oh, yes, his mother took care of that. Mr. Hasty's been gone, oh, it's been three or four years now. And by the time Garvey came home, Mrs. Hasty had the cancer. But she did the best she could before she died. She had the apartment added onto the house so Garvey would have a place to live.

They had to widen some doors for his chair and so forth—
My dad and Hal helped out on the construction. They said…"

Her voice trailed away and she peeked up at Lucy from
under her long, pale eyelashes. "Oh, I don't know if I should
be talking this way. Listen to me, it's not my business," she
said, but then she turned another page in the book and continued.

"They said the day the will was read, Mrs. Sloat had a fit,
came home and took an ax to the addition. It was all framed
out and all—she didn't do much damage, but she was so
angry. See, Mrs. Hasty didn't tell nobody before she died
that she changed the will and left everything to Garvey."

"The motel too?" Lucy asked, astonished. "After she built
it for Mrs. Sloat?"

"Motel, the big house, the furniture, all the land, the cars.
Everything but the silver and china, because what's a bach-
elor going to do with that, after all?"

"But then…"

"She put in a special provision. Mr. and Mrs. Sloat get to
live in the house their whole lives, and they get a share of the
profits from the motel as long as Garvey owns it."

"But what if he sells the motel?"

Ruby rolled her eyes. "And what's he gonna do then?
Live off stuffing those trophies? I think it was smart of Mrs.
Hasty, because this way, they all depend on each other. She
kept the family together."

"But…" Now it was Lucy who lowered her voice. "They
seem like they'd as soon never speak to each other."

"Oh, but it was way worse before. Now they *have* to get
along."

"I guess." Lucy thought about that first day, the expression
on Mrs. Sloat's face when Garvey cursed her: that cold smile
laced with triumph. The two of them, pitted against each

other for the rest of their lives... What would their mother think if she could see them now?

"So," Ruby said, setting the well-thumbed scrapbook down on the step next to her. "What happened to *you?*"

Lucy spent Saturday afternoon in her tiny hidden garden. She cleared an area several feet square and began creating a low wall by setting oblong stones into the dirt. As she worked, memories of Reg's hands on her body warred with thoughts of the long-running battle between Mrs. Sloat and Garvey. This job was supposed to be an escape, a way to put the pain of her mother's death behind her; instead, she found herself right back in the crossfire of human emotion. Was there nowhere on earth for Lucy to escape, to start a life free of anguish?

When the sun began to set, she washed her hands under the spigot by the shed and wiped them on her dress. Feeling the coins in her pocket, she took them out and counted; today had netted her another eighty-five cents. Weekends seemed to mean bigger tips. Mrs. Sloat said she was keeping Lucy's account for her, but Lucy had her doubts. She had no leverage, no way to ensure she was paid for her work. She had to assume it would be up to her to save enough for a fresh start.

That night in her room she found a loose section of floorboard that could be eased up to reveal a small hole in the wall where the plaster had crumbled away. She put the money there and dreamed of her little stash growing, stacks of shiny coins filling the wall.

Sunday dawned warm and clear, but her hopes for getting back into her rock garden were dashed when Mrs. Sloat met her on the way back from the motel.

"Don't put that cart away yet. It's high time you got started on Garvey's room. Here," she added, pulling a key from her pocket. "Keep this. Now you can go in there anytime you want, and you won't have to wait for him to get to the door."

Lucy pocketed the key wordlessly, afraid that anything she said would provoke Mrs. Sloat.

She wolfed down the plate of ham and biscuits Ruby made for her, then dragged her cart around the side of the house and up the ramp. When knocking brought no response, she used her key, entering the room cautiously, not surprised to see Garvey working at his desk under the light of a bright Tensor lamp.

"Who said you could come in here?" he growled, turning his chair around to face her. Today he was wearing a blue plaid shirt with short sleeves that strained around his biceps. His arms were far more muscular than she'd realized, sculpted by the effort of wheeling himself up and down the ramps and over the uneven grounds, the gravel and sunburned sod. He wore pressed canvas trousers, a snowy-white undershirt under his shirt. Someone was keeping his laundry nice. Lucy kept expecting it to show up in her pile, but so far it hadn't.

"No one said. But I need to get started on your room. Mrs. Sloat wants it done today."

"She can't tell me what to do in my own house. I don't want you in my room."

Lucy dragged the cart into the room and took the folding step stool from its hook. "I'm just going to start on the walls," she said as calmly as she could, hoping he wouldn't see the way her hands were shaking. "You won't even know I'm here."

She set up the ladder in the corner farthest from Garvey's desk and fetched a rag and the bucket of sudsy water. She had purposely put on her longest dress, the only one that was too big rather than too small, so that it wouldn't ride up high on her legs as she worked, but she still felt self-conscious as she started on the wall. Her first swipe at the plaster coated the rag with grime, and the water quickly turned black. Water sluiced down her arms and onto her dress, her bodice getting uncomfortably damp so that it clung to her body. When she got down off the ladder, she'd only cleaned a couple square feet of the wall.

Garvey hadn't budged. He was staring at her unabashedly, his arms crossed over his chest. "They teach you that in that place? How to do the shit work no American'll touch?"

I'm American, Lucy thought, but she refused to let him rattle her. "May I please use your sink? If I have to fill this from the hose, it's going to take me a lot longer."

Garvey only snorted, so Lucy emptied the bucket out the front door and crossed in front of Garvey to get to his private quarters, feeling his eyes on her the whole time. His bedroom was spotless, the bed precisely made up with the plaid spread she'd glimpsed that first day. A tall stack of books teetered on his nightstand, and she wished she could read the spines, but she didn't dare.

The bathroom had a curious shower attachment and a steel bench; the tiled lip of the shower was only a few inches tall. Lucy caught herself wondering how he got from the chair to the bench and felt her face flame with embarrassment. She filled the bucket and carried it back to the ladder. Still, he stared.

Lucy couldn't stand it. "You just going to watch me all day?"

"If you're going to come in here against my wishes, disrupt my work, make it impossible for me to concentrate, I guess I'll do whatever I damn well want."

Lucy dipped her rag and started on the wall again. At this rate, it would take all afternoon to get halfway around the room. "Well, I'm not stopping you. If you don't want to work, I guess that's your choice."

She scrubbed until the water was filthy. This time when she returned with a bucket of fresh water, she paused before climbing the ladder. "If you're just going to sit there, you could at least talk to me."

Garvey laughed bitterly. "About what? Trust me, the only thing you and I have in common is the misfortune of living on this cursed patch of land. You just do your work, think your pathetic little thoughts, and leave me in peace."

He was silent after that, and eventually he turned back to his work, but throughout the long afternoon, Lucy felt him watching her. When evening approached and the light grew too dim to keep working, she had done all but the wall above his desk. Her arms ached and her back hurt, but as she pushed the cart out the door, she took a final look around the room and felt a sense of accomplishment. "I'll finish the rest soon," she said.

"I really wish you wouldn't bother," Garvey sighed.

But some of the vitriol had left his voice, as though the effort of despising Lucy had softened him.

Despite her weariness, Lucy felt unaccountably buoyed, and after dinner she set about cleaning her own room.

After pulling nails and clearing cobwebs and sweeping, Lucy looked around the tiny space and wondered if there was any hope for it. In Manzanar she learned to be on the lookout for spiders and mice and rats and lizards, even scorpions that found their way through cracks in the floors and walls. Somehow, the threat in this old house seemed even worse. In the night, it seemed likely that things were hiding behind the wall. Things that skittered and slithered and beat their papery wings, things with claws and teeth and hairless tails, tiny ears and gaping mouths and a dozen legs and slimy tongues.

The last thing she did before turning in was to take the pile of nails and broken lath and plaster out to the fence, stumbling in the darkness. She tossed it on top of the junk pile and turned back to the house. A light was on in Garvey's apartment and she stared at the window for a moment, seeking his silhouette through the shade.

At the back door, Mrs. Sloat waited, bracing herself with one hand against the frame, watching Lucy approach. She smelled like liquor even from several feet away, and Lucy wondered where she'd gone all afternoon. Yesterday's errand to see the fish man had taken far longer than a forty-mile round-trip ought to require.

"Now, how would you have gotten back in if I locked the door?" Mrs. Sloat said mockingly, holding up her ring of keys. They made a pretty tinkling sound.

"I don't know, ma'am."

"You coming from Garvey's? Having a little fun?"

"No!"

They stared at each other, Lucy shivering under Mrs. Sloat's drunken scrutiny. Finally the woman sighed and pushed away from the door. "Well, come on, now. I don't have all night."

Inside, the house still smelled of frying. Mrs. Sloat staggered toward the stairs, and Lucy headed for her room, finding her way in the dark.

30

IN THE MORNING SHE FOUND A TIN PICNIC
chest in the kitchen sink. Inside, a string of fish, silver scaled
and gape mouthed, lay on a bed of melting ice.

"Mr. Dang caught smallmouth bass yesterday," Mrs. Sloat
said blandly. She was sitting at the table, a glass of water resting on top of the folded newspaper. Lucy wondered if she
even remembered their exchange of the evening before. "We
can do these with cornmeal tonight."

Lucy started to gather the breakfast things, but Mrs. Sloat
stopped her.

"I'll take care of breakfast this morning," she said, getting
up slowly, her hand to her temple. She went to the counter
and poured coffee into a thermos. "You take this to Garvey.
Spend a little time with him. Keep him company."

"I don't think I should," Lucy said carefully. "I was there
all day yesterday—I'm not sure he wants to see me again so
soon."

"We've spoken. He understands that your responsibilities include attending to him," Mrs. Sloat said impatiently. "You shouldn't have any more trouble from him."

"But I don't…"

"You're here to make his life easier," Mrs. Sloat said shortly. "He should be grateful. Besides, you're still a woman, despite—" She waved her hand in the direction of Lucy's face. "And he's still a man, though not much of one, unfortunately."

Lucy left the kitchen, her face flaming with embarrassment. She needed a moment to think. Outside, the morning was cool, dew on the grass and wild poppies opening to the first rays of sun.

Mrs. Sloat wanted her to wait on her brother, to serve him—but why? Only to humiliate him further, to underscore her limitations? It was as if she wanted to taunt him, to taunt them both. *You're still a woman, and he's still a man.*

Lucy felt the flush creeping across her face. No man would want Lucy, not even a man like Garvey.

She stood at the bottom of the ramp, debating with herself. She could refuse, she could defy Mrs. Sloat. And Mrs. Sloat could send Lucy back to Manzanar with no notice. There would be no second chance after that; Sister Jeanne had made it clear that this was her one opportunity.

But if Lucy could save enough, she could set out for the east, some busy city where a strong back and a little luck would be all she needed to start a life. She just had to endure long enough.

She'd endured worse, hadn't she?

Lucy walked past the oleander, up the ramp. She didn't bother knocking, but fitted her key to the lock. It was warm from being carried in her pocket. The door swung open and she stepped inside.

Garvey was sitting at his worktable, as usual. "Why the hell can't you just leave me the fuck alone," he muttered, wheeling himself around.

Lucy set the thermos down on a small table in the bay window and reached for the broom and dustpan that were leaning next to the door, blushing furiously as she tried not to meet Garvey's eyes.

"Mrs. Sloat wanted me to bring your coffee," she said, not knowing what to say next. Another girl would know what to do. Even *she* would have known what to do, before. She thought of Jessie, those first sweet kisses. Lucy had marveled at the knowledge that lay inside her, dormant until the day he took her hand in his: how to walk with her hips gently swaying, how to turn and smile over her shoulder, how to lean into his neck so they fit together perfectly.

"The floors must be hard for you. I can have that done in no time. I can sweep today and then if you want, one day later this week I can wax. I'll have to move the furniture but I can do half at a time, I don't mind—"

"I don't need you," Garvey said, his voice hoarse and ragged. "I didn't ask you to come here."

Lucy took a small step closer. So he wasn't going to make this any easier for her. "But I have to. Mrs. Sloat said she talked to you, she said…"

"Oh, God," Garvey said, and turned back to his table. The pelt he'd been working on all week was now stretched over a wood-and-wire form, only its mouth still rolled back on itself. He stared at the thing's gruesome, gaping face. "Oh, *God.*"

There was such revulsion in his voice. Was it so painful to look at her? She knew that her face twisted something inside him, provoked him. It had never been because she was Japanese—she saw that now as he clutched the edge of his worktable with both hands, the skin of his knuckles whitening at the power of his grip.

They were both damaged. Both unwanted. Was it the reflection of his own misery that Garvey saw when he looked at her? Couldn't they forge some sort of alliance—the kindness of silence, the knowledge of kinship? Couldn't some small bond be knitted from the strands of the terrible things that had happened to each of them?

But if the answer was no, she would not let Garvey intimidate her. She watched his quaking shoulders, his agonized face, and hated him for finding her wounds uglier than his.

"Please," she said carefully. "Your sister sent me...."

Garvey's fist crashed down onto the worktable, causing objects to jump and skitter. Something fell to the floor, and Lucy knelt to retrieve it. A small, pale, round thing, it rolled away from his chair and out of sight, into the small space between the cabinet and the floor.

"Don't," Garvey said sharply. But Lucy was already crawling after it on her knees.

As Lucy lowered her face to the floor, she saw the spinning spokes of the chair's wheels out of the corner of her eye, catching the sunlight. There—all the way against the wall—the little object glowed milky-white.

Lucy's dress had been clean this morning. She had done her own laundry on Friday, pressing her three dresses with care. The neat pleats and crisp collars mattered to her the way the sparkling mirrors and perfectly made beds and orderly kitchen cupboards mattered, as proof that Lucy was better than any task life put in front of her. But the dress could be laundered and pressed again.

She lay flat on her chest and extended her arm as far as she could under the cabinet. No good. Her fingers grasped at nothing as she strained against the lip of the cabinet, her shoulder blocking her reach.

"Stop it. Stop it," Garvey said roughly. "Use this, for God's sake."

Lucy backed out, aware of how she must have looked, prone on the floor. Her skirt had ridden up, and she tugged it back down, embarrassment flooding her face. Something touched the top of her hand. A long stick with a metal hook at the end. Its point was dull, but it looked like a miniature version of Blackbeard's arm, an image that came from an illustrated copy of Peter Pan that she had once owned.

"*Use* it."

Lucy accepted the tool Garvey was holding out to her. She pushed it under the cabinet and hooked the end around the white object and coaxed it forward. It rolled easily over the floor, and in seconds it was in her palm, smooth and cool against her skin.

It was an eye. Made of glass, only half an inch across, perfectly colored with a blue iris, a coal-black pupil. Like the eyes that belonged to the beautiful doll Lucy had received for her eighth birthday, the doll that had been given away as they prepared for evacuation.

But without the benefit of long-fringed lashes, without the closing plastic lid, the eye looked naked, almost…obscene. Lucy didn't want to touch the thing. She held it out to Garvey, brushing his fingers with hers. He seized it and jerked away from her as though even that slight touch repulsed him.

"What is it for?" she asked.

He didn't respond, but began moving things around on the worktable. He found a little ceramic dish and dropped the glass sphere into it; it made a tiny ping. A pleasant sound.

"Are you almost finished with your…squirrel?" It was a

guess, based on what she could see of the creature taking shape on the fragile form.

Garvey turned on her, his fury unabated. "Does it look finished?"

"I'm sorry. I didn't know. I just thought…"

He picked up the animal by the wooden base to which it was clamped, and thrust it at Lucy with the mouth facing up. The teeth were set into some sort of clay or modeling compound, and the rough outline of a tongue and the roof of the mouth had been sculpted inside the form. Over that assemblage, the creature's lips were peeled back wider and farther than Lucy would have thought possible—a nightmare scream, with the snout bunched up under wrinkled flesh.

"There's ten, twelve hours left on this, easy."

Lucy felt nauseous, and wondered what would happen if she were to vomit here in this room. The odor would get into the floorboards. Garvey would hate her even more. She swallowed down hard.

"I'm sorry," she said again, whispering.

"You don't even know why she sent you over here, do you?" Garvey said, placing the thing gently on the worktable. "You have no idea what she means for you to do."

Lucy stared at the floor, the distance between her shoes and his chair. She felt her pulse in her throat. Her fingers touched the key in her pocket.

"My *sister*…"

More time passed. The smell in the room held a very faint, odd note, mostly unpleasant, the smell of meat left out in the sun. But Lucy's stomach had settled back down and her breath came more easily.

"Look at me."

She did, briefly. Garvey's expression was hard, but Lucy

couldn't help noticing that his hair was soft and silky, his face smooth from his shave.

"*Look* at me, I said."

Lucy forced herself to keep her gaze on him. She focused on the space between his nose and mouth.

"Do you think any woman could want this? Could want *me?*" Garvey demanded. "*Do* you?"

Lucy ground her teeth against each other, hard enough to make her head pound. What was she supposed to say? Did he not see her standing in front of him, wrecked and ravaged?

"You want to know about what happened to me? How I ended up like this? There isn't much to tell, unfortunately. Boom. A shell blew up, they fired on us. I didn't feel anything. I just knew I couldn't move. I figured I was dead or almost dead. Guy next to me, he went down with his guts hanging out of his stomach. I watched him trying to stuff them back in. He was two feet away, his hands covered with blood, he kept pushing at himself, trying to talk. After a while it was just me and him, everyone else was dead or went on ahead. It was so…quiet."

"Did he die?"

Garvey shook his head slowly. "What—what the hell kind of question is that? A shell took out half his guts. The rest were—it was like at the butcher. Picture a string of sausages. Can you do that? Lucy? He. Died. With. His. Hands. *In. His. Own. Bowels.*"

"I'm sorry," Lucy whispered again, but she wasn't sorry. She was angry. Did he think she had never seen anything horrifying? "But *you* lived."

Garvey's eyes narrowed and his lips thinned. "You're done here. Get *out*—I'm not asking again."

"Or what?" She was trembling, her insides hot with shame and anger and emotions she couldn't name.

He snatched something from his workbench, metal glint-
ing, and brandished it at her. A knife—curved, wicked, at
home in his hand. Lucy jumped, more from surprise than
from any real threat. And then she backed away. Two paces,
three, all the way to the door. Her hand groped for the knob
behind her; she never took her eyes off Garvey.

He would never cut her, she was sure of it. But something
dangerous had showed itself nonetheless, and its energy arced
between them like lightning on a lake.

31

IT WAS LUCY'S JOB TO CLEAN THE DOWNSTAIRS bathroom in the big house every day, since nearly every guest used it when checking in, a practice made necessary by the long drive to Lone Pine from Fresno or Bakersfield. Lucy knew every inch of the room by heart. Each day she wiped down the mirror, faucet and sink. She placed the cake of soap on the windowsill while she cleaned the porcelain soap dish that jutted from the wall. She swabbed out the toilet and wiped every surface.

Still, as she sat in the tub full of water as hot as she could stand it, she imagined that every surface teemed with germs and filth. Bacteria were oddly harmless-looking things in the textbook photos—little tubes like so many Mike and Ike candies—but Lucy knew they could poison you. Who knew what bacteria were waiting to burrow down your neckline or into your eyes and ears, to tunnel through your pores into your organs, your brain?

Only in the water did she feel safe, despite the heat making sweat trickle down the back of her neck. She washed with a rough rag and the lye soap Leo used to remove motor oil from his hands, scrubbing until her skin stung and turned the red of an overripe tomato. It took a long time for her to feel clean enough, and then she stayed as still as she could in the water, trying to feel nothing at all. At one point Mrs. Sloat knocked on the door, but after Lucy ignored her long enough she finally went away.

Lucy drowsed, the bathwater lapping gently over her stomach, her breasts. Her arms floated, her hair swirled around her face. She sank lower, her ears under the surface; only her nose, lips and eyes remained exposed, and she listened to the groaning of the house, magnified by the water. Only when every bit of heat had left the water, and her knees, bobbing above the surface like pale islands, were pocked with goose-flesh, did Lucy finally get out of the tub.

She put on clean clothes and used her damp towel to pick up the dirty clothes, and took them to the laundry. Sharon and Ruby had arrived and the aroma of fried onions filled the air, but Lucy avoided the kitchen, slipped out the front door, fetched the cleaning cart and got to work.

Lucy welcomed the ache in her muscles from washing Garvey's walls the other day. By the time she finished the last room, she was out of breath, sweat dampening her dress and dripping in her eyes. She hadn't bothered with gloves, and her hands were raw and itching. Her scars throbbed, her whole face pulsing with the rhythm of her shame. But at least she had managed to keep her thoughts at bay.

It reminded her of something Sister Jeanne had told her when her pain was at its worst, when she'd stopped screaming only because she lost her voice. Jeanne told her she had known a wounded soldier who described his pain as a burning sheet of foil, a thousand degrees, curling from the heat. When the pain was greatest, the foil glowed as though the sun was shining down directly on it. When the pain lessened the surface seemed to dull, like tin or tarnished silver. Jeanne said this was as good a way to think about it as any, and that Lucy should practice envisioning her pain this way, folding this sheet of foil into a tiny square using only her mind. That she should fold it over, and over again, and over and over until she made it small enough to bear.

Lucy dragged the bucket to the backyard one final time, drenching the parched soil around the roses before she went to the fence at the edge of the forest and sank to her knees, exhausted from the afternoon's cleaning. Weeds and bits of dead grass poked her knees. She didn't care. The pain was everywhere. It was in the pads of her fingers and the rough ends of her hair, the dry skin of her knees and heels and the soft flesh of her stomach. It was inside—where her organs were, the muscles and veins and fat.

She shifted from her knees to her haunches. The buzzing of insects had swelled as the sun grew high in the sky. The sounds of the meal—conversations in the dining room, kitchen sounds, cars pulling into and out of the parking lot on the other side of the building—seemed safely distant. No one would search for her here. No one would search for her at all. She was neither expected nor wanted until morning, and if she didn't return at all until then, she doubted anyone would care.

After a while, Lucy allowed her eyes to flutter closed. She dozed, in between waking and sleep, listening to the night sounds. An insect buzzed near her ear. A rustling in the brush signaled some small animal startled into flight. Sister Jeanne had once given her a prayer card bearing a picture of Saint Francis, surrounded by small creatures—a doe, a pair of rabbits, ducks with ducklings. Lucy wished for animals to encircle her now, to beg with their dumb eyes for her caress, for her kind word. There had to be something in this world that needed her.

Later, much later, the last of the cars pulled out of the parking lot. Sharon's truck belched exhaust as it trundled into the road. Then the house was quiet. Afternoon faded to evening as Lucy dragged herself farther into the woods, sitting with her back against a tree. She was hungry, but the thought of meeting Garvey or Mrs. Sloat or even Leo in the hall was too much to bear. The light in the upstairs rooms went out. A little later, so did Garvey's. The moon was three-quarters full but weak, its light thin and treacherous. Lucy picked her way with care across the backyard, avoiding by memory the biggest holes, the clothesline poles. Her keys were in her pocket, but the back door was unlocked. How quickly the house had adapted to her; she had become the one who locked up at night.

To her room, sliding her feet along the waxed floor. Hands trailing the wall, like Mrs. Sloat. Silent; no one in the house would know she was there.

Her door was open a few inches. Lucy wondered if Sharon had looked inside. She would not have found the loose board, the stash of money, but she might have been surprised at what Lucy had accomplished. It still smelled strongly of bleach. That was a comfort as Lucy shucked off her ruined dress and slipped her nightgown over her arms. Tomorrow she would wash the dress, the rags, even the nightgown, and she would bathe again. And again.

Lucy fought the images that flickered at the edges of her mind—the smooth glass eye rolling in her palm, the anguish in Garvey's eyes—but she was able to keep them away. *No,* as she breathed in. *No, no, no,* as she exhaled.

★ ★ ★

The next time Lucy went to Garvey's room, to collect his laundry, the door was locked. When Lucy tried her key in the door, it wouldn't budge. Garvey had lodged something— a dresser, a chair?—against the door.

When Lucy reported back, Mrs. Sloat's lips narrowed and she fumed for a moment before disappearing up the stairs. A moment later, she came back with Leo, puffy faced and sleepy looking—and holding a rifle.

"Don't worry, he's not shooting anybody," Mrs. Sloat smirked when Lucy gasped. "Only talking some sense into my brother."

Still, Lucy was relieved when half an hour passed with no shots being fired. Leo returned first and glared at his wife with disgust as he passed her in the kitchen. "Last time I do your dirty work," he muttered. When Lucy tried the door again later, it was open—but the apartment was empty.

Lucy got to work. After starting the laundry, she began dusting the tops of the shelves, the objects that Garvey couldn't reach. It was almost lunchtime when she finished, and she was carefully arranging a tray of what looked like tiny bottles of paint when the door opened and Garvey rolled into the room.

Lucy braced herself to be yelled at, but Garvey didn't even look at her. His chair was dusty, and a few wisps of weeds were caught in the spokes. Had he really tried to take the thing out across the yard—into the woods? Lucy realized then just how trapped he really was: he couldn't even go through the forest to the creek, or to the path that led to grazing land on the ranch across the street, as Lucy had on occasion when she wanted to be alone.

The wheels tracked dirt across the floor Lucy had just swept, but she said nothing, holding her breath to see what

Garvey would do. The last time she had stood in this room, he'd drawn a knife on her and practically chased her out.

He pulled something from his pocket and laid it on the worktable: a plump gray-blue quail whose brown belly was streaked with white. Lucy had no idea if he'd shot it or trapped it or bought it or even found it dead in some sunlit vale, but as he prodded it gently with a finger, sliding its small, pretty body this way and that, she knew instinctively that he was figuring out where to make the first cut. After a few unhurried moments of consideration, with his left hand he picked up the curious knife with which he had threatened her, the one with the blade shaped like a beak.

Lucy ventured closer, unable to resist. She peered over his shoulder at the bird. In the light from Garvey's gooseneck work lamp, it looked almost alive—as though it had died only moments ago, as though its blood was still warm. Garvey smoothed its white-tipped feathers tenderly, caressing the delicate ruff at its throat, and Lucy felt the pulsing excitement of discovery, a ravenous curiosity about the gateway between life and death through which the tiny creature had passed.

"Can I do it?" she asked breathlessly.

"Can you do what?"

"Cut it open."

Instead of answering, Garvey put the tip of the knife to the top of the breastbone, his hands steady. Slowly, surely, he drew down, and the bird's flesh split. When he reached the end under the tail, he peeled the skin away tenderly, revealing its glistening pink innards. There was no blood, which surprised Lucy, and then it didn't.

"No. You can't," Garvey said. Then he set the split bird carefully on the table. "Not yet, anyway. You have a lot to learn first."

32

YEARS LATER, WHEN LUCY THOUGHT BACK over her time at Lone Pine, it was the months that followed that she thought of as the happiest of her life. She did her work each day, the smells of ammonia and bleach becoming as familiar to her as once was her mother's perfume or her father's pipe smoke. As spring was overtaken by summer, Mrs. Sloat divided her time between motel business and trips to Owens Lake several times a week. Sometimes she returned with fish; sometimes she didn't. Twice, Lucy glimpsed Mr. Dang when she went into town on errands with Mrs. Sloat. Both times, he wore a necktie and a hat, despite the heat. Lucy had a hard time imagining him on a boat in his shirtsleeves, checking his lines and dipping his hand into a bucket of bait.

Ruby and Hal ate their weekend meals with Lucy and took her for drives in their mother's truck. They made her laugh with their clowning around. The stash of coins and the occasional bill grew in her secret hiding place, each addition bringing her closer to her dream of escape. And best of all was the time she spent with Garvey, learning and assisting at his bench after her work was done each day.

As time passed, Lucy learned to relax around him, and his silence gave way to measured conversation, and later to longer stories, from his boyhood adventures in the foothills and hunting camps, his college years, the football games and fraternity pranks. Hours could pass before Lucy noticed the sun sinking in the sky or her stomach growling in hunger.

And the animals: Lucy watched Garvey study them before he took them apart and slowly, with tender and fastidious attention, put them back together. He coaxed emotions from them that they'd never experienced in life, using his scalpels and thread and forms and glues and paints to create poses and expressions that were somehow knowing and sly and mischievous. Garvey's animals were not only livelier than their former selves, but transformed by his hands into nearly mythic beasts.

Lucy watched Garvey when she was supposed to be studying the way he notched a jaw or slit the dry tissue of a nose. Tragedy had transformed her, but it seemed that Garvey was teaching her that her transformation was not yet complete. That like the limp, lifeless corpses that he began with, there was, buried inside her, the potential for wondrous and surprising things, things that only he could see.

Their lessons slowly took on a new rhythm. Garvey would have the tools and supplies laid out when she arrived, but instead of beginning right away, they would talk for a while. Lucy told herself it was only a courtesy, nothing more. But there were days when talking took the entire afternoon, when they never got around to the animals at all. Or when, as he guided her hand along the knobby curve of a spine or the smooth-sanded surface of a base, his fingers lingered on hers.

One warm June day, Mrs. Sloat came to the doorway, which Garvey had propped open to let air into the room. She was wearing a town dress and a slash of lipstick.

"Lucy," she snapped. "I need you to come pick up the drapes from the cleaners and help me hang them."

Mrs. Sloat liked to have company when she did errands. Often she sat in the car and had Lucy go into the store. She was shy about her limp, less steady than she was at home, where she'd navigated every hall and step a thousand times. Lucy had become accustomed to their trips to town; people no longer gaped and whispered as they once had. The clerks and stock boys even greeted her like a local.

Lucy had no desire to stop what she was doing, but she knew Mrs. Sloat wouldn't take no for an answer. She sighed and set down the tiny paintbrush she had been using to touch up the color along the gums of a pretty two-point buck shoulder mount.

"She's busy," Garvey growled.

There was a silence. Lucy glanced back and forth between Mrs. Sloat and Garvey, who didn't bother to look up from the striped trout he was working on. Today's painting lesson had filled the air with acrid fumes, and after a moment Mrs. Sloat sneezed twice in rapid succession.

"Seems like you can't tolerate the air in here," Garvey said. "Maybe you ought to be on your way."

"Not without my *employee*," Mrs. Sloat huffed.

The change in Garvey was instant and breathtaking. He jammed his hand down on the wheel so fast that metal scraped on metal and the chair shuddered and turned. It was as though he meant to propel himself out of the chair. In that moment, Lucy wouldn't have been surprised if he'd stood on his ruined legs and gone after his sister, and she must have felt it too, because she stepped back, nearly falling.

"Whose employee? *Whose* fucking employee, Mary? It seems to me that you've been forgetting something important."

"I only said—"

"Everything in this house, every inch of this land, every miserable dollar in the bank is *mine*." He was bellowing, spittle flying from his mouth, his fists clenched.

"Stop it, Garvey, the guests—"

"Let them hear! Let them all hear! Let them shut this place down, I don't care anymore."

"Watch what you're saying," Mrs. Sloat said, regaining her composure. "You can't treat me this way. You can't run this place without me. You can't even go up the stairs."

Garvey opened his mouth in retort, but Mrs. Sloat was back in the fight, and she pulled herself up to her full height, towering above her brother.

"Don't forget, the money's not really yours. It's in your *trust*. You think if I walk in that bank and tell them my brother's losing his mind, they won't shut down your allowance like *that?*" Mrs. Sloat snapped her fingers for emphasis. "It's all legal, Garvey. There's not one damn thing you can do about it."

"But Lucy doesn't—"

"Do you really think she wants to be your assistant?—your *protégé?* I have news for you, oh brother of mine, she might not look like much, but on the inside she's every bit as cagey and coldhearted as any other woman. She's looking out for one person and one person only—her*self*."

Mrs. Sloat glared at Lucy, then walked out of the room. Garvey watched her go, and then rested his head in his hand.

"God," he said softly. "What a fucking mess."

Lucy sat frozen in her chair, unsure of what to do, embarrassed almost to tears by Mrs. Sloat's insinuations. "It's true, then?" she asked. "She could do that to you? She could take what's rightfully yours?"

"No, no, it's—well, it's complicated. My mother was trying to be fair to everyone, I guess. And instead she set it up so my sister and I can never escape each other." He rubbed his face. "You should have seen her, when she went off to college—most beautiful girl around. Could have had anyone she wanted—"

He stopped abruptly, and Lucy knew immediately that he thought he'd offended her. "No, no," she whispered. "It's all right."

"No. It's not. Lucy... Look at me."

Her gaze traveled a slow path from her hands twisted in her lap up to Garvey's face, full of anguish but still handsome, still perfect. What a pair they made; Garvey as good-looking as a movie star, stuck with a body that didn't work—and Lucy, lithe and strong from her work, but doomed with a face that would always turn people away.

"The things I said to you," he said softly, "when you first came here. I was... I was horrible to you. I'm so sorry."

"It doesn't matter. It's all right." Lucy tried to blot out his apology with her words; she couldn't bear for him to show himself to her this way.

"It matters. Everything matters." Garvey took a deep breath but didn't look away. "You matter."

Lucy didn't dare reply. Garvey's eyes, moody-gray on a good day and nearly black when he was angry, were unreadable. He reached out a hand, his fingertips brushing her forehead so gently she could barely feel his touch.

His fingers traveled down the outline of her scar, achingly slowly, as though he sought to know her through his touch.

He was not repulsed by her ugliness, and Lucy's breath caught in her throat as his fingers fluttered against her eyelashes, as his thumb found the corner of her mouth, and gently slid along her lips.

Lucy closed her eyes and placed her hand over Garvey's. She held it hard against her mouth, her lips pressed against his palm. She couldn't bear to let go. It had been so long, so terribly long since she had touched anyone, since she had felt another human's warmth.

Garvey's other hand touched her cheek—her good cheek, the smooth one, the perfect one—and then his fingers were in her hair, pulling her closer, and Lucy made a sound like a sigh that was really a plea, the desperate voice of her longing for the kiss she had never dared to imagine until just this second. Garvey's lips on hers were tentative but hungry, and Lucy assured him with her touch, her arms around his neck.

Her body was trembling when she pulled away from him. He looked stricken. "I—I'm sorry—"

"No," Lucy whispered. She put a finger to his lips to silence him, and went to the door, which Mrs. Sloat hadn't closed all the way. She pushed it shut and turned the bolt, then came back to stand in front of Garvey's chair, her knees touching his. When she lifted her dress up over her head and let it fall to the floor, her skin prickled in response and her blood surged with longing.

"Lucy," Garvey said. He was so close she could feel his breath through the thin cotton of her camisole. "What are you doing…?"

She reached for one of his hands, and pressed it to her rib cage. His hand fit perfectly, wrapped around the curve of her waist. His fingers splayed across her skin, gentle and warm.

"The other," she whispered. "Please."

And he did. He lifted his other hand and placed it next

to the first, encircling her waist with them. He let out a groan—of pleasure, pain, longing; Lucy had never heard a man make such a sound but discovered that she understood this new language perfectly.

"Lucy. You know I'm— I can't—and you're—"

"Shhh." She let her eyelids drift down and concentrated on the place where her body met his. "Just...this. Just for now."

After that they didn't speak.

33

San Francisco
Friday, June 9, 1978

PATTY TRIED JAY'S OFFICE AGAIN.

"I'm so sorry, Patty, I don't know what to tell you." If Jay's secretary was getting exasperated, she didn't show it.

"I called the airline. They said his plane landed almost an hour ago."

"But they could have taxied for a while, there might be traffic. I really do expect him to be here in the next half hour or so."

"And you'll have him call me first thing?"

"I will, I promise." She hesitated. "I'm really looking forward to the wedding, you know. We're all just so happy for you and Jay. You're perfect for him."

"Oh." Patty was so surprised that for a moment she forgot her panic. *Really?* she wanted to say. Instead, she bumbled through an effusive thank-you and hung up, then set the phone down and forced herself to take a few deep breaths.

Okay. Jay would be in the office soon, he'd get her message (messages, three of them), he'd call her back and he'd know what to do. His best friend, Bryan, was an attorney; he'd probably know who to call. If she could just be patient another half hour, they would take the next step together.

There was a soft tapping at the door. Patty jumped—could it be Jay? Surprising her, stopping by the house first before he went to work? She ran to the door, but this time, before opening it, she looked through the peephole.

A middle-aged man in a red windbreaker, Levi's and cowboy boots waited, eyes hidden behind aviator sunglasses. His haircut looked expensive. He didn't look like a cop, but Patty had had about all the surprises she could stand for one day. She hesitated, wondering if he'd heard her footsteps, thinking she'd just retreat back into the house.

"Lucy," the man said. His voice through the door was muffled. "Lucy, are you there?"

Patty was sure she had never seen the man before in her life. Curiosity overwhelmed her better judgment, and Patty opened the door.

His expression changed to one of surprise.

"I'm sorry, I was looking for the home of Lucy Takeda."

"You've found it. I'm her daughter. Patty."

His surprise deepened, and then he smiled. "I'm so sorry, I didn't know—please, forgive me. I'm a friend of your mother. Jessie Kadonada."

He wouldn't stay more than a few minutes. Patty offered him tea, coffee, a glass of water, but he kept looking at his watch.

"I really ought to get back on the road," he said. "I have a long drive."

He lived in Portland, he'd explained, and he was here on business. Patty thought it odd that he'd driven—Jay, who traveled for business two or three times a month, always flew, even if he was only going to Reno.

"Any idea when your mother might be back?" he asked.

"She got called away sort of unexpectedly. Was she expecting you?"

"Yes, we made tentative plans to meet. Of course, it's possible I misunderstood...."

They looked at each other; Patty got the sense he was choosing his words as carefully as she was. She wanted to tell him that she'd seen his photographs in Forrest's album, that she could see the resemblance between the shy boy and the man he'd become. But then she would have to explain how she had come across the album. Jessie didn't mention Forrest; if he knew about the man's death, he was covering it well. He really did seem like a man paying a casual visit to an old friend.

But it still seemed to Patty too coincidental that he had come to town only days after Forrest had been killed. Especially because now she knew that her mother had lied when she said they had lost touch. He knew where she lived; he knew details about her life.

There was something here that didn't fit, and Patty didn't want to let him go before she found it.

"Did you move to Portland right after the war?" she asked, trying to keep her tone light and conversational.

Jessie's expression fell for a fraction of a second. "No. My dad took a job in Chicago. We left Manzanar in the spring of 1944. We were lucky, we got out a lot sooner than other people did. I finished up high school there, went to Northwestern, got my degree in business. I worked in Chicago for a long time. I only moved a few years ago, got a job offer I couldn't turn down."

"Oh." Patty couldn't think of anything else to ask, to keep him talking. "Well, I would be happy to give my mom a message, if you want."

"Yeah, maybe I can catch up with her next time I'm in town. Have a drink or something." Still, he didn't move toward the door. "Patty…"

"Yes?"

"Just…" He cleared his throat. "Your mom is a very special lady."

"Thank you," Patty said, flustered. "I mean, you're right, she is. Mr. Kadonada…sometimes, I feel like there's this whole side of her that I don't even know. She doesn't talk about the past much."

A pained expression passed over his face. "Don't judge her for that. Please, Patty. The war changed all of us. None of us came out of it whole. But that doesn't change the way she feels about you, it doesn't limit how much she loves you."

"How can you know?" Patty didn't mean for her words to come out as harshly as they did. "You don't know her anymore. You don't know who she is now."

Jessie shook his head. "No, I suppose I don't. But I know who she *was*. Your mom was…well, she was perfect. Graceful, and funny, and beautiful, and kind. She got me through—if it hadn't been for her, I don't know if I could have survived."

They were both silent for a moment, and then Jessie put his hand on the door.

"Thank you," he said formally.

"I would be glad to give my mother a message for you."

"It's not necessary. I'll call soon."

As Lucy closed the door behind him, she felt as though she had failed to ask the right questions. If Jessie Kadonada knew something about Forrest, about his death and Lucy's involvement, he'd kept it well hidden.

Patty paused in the short hall leading to the kitchen and looked back on her mother's living room: the plastic-covered furniture, the carpet that bore the even track marks of its thrice-weekly vacuuming, the drapes and lampshades and potted plants. Lucy's life was solitary and careful and orderly and so empty it echoed. But once, it had been different. Once, it had been marked with beauty and passion and bravery. Somewhere, deep inside Lucy, that girl still lived, her sacrifices making it possible for Patty to thrive. And that was worth honoring, wasn't it? Worth defending?

Jay called moments after Jessie left. He'd gone straight to a client's office from the airport, and had only just now picked up his messages. Patty gave him the condensed version of events, leaving out Jessie's visit, and Jay called his attorney friend immediately and set something up. With any luck, they'd have Lucy home tonight.

It was obvious that Jay had a lot of questions—it wasn't every day, Patty supposed, that a man's future mother-in-law was taken in for questioning for a murder—but he'd merely told Patty that he loved her, that everything would be all right and that he would see her over at the police station with the attorney at four-thirty.

Patty sat down and tried to figure out what to do next. When Torre and Officer Grieg had left earlier, they were weighed down with most of Lucy's taxidermy tools. The implements were sealed in plastic bags, but Patty still recognized the knives, the clamp and the hide stretcher. Could they really think Lucy might have used them to murder Forrest?

Grieg had also taken some of Lucy's clothes, including a blouse that had been in her laundry basket. Was it the one

she had been wearing the other day, when Forrest was killed? As hard as she tried to remember, Patty couldn't.

It felt as though the cops were building a case against her mother one piece at a time. Between their insinuations and Lucy's revelations about her mother, Patty was feeling doubt beginning to take hold. Even if each step the police took was a false one, even if Lucy was innocent of everything but keeping her past a secret, they could still make her look guilty.

Patty had to find a way to stop them.

An idea had been forming in her mind ever since she'd seen the photos of a much younger Benny Van Dorn partying in the cramped motor pool office all those years ago. Sometimes a person could leave the past behind, as Lucy had done for so many years. But sometimes, outside factors made that more difficult. Such as, for instance, if a person held an elected office.

Patty made a quick call to the number listed in the phone book for the district headquarters and used the working-on-an-article ruse again. Benny Van Dorn's assistant seemed happy to tell Patty that he would be in the office that afternoon, and that he would be able to spare her a few minutes for her article about the Ocean Avenue development.

She made a quick trip to Kinkos to copy some pages from Forrest's photo albums, and at a few minutes before three, she was ushered into Van Dorn's office.

Patty fixed what she hoped was a confident smile on her face. "Supervisor Van Dorn?"

He looked up from his desk and took off his glasses, then stood with some effort and came around to greet her. He was several inches over six feet, swollen and florid, his jowls disappearing into a too-tight collar. He smiled and extended his hand. Patty shook it; the flesh was warm and tight, as though all the blood had rushed to his extremities.

"Hi. Janice Stapleton, the *Chron*. I'm not supposed to say this, but I live in Ingleside and I voted for you." She laughed coyly. "I was hoping you could spare me a few minutes for a piece we're doing on Ocean Avenue. I spoke to your assistant about it?"

Patty allowed her hair to fall forward, the ends resting above her cleavage, more of which was exposed than she would ever ordinarily allow. She'd left two buttons of her blouse unfastened and spent a little extra time on her makeup.

"Of course, of course, sweetheart," Van Dorn said, letting his gaze rove freely to her breasts.

Was it really so easy? Patty, who had never consciously flirted in her life, who still got flustered whenever Jay snuck a caress in a crowded elevator or under a restaurant table-cloth, flicked her hair over her shoulder. "I appreciate you taking the time to talk."

"Well, here, sit, get comfortable."

Patty took the seat he offered, and he closed the office door. He went around the desk and lowered himself back into his own chair, grunting from exertion.

Now that they were ensured privacy, Patty didn't bother with the fake smile. She pulled the copies of Forrest's photo album out of the envelope and spread them in front of Van Dorn.

There he was, thirty-five years ago—with his hand between a young woman's knees as she sat next to him on a couch. Here was a shot of him and Rickenbocker, toasting with highball glasses while a young Jessie Kadonada stood like a ghost in the background. Half a dozen more, with Van Dorn featured in each, drinking and laughing and exploring the flesh of young women and, in one case, with his arm slung around Jessie's shoulders.

"Reg Forrest is dead," Patty said. She spoke quickly, know-

ing she had very little time. "The police are questioning my mother. My grandmother was Miyako Takeda." She tapped her index finger on the photograph of her mother sitting on Rickenbocker's lap. "My mother is Lucy Takeda. I believe you knew her."

Van Dorn's convivial grin vanished and his brow wrinkled with confusion and irritation. "Hey. What the hell is this?"

"I want the investigation stopped. I believe there is some question as to whether Forrest's death was a suicide. I want you to make that official."

"It was your mother who offed him?" Van Dorn demanded. "I should have guessed."

"*No.*" Patty stabbed her finger on Rickenbocker's image. "She's innocent. I don't know who killed him, and it doesn't matter. I just want her left alone."

Van Dorn raised an eyebrow. "You sure about that?" he said. "What I hear, they have a couple people ready to swear she was there that morning."

So he'd been following the case.

"I know you and the police scratch each other's backs," she said quietly. "You may have to call in a few favors, but I'm guessing you'll be willing to do that."

Van Dorn laughed. "Why's that? 'Cause you've got a few shots of me at parties with pretty girls? You think every man in the district isn't going to take one look at those and wish *he'd* been there?"

Patty pointed to Jessie's frightened, pale face in the photo of Van Dorn and Rickenbocker. "Jessie Kadonada was abused by Reg Forrest. *Raped.* Repeatedly."

Van Dorn's face reddened, his soft jowls quivering. "So? What does that have to do with me?"

"Well, for one thing, you were there. You knew it was going on. You didn't do anything about it."

"So you say," Van Dorn said, starting to get up again. With considerable effort, he pushed back his chair and gripped the desk, struggling to lift his mass.

"And for another," Patty continued, "you abused him too. You took advantage of a position of power to indulge your perverted desire to have sex with children."

"I certainly did not!" Van Dorn was so taken aback that he sat back down. "I never touched that boy."

Here it was—the moment for Patty's great gamble, the lie that could change the rest of her and her mother's lives. "Jessie Kadonada is willing to say you did."

The color seemed to drain from Van Dorn's face. "I don't believe you."

Patty shrugged. "Believe what you want. I talked to him just today. He's very successful now, a sales manager up in Portland." Now that she'd gotten started, the embellishment was easy. She justified it by reminding herself that she was protecting Jessie as well as her mother. Regardless of the truth, both of them had reason to hate Forrest, and either of them could have killed him.

Or maybe Forrest really had done it himself. Patty wondered what it must have been like to live with himself all those years, knowing what he had done. Forrest had once dreamed of being in the movies; instead he'd ended up in a broken-down apartment, spending his life in a stinking basement, alone. Was he haunted by Jessie Kadonada's face? Did he see him crying in his dreams?

How tempting would it be to end those memories once and for all?

"You slant-eyed, devious little cunt," Van Dorn muttered. "You know your grandmother couldn't wait to open her legs for George, don't you? She was hot for him like a bitch in heat."

"That's a lie."

"And your mother, she would have been next. She came looking for it, you know. She came around one night when we were partying. Gave George a taste of her sugar. Couldn't wait to have what her mama had."

"You're wrong," Patty muttered, but it came out in a whisper. She stood, her legs trembling, and picked up her purse, digging her fingers into the leather to steady them. "You can keep those copies. I have the originals. If the case isn't closed by tomorrow at noon, I'm taking them to the papers. Oh, and by the way, I'm not really a journalist, but I think the *Chronicle* might be interested in what I have to say anyway."

"That's not a lot of time," Van Dorn said, making no move to pick up the photographs.

"Then it's a good thing you're such a powerful man."

34

Lone Pine
September 1943

LUCY AND MARY LEFT LONE PINE IN EARLY autumn, when the pregnancy could no longer be easily hidden with loose clothing. Lucy took only what fit in a single suitcase, just as when she left Manzanar. She wished she had brought one of the tiny trophies she'd worked on with Garvey—a little canyon wren mounted on a piece of driftwood ornamented with a tiny porcelain blossom, or a pair of white-bellied pocket mice whose paws were joined to suggest a waltz. But Mary had planned their departure in secret. No one knew about the baby but the two of them, and Mary packed their bags and wrote a letter to Garvey while Lucy slept. After she woke Lucy before dawn to announce that Sharon was waiting in the drive, ready to drive them to Bakersfield in the High Boy, she insisted on standing watch while Lucy dressed, never letting her out of her sight. And when Lucy cried for the first hour of the three-hour drive, Mary ignored her tears and stared out the window. Sharon kept her mouth shut and an inscrutable expression on her face.

Mary—she had insisted Lucy start calling her by her first name—knew of a place in San Francisco where unwed mothers could wait out their pregnancies. "Don't be getting ideas," Mary added before the truck had even disappeared down the street. "If I find out you've been in touch with Garvey, I'll call the lawyer so fast neither one of you will know what hit you. I'll tell him Garvey's not right in the head."

"That's what you wanted from the start," Lucy spat. Mary had trapped her, and she could see no way out. "A way to make him look bad so you could have the motel and all the money."

"Not all of it." Mary smiled, that old familiar cat-with-the-canary smile that Lucy had learned to fear more than her temper. "He'll always have a place to live. Mother would have wanted that. We'll provide for him."

"You *know* that's what hurts him the most," Lucy said, unable to stop herself, even though she knew she was only adding fuel to the fire. "Having to depend on anyone else."

"Of course I know that."

"But—he's your *brother*. How could you *do* this?"

In the distance, the whistle of the approaching train played its long, lonesome note. Travelers gathered under the station's arches along with people coming to greet their loved ones or say their farewells, the excitement of reunion mixing with the melancholy of separation. For Lucy, there would be neither—no one to miss her, no one to cherish her return.

The chilly smile never left Mary's face. She picked up her suitcase and started walking down the sidewalk toward the platform. Lucy stumbled, trying to keep up.

"He was always the golden boy," Mary said. "Everyone

loved him. He should have died in the war. But he came back, and now he has to pay the price."

Once they were settled in San Francisco, an edgy peace took hold between them. There was a library branch a few blocks from the rooming house, and Lucy spent most of her afternoons in the reading room, losing herself in any story that could make her forget for a while. Mary left for hours at a time, but Lucy wasn't sure where she went. Sometimes she'd glimpse her staring into shop windows or buying a pastry at a bakery. Lucy was amazed that in a city as busy as San Francisco, she would ever see Mary at all; it seemed as though the crowds and streetcars and traffic would swallow them both up. But late every evening, they both found their way back to the room, to another meal spent mostly in silence, another night when Lucy woke to find the city's gilded glow seeping into their room, casting its frenetic energy across the worn carpet like rice spilled from a jar.

Sometimes, when Lucy couldn't sleep, she went up to the roof and stared out at all the tall buildings, the sky hazy with the glow of the city. She sat so still that the pigeons, unsettled by her arrival, eventually touched down and flocked around her. As the weeks passed, they learned to anticipate her arrival, especially after she started bringing them morsels left over from dinner.

Sometimes, the words Lucy whispered to the pigeons were the only ones she uttered all day, other than the terse conversations she had with Mary. The frequency of her visits with the pigeons became a barometer for her loneliness. A hundred times, Lucy thought about running away. But where would she go? She had nothing, not a dime to her name. Mary had known about her secret hiding place all along, allowing Lucy to keep adding coins and bills to her stash until the night before they left, never letting on that she knew. Now she kept their accounts at the rooming house and diner, and stored her money in a cloth wallet that she wore around her neck, even while she slept.

There was no way to escape. And even if she could, the penalty for leaving was one that Lucy could never bear. She wouldn't give Mary a reason to hurt Garvey further. So she waited. She just had to endure a little longer. And endurance was one thing Lucy knew how to do well.

Mary told everyone they met that Lucy was her ward. No one asked questions. The people here were nothing like Lucy's old neighbors in Los Angeles. They were not friendly. They seemed willing to take Mary's explanations at face value, and if they didn't seem repulsed by Lucy's damaged face, they didn't seem the least bit interested either. Lucy watched the other girls in the building grow bigger and bigger until one day they simply disappeared, and she would know they had given birth and gone back to whatever lives they'd had before, or whatever new ones they were able to carve out for themselves.

Finally, the baby arrived, making remarkably little fuss during her arrival, as though she knew her conception had already caused enough problems.

A few nights later, they packed their suitcases. In the morning, Mary would go to the train station for the first leg of her journey back home, but before she left she would give Lucy the money she owed her and the key to her new apartment, a shabby studio near Mission Dolores. She seemed surprised by Lucy's decision to keep Patricia—Lucy had chosen the baby's name from a little booklet one of the girls had left in the rooming house parlor—but also indifferent. For her part, Lucy's decision had been made after one glimpse of

Patty's tiny mouth, her black eyes bright with life, her little hands shaped like starfish. Besides, she could never have left Patty at the orphanage, knowing that the staff wouldn't try to place a baby with mixed blood. Lucy refused to doom Patty to the life she herself had narrowly escaped.

Lucy had little to offer, but it would have to be enough. She would find a job, someone to watch Patty while she worked; their needs were few. She would take care of Patty and she would not be afraid and she would not allow fate to swallow them as it had her own mother. She would survive as she always survived. *I can,* Lucy had whispered to herself the first time she held Patty in her arms. *I can.*

Lucy waited until Mary was asleep to make one last visit to the roof. The baby was asleep and would, if the experience of the last few nights served, remain asleep for at least a couple of hours, more time than Lucy needed.

Lucy climbed the twisting staircase, out into the drizzling, misty December night. Fog obscured the buildings all around, creating glowing coronas around the windows where lights burned all night long. Lucy looked out over the rooftops, across the financial district, toward the sliver of the bay that she could see on clear days. In the tenement a block down Franklin, she imagined figures silhouetted against windows, and wondered, as she had every night of the past three months, what Garvey was doing at that moment back in Lone Pine.

Lucy took her customary place on the parapet at the roof's edge and immediately the moist air surged into her ears, her eyes, her lungs. It was a small inconvenience. She wouldn't be here long. She dug in her pocket for the packet of saltine crackers she had taken from the diner. She crumpled one in her fist, shaking out the crumbs at her feet. It took only a matter of seconds for them to come, four of them this time, but there was only one she wanted.

A large bird perched near her feet, with wings checkered in blue-gray and mottling on his smooth white head. Lucy couldn't be sure he was a male, but Garvey had taught her a few things to look for—overall size, size of head, relative aggression with the other birds.

Tonight, the bird came strutting toward her, his feathers sleek and glossy, head angled jauntily, emitting his warbling coo, repeating the same stanza over and over. Lucy broke another cracker and set a piece in the middle of her palm. He hopped into her hand while his companions cawed and circled.

As he finished the last bit, Lucy stroked his crown down to the nape. He'd allowed this intimacy only for the last few weeks. Lucy had worked hard to get him this far, because she knew their time together would be ending soon.

The bird seemed to lean into Lucy's caress, his smooth, pretty head curved against her fingers. His warble softened to a purr, and Lucy wrapped her fingers tenderly around his body, feeling his heartbeat under his warm breast.

Then she began to squeeze. She meant to smother him, to keep squeezing until he lay limp and lifeless in her hand. She had planned this for weeks: her final gift to Garvey. She would beg Mary to take him back, wrapped in a napkin, a thing of beauty for the joy Garvey had given her, preserved forever in death to remind him that they had each loved, once, no matter what came after. She'd imagined Garvey preparing the bird's perfect pelt, arranging his wings in flight, suspending him in the room where they had spent so many happy hours together. When Garvey looked at the bird, he would think of her.

She squeezed, and the bird blinked his bright, glassy eyes—

and suddenly her hand went limp and tears came to her eyes. She couldn't do it.

He bobbed his head, no worse for wear, and hopped down onto her knee and from there to the asphalt roof. He pecked at a speck, lost interest and wandered off, joining the other birds who fluttered and jostled a few feet away. A moment later they all swooped into the air at some invisible signal, the air filled for a second with the thrum of their beating wings. Then they flew away as one undulating cloud, disappearing below the rooftop, dipping and diving into the city's canyons below.

Lucy stood and dusted the cracker crumbs from her hands. It was all right. She and Garvey needed no mementos of each other. They had healed each other, sealing over the hurts they'd borne before and guarding against the ones to come.

When she walked down the stairs to their room, Lucy heard raised voices inside.

She threw the door open and was astonished to see Garvey in the green armchair next to the window. For a second she thought he was a vision, a miracle. But he was real. He had come for her. She raced across the room and knelt in front of him, put her head in his lap and wrapped her arms around his waist, sobbing his name.

He shoved her violently to the floor. Her chin hit first, jarring her head, and as she struggled to sit up, her vision wavered. "What—"

Garvey was gripping the sides of his chair, his face distorted with rage. "Don't touch me," he muttered. "Don't."

"I had to tell him." Mary was sitting on her bed holding the baby, who was awake and blinking. "About Hal."

"*Hal?*" Garvey demanded. Up close, Lucy could see that he hadn't shaved today, something that hadn't happened in all the time she had known him. His beard came in thick and ginger-brown. His shirtsleeves were rolled up to his elbows despite the chill in the room, and the tendons in his arms bulged as though he couldn't contain his fury. "All this time, it was *him?*"

Lucy gaped, at a loss for words. In the corner, she saw a burly stranger standing with his arms folded, watching silently.

"How…how did you find us?" Lucy asked.

"Sharon called when she got the telegram." Garvey sounded sickened. "You really thought she'd keep it from me, Mary? I've known her my whole life."

Mary shrugged, jostling Patty, who squeaked in protest. "It wasn't her business. I paid her to pick us up, that's all."

"I guess some people aren't for sale, even for *your* money."

"Garvey, listen to me," Lucy implored. "There's nothing— has never been anything—with Hal."

"Think hard before you say anything else," Mary snapped at her. "Hal's just a dumb kid. Everyone will understand what happened between you and him. You didn't mean anything to him. He'll have forgotten you by his twentieth birthday. But if you try to convince people that Garvey…"

Lucy looked from one sibling to the other: Mary calculating and cold, Garvey's face contorted in anguish. It was all she could do to stop herself from crawling to him, begging him to listen. "But I *never*—"

Mary cut her off. "You want to keep this baby, that's your choice. But before you say one more word, understand this. If you insist on telling some crazy story about you and Garvey, if you bring a baby back to Lone Pine and say it's his, he stands to lose everything. The age of consent in this state is eighteen—he could go to jail. You think I can't prove how old you are, Lucy? I've known since the day you came. It's in your *papers,* Leo was just too dumb to ever read them. And all I need to do is tell the lawyer."

The room was silent except for the baby's whimpering. "Garvey," Lucy whispered, pleading.

"Is it true?" he demanded. "Just tell me that—only that."

Lucy could read the hurt, the uncertainty in his eyes, and longed to tell him it would be all right. They could stay here in the city, the law would never pursue them this far. They could turn their back on the motel, the house, the inheritance, and be a family—the two of them and the baby.

As soon as the beautiful fantasy flickered to life it was snuffed out. She and Garvey had been dealt harsh hands. They were broken—he couldn't even walk the stairs to this room on his own. He couldn't ride a streetcar or go up a flight of steps. He'd never find work. And every stranger who saw her face recoiled. They would never survive here together.

She blinked back tears, and her fingers twitched with longing to reach for him, to touch him. But at the last minute she twisted her hands into fists, and got to her feet. She turned her back on him before she spoke.

"It's true. I'm sorry, Garvey. The baby's Hal's."

"I don't believe you." His voice, cracked and broken.

Lucy took Patty from Mary and buried her face in the baby's warm neck, already as familiar as her own skin. "Believe what you want, but Hal and I… It just happened."

Mary waited, quiet for once, the amusement wiped from her expression. The baby suckled air, whimpering, her small and perfect mouth brushing against Lucy's cheek.

"Come get me, boy," Garvey demanded, and the young man stirred from the corner of the room. "Get me the hell out of this place."

Lucy kept her face pressed to the baby, her eyes shut tight, to give him this last bit of dignity.

There was nothing else she could give.

35

BY FIVE-THIRTY, THE POLICE STATION HAD emptied out dramatically, and Patty had to fight a sense of panic that her mother was going to end up spending the night in jail. Or wherever they were keeping her.

Patty and Jay had been drinking coffee from a machine and sharing a packet of cheese–peanut butter crackers when the attorney came out to the waiting room to give them the news that the case had been dropped.

"There'll be paperwork," he said, tugging his tie loose, "but essentially that's it."

"I don't understand," Jay said. Relief made Patty feel a little dizzy, but she forced herself to stay composed. She hadn't told Jay about going to see Van Dorn. She'd given him a condensed version of what her mother had told her about Manzanar, leaving out the part about the abuse her grandmother had suffered, about the man she had killed. Talking about it in the police waiting area felt like tempting the Fates, and Patty told herself she would share the whole story later, when she and Jay had some privacy. But as the attorney explained that Forrest's death was going to be ruled a suicide, Patty wondered if it would be better just to try to forget the whole horrible story. She thought about the albums hidden underneath her wedding dress and realized that she could simply get rid of them, destroy the evidence. Maybe her mother had been right to try to shield Patty from the darkness of the past.

When the attorney left, Jay pulled Patty into a hug. "See?" he said, smoothing her hair back from her face. "Nothing to worry about. All a big misunderstanding. Your poor mom—I hope she isn't too upset."

Soon after, Torre emerged to say that he was sorry it was taking so long, but he wasn't much of a typist, and twice already he'd had to crumple up the forms with all their carbons and start over. If they wouldn't mind waiting just a few more minutes?

And Patty had said she didn't mind at all. The men shook hands and Torre retreated, his footsteps echoing down the hall.

"Just a little longer," Jay said softly, and Patty let herself believe it was over.

Lucy was remarkably unruffled—and hungry. They stopped for takeout from a Greek restaurant on the way home and while Jay piled food onto paper plates in the kitchen, Patty took advantage of the moment of privacy to tell her mother about Jessie's visit.

"I should have told you I'd been in touch with him," Lucy said apologetically. "He calls sometimes when he's in town.

It's nothing, really, but with the police and everything, it just didn't seem like the time to try to explain."

"Does he know?" Patty asked. "About Mr. Forrest?"

"I'm sure he does, by now," Lucy said, not meeting Patty's eyes. "It's been in the papers. Patty, I'm not sure what impression he gave you, but Jessie and I aren't close or anything. We just—we have some history together, that's all."

"Okay," Patty said, figuring that if there was more to the story, she wouldn't ever find out from her mother. "There was one other thing I have to tell you. The police found the box. With all the pictures in it, the one you were showing me. It's my fault, sort of. I went looking for it…. I found it in your closet, and when they got here, I didn't have time to put it back."

"Oh," Lucy said. "Well, they'll probably return it eventually. They said I'll get my tools and things back."

"You're not mad?"

Lucy smiled. "No. I don't know why I never showed you any of it before."

"I was wondering… There was a letter. Signed 'G.' Was that from someone important to you?"

Something flashed across her mother's face: a fraction of a second of unmasked emotion, regret or longing, something bittersweet. Then Lucy smiled and the moment passed. "Oh, that was from Garvey Hasty. He owned the hotel. Mary's brother. He's the one who taught me taxidermy."

Now that you know everything I can teach you, I have nothing more to give….

"It sounded like he cared about you a lot."

"He was like a mentor, I suppose. He was a veteran, he was wounded in the war. Got around in a wheelchair. Wow, that smells good, doesn't it?"

Patty wanted to ask more about him, but her mother

clearly didn't want to talk about it and Jay called from the kitchen to ask for help serving the meal.

It was nearly midnight when they finished dinner, but no one made any move to get up. Talk had circled around Lucy's childhood, and she'd told stories Patty had never heard, about her school days and visits to her father's factory, about her mother's best friend and her cats. Patty felt wistful that she had never been able to coax these stories from her mother as effortlessly as Jay did, but mostly she was fascinated, holding on to every anecdote, every detail.

"What did you do after the war, Mrs. T?" Jay asked. "Patty says you lived somewhere up in the desert."

Lucy set her fork down on her paper plate and dabbed at the corners of her mouth with her napkin.

"She worked as a maid, I told you that," Patty said quickly, putting her hand on Jay's knee, willing him to let the subject go. She didn't want this remarkable evening to end with unpleasant memories for her mother.

But Lucy seemed fine. "That's right, I did. In a motel in Lone Pine, not far from Manzanar. One of the nuns helped me get the job."

She looked at Patty and smiled tentatively, holding her gaze as something passed between them: acceptance, forgiveness, permission to let things go.

"I worked for a family. The work wasn't too hard, and they had a little taxidermy business on the side. That's how I learned, in my free time, helping out with the grunt work at first before they let me do my own projects."

"And you met Patty's father there?"

"Jay," Patty said sharply.

"I'm sorry," Jay said quickly. "It's none of my business—"

"No, it's all right." Lucy smiled at Jay, taking a sip from her wine. It was the first time Patty remembered her mother having more than one glass. "I did meet him at the motel. He did maintenance on the grounds. It was one of those things, both of us too young to know what we were getting into. Luckily, as soon as she figured out what was going on, the lady I worked for brought me here and took care of me until Patty came. Her name was Mary." She looked down at her hands. "She changed my life."

"Wow, Mrs. T. That must have been tough," Jay said.

Patty didn't want to break the fragile thread of her mother's recounting, but she had to know.

"What was his name, Mom? The boy?"

"Hal," she said. "His name was Hal."

Patty tested the name in her mind. *Hal,* her father. She waited for some thrill of recognition, some sign that he lived on inside her, that his blood beat in her veins. But she felt nothing.

"Did you ever see him again after that?" Jay asked. "Do you know what happened to him?"

"I found out later that he died in a car accident, not long after Patty was born."

"Oh, that's awful, Mrs. T." Jay covered Patty's hand with his own. "I'm so sorry."

Lucy waved her hand dismissively. "Don't worry, it was a very long time ago. I was so busy in those days, working and taking care of Patty. She was a good baby, though. Such a good little baby." Lucy beamed at Jay. "Just think, soon you'll have kids too. Grandchildren!"

As Jay and Lucy went on about the future, Patty remembered that earlier in the day, in the police station waiting room, she had thought that the first thing she would do when Lucy was released would be to ask her point-blank if she had gone to Reg's Gym that morning. If she'd taken his life. Patty had felt she was owed an answer, that she'd earned it.

Now she was content never to know. Her mother had been caught in life's crosshairs and she'd survived it all—and made a life for Patty too. Patty was ready to call all her mother's debts settled.

Let the future come, she thought. *Let it come.*

"I love you, Mother," she said. Her face flushed—she'd had a little more rosé than she realized. "I love you, Jay."

"Okay, okay," Jay laughed. "How about I let my two best girls get to bed."

He kissed Patty in the doorway to her room and she got into bed without undressing. She could hear Jay joking with her mother, saying good-night. She heard him push the chairs back under the kitchen table and stack the dishes in the sink. Finally, she heard the front door close, and the house was silent, and she stretched deliciously and let sleep take her.

36

San Francisco
Saturday, June 17, 1978

LUCY PULLED UP TO HER HOUSE AS THE LAST
rays of the sun pierced the clouds over the rooftops, landing
in untended lots and lush gardens and the row of carefully
chosen stones lining her front walk. The setting sun turned
them pale gold. On warm days the stones baked in the surrounding earth. In spring they glistened wet and gray like
the bodies of the sea lions down at the pier.

Lucy was anxious to get out of her high heels and girdle,
and the polyester dress, the tag of which had been itching
her neck since ten o'clock this morning when the photographer arrived.

All the discomfort was worth it, though. Patty had been
a beautiful bride, unexpectedly graceful in her confection
of a dress, her hair in curving waves around her face, a thin
sequined band holding back her bangs. She rarely let go of

Jay's arm, and the two of them never stopped smiling. They were *happy.* Truly happy, and Lucy had spent the day swept up in their delight and love.

As she watched Patty dance with Jay on the candlelit dance floor, Lucy had thought about the first hours of Patty's life. Lucy had waited alone in the chilly halls of Saint Francis Hospital while Mary recovered from childbirth. Lucy listened to the screams echoing up and down the tiled halls, and finally, exhausted by the waiting, took a walk to the viewing window. There, in neat rows of bassinets, were the newest babies fate had seen fit to toss onto the unwelcoming shores of this life. On either side of Lucy, two new fathers regarded their babies with what seemed like equal parts terror and pride.

She scanned the white cards until she found the one: Baby Girl Sloat. There. The little bundle shifted, a tiny arm stretching and a sweet mouth opening in a yawn below a shock of inky, untamed hair, and Lucy fell in love. In the passing of a single second, she realized she could never allow Mary's daughter to be given over to the orphanage, where her mixed race would ensure that she was never adopted.

"I will save you," she mouthed silently. She watched the baby sleep for a while, her promise taking shape in her mind, the life she would create for them both.

Several months earlier, Mary had come to Lucy while she was cleaning room four. "I want to talk to you about something," she said, locking the door behind her.

Lucy had been on her knees, dusting the baseboards. She got to her feet, smoothing the wrinkles from her dress. They looked at each other for a moment. Then Mary extended one clenched fist and uncurled her fingers one by one, revealing every dollar that Lucy had managed to save.

"You picked a good hiding place," Mary said. "Just not good enough."

Lucy could have her money back, three times over—enough for a bus ticket and a few months' rent—and all she had to do was go with Mary to a place she had heard about, where they could wait until the baby came. Mr. Dang would never know. Leo would never know. Everyone in Lone Pine, including Garvey, would think that Lucy was off bearing his bastard child, and when Mary returned to town, she would take up where she'd left off—and hire a new maid.

The baby would be placed in an orphanage, Lucy would be free to start a new life in the city, and if all the residents of a dusty desert purgatory figured they knew the story, and only got the characters wrong, what would it matter? Lucy's future wasn't in Lone Pine.

"I won't do it," Lucy had said, horrified. "I won't have him thinking...that."

"Oh, Lucy," Mary said with cruel amusement. "You went and fell in *love,* didn't you? I suppose I should have seen it coming—the two of you, it's sort of sweet."

She smoothed the stack of bills she held in her hand and tucked them into her purse. "Of course...there aren't a whole lot of places a girl like you can go with no money and no job."

Would she really do something so heartless? Lucy wondered. "I'll call Sister Jeanne," she said uncertainly.

Mary snorted. "Good luck, then. You know they're sending all the orphans back where they came from. Poor Sister Jeanne has her hands full, I'm sure. Why, I bet she doesn't even know where *she's* going to go when this is all over."

Lucy felt sick. She'd been cornered, outfoxed, and neither of them had even mentioned the worst possibility of all.

"I could tell Garvey," she whispered.

"Yes, I suppose you could. Let's think about that for a moment, shall we? No doubt Garvey would tell Leo right away, and Leo would have no choice but to divorce me. The judge would dissolve the family trust, make us sell off the assets. He'd give Leo the lion's share. Oh, I'd do all right, I suppose…. I'd have a little cash to start over. I'd have to get a job. I could be a maid, like you. Wouldn't that be amusing?"

She laughed and then her nostrils flared and she glared at Lucy. "But Garvey? That's another matter. The motel would be gone—he'd have to watch someone else run it, on the land that once belonged to him. I suppose he could rent out rooms in town, try to keep his taxidermy business going. But without you…do you think his heart would really be in it? Or wait—were you thinking he would actually take you with him? *Marry* you, perhaps? Oh—that would be one for the history books, wouldn't it?" She laughed again, the sound chilling and mean. "I'm sorry, Lucy, I'm just trying to picture that wedding announcement. The photo of the happy couple. You…you could sit on his lap, wearing a white dress, while he wheeled you up over your new doorstep, into the pathetic single room that you'd have to share with all your little animals. Only…"

She twisted her mouth in mock dismay. "I don't suppose you've ever had a chance to look at the Mountainview's books, have you, Lucy? No, of course not. Well, it may come as a harsh surprise to you to know that the income Garvey generates wouldn't even pay the light bill here. He fancies himself an artist, I know, but *art* doesn't put food on the table.

He can stuff those carcasses all day long, and he still wouldn't be able to support the two of you."

Mary rubbed her hand over her barely swollen stomach. "So when you think it through the way I have, I think you'll have to agree that the very best thing for all of us is to get through this together and then part ways as friends."

She lingered over the word *friends* and reached for Lucy's hand, giving it a quick, hard squeeze before unlocking the door and leaving. Lucy stayed in room four for a long time, trying to find a way out of Mary's scheme.

If Mary had been a different woman, Lucy might not have begrudged her those stolen hours with Mr. Dang. Two lonely people; they'd both known their share of cruelty. Maybe it was the sting of being unwanted, being reviled, that brought Mary and Mr. Dang together. Maybe they found a little pleasure; maybe it was only commiseration. Lucy didn't know and she didn't care. If Mary hadn't been born lacking compassion, life had scoured it away and filled the hole with bile, until she could only be happy when others suffered.

And this time she had found a way to make sure they suffered spectacularly.

She had won. Garvey could never know the truth, because the truth would break the fragile balance of his life. Lucy felt her legs go weak as she realized what she had to do, and held on to the handle of her supply cart for support. She would go along with Mary's plan, she would walk away from this place and the man she loved and she would never look back.

She would do it for Garvey, and if it broke his heart, at least hers would have broken first.

As the garage door rolled up, Lucy noticed a figure standing motionless outside her front door. She pulled in slowly, turned off the car, sat for a moment. She scratched at her waist, where the band of her panty hose cut cruelly into the soft flesh of her stomach, and thought about what to do next.

There were only a few people she could think of who would come to see her on an evening like this—or any evening at all, really—and two of them were on their way to the Saint Francis hotel to start their lives together as a married couple.

"Jessie," she said as she approached the door, her heart pounding under the pink lace of her dress. How many times had she imagined this moment, the first time she lay eyes on him after all those years? He was different, with the thickset body of a middle-aged man, silver in his hair, an expensive shirt and gold watch. But he was the same too, around the eyes, the shy smile. "What are you doing here?"

"I was in town for work, but I decided to stay an extra day. I was hoping to see you in person."

"You saw me in person," she said. "Didn't you? That morning at the DeSoto."

"But you didn't see me. You were only a few minutes behind me, Lucy. I'd made it all the way up the stairs to the lobby when I realized I didn't have the stunner with me. I dropped it after I shot Reg. I was going to go back when I saw you coming through the revolving door and I panicked."

"Why did you have to tell me you were going to do it? Why'd you ever call me, Jessie?" she asked. "Were you hoping I'd stop you?"

"No, no. I'd never put that on you, Lucy. I'm so sorry I involved you at all. I should have waited until after it was done. I just…" His eyes grew shiny, and he brushed at them impatiently and cleared his throat. "I just wanted to hear your voice first, I guess. You could always make me feel like everything was going to be all right. Even then. Even after

I told you I was going to see him, you made me feel like it would all be okay."

"You hung up on me," Lucy said, aching to think of him in some hotel room, alone, deciding to do this thing. Reliving all the hurt and all the shame for the hundredth time, the thousandth, the millionth, and deciding that he would finally end it.

"Only because I knew you'd try to talk me out of it."

"I would have." Not because killing was wrong, but because it was a risk; he was gambling everything, whatever was left of his life. And what guarantee was there that in taking Forrest's life, he could extinguish the pain? Lucy looked at his face, searching for proof that he'd succeeded. "Are you all right?"

"Yes. I am. I really am." He touched her arm lightly. "But what about you? Lucy, when I think of what I put you through…that you saw what I did. Saw *him*."

For a moment, Lucy felt it all again, the shock, the regret, the fear. Forrest had been slumped in his chair, blood cascading down his face, his mouth slack. He looked nothing like he did back then. He'd looked so *old*. Staring at his still body, his gut hanging over his pants, his feet splayed in their dirty white sneakers, the cramped room smelling of sweat and feces, Lucy almost felt pity for him.

It had been nothing like the night at Rickenbocker's room. Then, she'd felt like Nancy Drew, stealing along the back of the staff buildings, stealthy, with her mother's scarf wrapped around her hair. She saw the way he looked at her when he opened the door, his eyebrows raised in surprise, his smile hungry. She moved fast, carried by the momentum that took her through the door. She brought her mittened hand up and aimed well, her mother's good scissors heavy in her hand. And when it was done, when Rickenbocker sunk to his knees, clutching his neck and staring at her with his eyes bulging, she felt no pity at all.

He had swayed on his knees for a moment before falling sideways. It wasn't long before he was still. Blood made a puddle under his cheek. His eyes were open, but they seemed to look past her, as though he'd figured out her ruse and was searching for the real Miyako. He'd never touch her again, though; Lucy had made sure of that, and as she let herself back out into the freezing night, she felt no regret, only satisfaction.

She'd been young, too young to understand how it might play out. Miyako had known, though. She knew they'd come for her, and she knew they'd come for Lucy next. It would never end, and Lucy realized that her mother had done everything she could to save her...even if it meant causing her pain.

Rickenbocker's death had been for Miyako, and maybe that was why it never haunted Lucy, why she never regretted it.

"It's all right," she told Jessie, and she believed it. Forrest had hurt Jessie; now he was dead. It was not her place to forgive either of them, but maybe she could offer something else, the words she'd tried to live by herself. "Just look ahead now. The future is all that matters."

"I'm not sorry I killed him," Jessie said. "I'm only sorry I got you involved. Lucy...if it had gone any further, I would have confessed. I would never have let you go to jail for me."

"Then I'm glad it didn't go any further."

"Did your daughter tell you I came by? A couple days after?"

"She told me. She was very curious about my mysterious friend." Lucy smiled wistfully.

"She mentioned she was getting married. She's really turned out great, Lucy. You should be proud."

"Thank you."

"You know, all these years… Sometimes I would call information, just to find out if you were still here, still living in San Francisco. I guess I just liked knowing that I could find you again. But all that time I never knew you had a daughter."

"It's…it's a long story."

"I'm sure it is," Jessie said gently. "It can't have been easy."

"It wasn't. But it's all right." Lucy paused, wondering how much to tell him. "It might seem strange, but I never really told her about that time."

"I never talk about Manzanar," he said, the faint lines between his eyes betraying his age. "Maybe it's just easier, you know, when you've lived through something like that. But ever since I moved to Portland…since my divorce…I couldn't stop thinking about it. I had nightmares, I—I had a sort of breakdown. One day I bought that gun, but even then I wasn't really serious. I mean, I bought it in a *feed* store, for Christ's sake, it's made for stunning livestock. You don't need any ID. Hell, a kid could buy one. I didn't even know if it would work."

"When you called me that morning, you said you were just going over there to talk to him."

"I know. I've thought about that a hundred times. I mean, calling you… Maybe I still hadn't decided, I don't know. But once I got there, once I saw him sitting there, working at his job like he was anyone, like he hadn't done all those…things…well, right then I knew I was going to do it all along."

"Jessie. You know you have to be careful now. If they have your gun, they have your prints. Just because they closed the case—"

"I know." Jessie shrugged, and in the gesture Lucy saw

the boy he'd once been, and a thousand memories tumbled through her mind. The way he'd walk with his bat bag slung over his shoulder, like he couldn't wait to get on the field. The way he held her hand as they roamed the streets of Manzanar. "I know. But I'm not afraid of what happens anymore. He's gone. That's what matters."

He moved toward her and put his arms around her. For a moment Lucy stiffened, and then she relaxed. She rested her head on his chest and closed her eyes, and let him hold her.

When at last she drew away, there were tears in his eyes. "You look beautiful today, Lucy," he said gruffly. "Please give your daughter my congratulations."

Lucy watched him from her window, her fingertips resting lightly on the glass. He didn't look back as he crossed the street and got into a tidy sedan and drove away.

All these things from the past coming to a close. All these loose ends finally being tied up.

Lucy's back had been aching for hours. Too much standing in those ridiculous, shiny shoes. She stepped out of them right there at the window and left them on the carpet, and then she tugged off the panty hose too, and let them fall on top of the shoes. She could not recall another time that she had walked through her house barefoot.

In her bedroom, Lucy unpinned her corsage and set it on the dresser. She hung her dress and put on her nightgown and went back through the house, turning off lights. Jessie's visit had stirred up a confusing blend of emotions, on top of her exhaustion from the wedding.

It had been a long time since she'd made so much polite conversation. Jay's mother never let anyone get a word in edgewise. The men from his office seemed skittish around her, but their wives made an effort. Lucy appreciated that.

She wanted her daughter to be in good hands. Patty wasn't as wary as she ought to be.

Lucy got into her narrow bed and turned off the lamp. She pulled the covers up to her chin and stared at the bars of street light that came through the blinds and striped the ceiling. The crack was getting worse—each year it seemed to travel a few more inches. Nothing that some plaster and paint wouldn't fix.

Lucy let her eyes drift closed, and the image that came to her mind was from that long-ago moment in San Francisco when Mary had left for the train station and Lucy and Patty were alone in the tiny room she'd rented. She lifted a corner of the Woolworth's blanket and peeked at her baby. Patty was plain, even at a few days old. Her mouth was slack, her forehead broad, her cheeks ruddy and damp with sweat. Her tiny hands grasped at nothing. She would never know the thrill of turning heads when she walked through a crowd. She'd never move a boy to recklessness or a girl to bitter jealousy. She'd work for her rewards and suffer ordinary disappointments and, quite possibly, she'd always feel as though she was missing something she couldn't quite define.

One of the final wedding details to be worked out was Patty's walk down the aisle, since she had no father, no uncles, no older brother, no friend of the family to give her away. When Jay took the two of them to dinner one night a couple of weeks ago, Patty had said that she would just walk down the aisle by herself. She looked so wistful that for a moment, Lucy wished that she had done everything differently.

But Jay had toasted Lucy with his coffee mug. "Don't be ridiculous. Your mom can give you away. Can't you, Mrs. T?"

And so it was Lucy who walked with Patty today, holding tightly to her daughter's arm, unsteady in her satin shoes, trying to ignore the people staring at her. The altar seemed a mile away. *I can, I can, I can,* Lucy repeated in her mind, just like a hundred other times, and before long they arrived.

★ ★ ★ ★ ★

Acknowledgments

THIS STORY BEGAN THE WAY SO MANY OF MY favorites do: on the road with Juliet Blackwell. Over the years, many a boring stint on a plane or in a rental car have been enlivened by conversations with Julie, who I'm convinced knows a little something about every subject on the planet. "Just enough to be dangerous," I imagine her saying, but it was idle musing on the subjects of Japanese internment and Victorian taxidermy that inspired this book.

Barbara Poelle, my cherished agent, didn't even bat an eye when I told her what I wanted to attempt. Without her unflagging support, I doubt I'd have had the courage to imagine this story.

I am very grateful to Adam Wilson, my intrepid editor, for embracing this project, advocating for it and guiding me through the early stages. Then, when new adventures called Adam elsewhere, Erika Imranyi was entirely gracious about inheriting not just an author but a manuscript that needed serious attention. Erika and I went through several bruising rounds of revisions, and it means the world to me that she didn't give up until it was right. It is a privilege to work with her.

A few more thanks are in order: Leonore Waldrip for the brainstorming; Rachael Herron, Nicole Peeler, Mike Cooper and Bob Littlefield for the early reads and encouragement; Dave Madden, for writing a wildly entertaining book that changed the way I view research forever; The Pens Fatales and Murder She Writes for their friendship and support.

Special thanks to William Wiecek, Judy Hamilton and Kristen Wiecek. You are there when I need you, and I will never be able to thank you enough.

Garden of Stones **is very different from other books you've published. What led to your decision to write something new, and what inspired your ideas for the story and characters in the book?**

When I began writing several decades ago, I found I loved the freedom of moving between genres—crime fiction, young adult, dark fantasy—trying to craft the most compelling story possible. There is great excitement in treading on unfamiliar ground, and I think risk-taking can lead to captivating and unforgettable stories.

Garden of Stones came about over a series of conversations I had with my dear friend, author Juliet Blackwell. She is a native Californian, and knew much more about the Japanese internment camps than I did, having grown up in the Midwest. I found this chapter of our nation's history engrossing and horrifying, so I started thinking about how to explore it through fiction. My own novels often feature women—specifically mothers and daughters—at the heart, which led me to focus on their experience during this troubling era. Other story elements came about serendipitously, even small details like the Nancy Drew mysteries mentioned in the book—I'd unearthed an old copy of *The Mystery at Lilac Inn,* and I kept it on my desk as I wrote.

You've written about a very specific—and difficult— period in U.S. history. What drew you to this time and setting? What kind of research did you do, and what were the challenges you faced writing a historical novel?

When I began this project, I knew I had a daunting research challenge ahead of me. I read everything I could get my hands on: dozens of books, first-person accounts, journals, newsletters. I pored over photographs and covered the walls of my office with maps and illustrations.

I made the trip to Manzanar and spent a day at the restored camp, talking to the staff and viewing the exhibits. Walking among the ruins of the blocks and gardens I'd read so much about was inexplicably moving. I felt as though I was standing with the spirits of those who had lived there. I also visited a small museum in the town of Independence that had a wonderful collection of ephemera and memorabilia: letters, handicrafts, school photos, newspapers, dishes, clothes and furniture made by internees.

There are also many wonderful websites about the pop culture of the era; I spent an entire afternoon learning about 1940s cleaning products!

Did you find it challenging to write about a culture that's different from your own? What sort of research

did you do to ensure the authenticity of your characters and life inside the Manzanar prison camp?

I was concerned about this aspect of the book until I started reading the first-person accounts and interviews of internees. The perspective differed greatly between the Issei (born in Japan) and Nisei (born in America), and between those who were children and those who were adults. The accounts are rich with detail and helped me understand the values and priorities of the families and communities whose lives were affected by the war, which in turn helped me create credible fictional accounts. There was such a strong sense of patriotism among many of the internees, despite their treatment by our government and citizens. The determination to self-identify as American remained powerful in nearly every account I read, and I tried to reflect that in the novel.

In the book, you explore the lengths a mother will go to protect her children—even if it means hurting them. Some readers may find Miyako's actions cruel and unspeakable, while others may feel the consequences of doing nothing would have been far worse. Did you intend for Miyako to be a sympathetic character? What do you want readers to take from her actions?

Despite Miyako's struggle with her fragile mental health, she fights to hold herself together for the sake of her daughter. A woman with Miyako's challenges in modern America might find effective treatment and be able to lead a full and rewarding life. During the war, that was nearly impossible, and yet Miyako did the best she could for Lucy.

I think the interesting question is whether she failed Lucy in the end. I spent a lot of time considering how a girl who had suffered what Lucy suffered would grow up—what kind of woman she would become, and whether she would be able to forgive. I must admit that I'm not entirely decided, myself.

What was your biggest surprise as you were writing this novel?

I am very surprised at how familiar the adult Lucy felt to me as I began to write her. I thought I would have been much more tentative in describing her attitudes, emotions and actions. But she arrived, as characters occasionally do, completely formed, and I felt no hesitation as I wrote her scenes.

Can you describe your writing process? Do you outline first or dive right in? Do you write scenes consecutively or jump around? Do you have a schedule or routine? A lucky charm?

I am still searching for my best process, and I'm getting the feeling that search will last a lifetime! True to my restless nature, I try lots of different things. I've written with detailed outlines and none at all; in chronological order and jumping around.

I do keep a detailed guide for every book and series. This includes a table of characters with their most salient characteristics, a time line and a list of significant places. As for schedule…I adore the fact that this job lets me set my own hours. I work throughout the day—from first sip of coffee through the glass of wine that marks the end of most evenings. But I take breaks whenever I feel like it: to do chores, go to the gym or hiking, have lunch with friends, hang out with my daughter after school.

I have a variety of talismans in my office. There are three little plastic penguins, a mini Etch A Sketch on which my son wrote "I Love You" when he was 8 or 10, a tiara given to me by a writing friend, and the card that came with the flowers my brother sent to mark the publication of my first novel.

What can you tell us about your next novel?

I am working on a novel in which an affluent suburban family is forced to endure a terrifying event together. Over the course of two days, all of their relationships with each other are profoundly altered.

1. After Pearl Harbor, many Americans worried that citizens of Japanese descent, especially those living on the West coast, might be acting as spies and traitors. Are such fears understandable? Can you think of similar events in recent history? How can we avoid reacting as we have in the past, with suspicion and intolerance?

2. Miyako's husband was nearly twice her age, and her only friend is fifteen years her senior. What do you think drew them together? How does Aiko try to help Miyako, and do you think she succeeds? How did camp life affect their friendship? How might Lucy and Miyako's experience in the camp have differed if Renjiro had not died?

3. The Takeda family was wealthier than many who were interned. Do you think that made the transition to camp life harder or easier? In what ways?

4. George Rickenbocker, Reg Forrest and Benny Van Dorn created a sort of underground social network at Manzanar. How do you suppose they got away with it? How did internees figure into it? Do you think George and Benny were aware of Reg's involvement with Jessie, and if so, why did they tolerate it?

5. What finally drove Miyako to her desperate act in Manzanar? Do you feel she had other options, or was it the only way she could save Lucy?

6. In the deaths of George Rickenbocker and Reg Forrest, was justice served? Do you think Patty truly accepted the possibility that her mother killed Reg? Is she at peace with her mother's choices?

7. Patty grew up thinking her mother never experienced romantic love, but in fact, she did—twice: first with Jessie and then with Garvey. Why do you think Lucy continues to keep a few secrets, even after telling Patty nearly everything about her past?

8. Garvey is considerably older than Lucy. By contemporary standards, their relationship would be considered inappropriate. Do you think their relationship was genuine? Could they have survived in Lone Pine as a couple?

9. Taxidermy is more than an avocation for Garvey, and later, for Lucy. What is the symbolic significance of taxidermy in the novel? Why do you suppose each is drawn to it, and how does it bring them together?

10. Why do you think Jessie chose to contact Lucy and pursue vengeance after so many years? Had Patty not inter-

vened with Van Dorn, would Lucy have taken the fall for her childhood sweetheart?

11. Disfigurement is a recurring theme in the book. Besides Lucy, what other characters might be said to be wounded, either literally or figuratively?

12. There are several starkly different portrayals of motherhood in the novel. In what ways, if any, could each of these characters be considered good mothers?